BROTHER ISLAND

Borne Back Books
West Egg, New York

First Borne Back Books trade paperback edition August 2025

Cover Design: Damonza.com
Author Photo: Selfie

Manufactured in the United States of America

Publisher's Cataloging-in-Publication Data
provided by Five Rainbows Cataloging Services

Names: Gibbs, Chad Alan, author.
Title: Brother island / Chad Alan Gibbs.
Description: Auburn, AL : Borne Back Books, 2025. | Summary: Izzy Brown attempts to solve a fourth mystery while struggling with anxiety and opioid dependency. | Audience: Grade 9 & up.
Identifiers: LCCN 2025915296 (print) | ISBN 979-8-9856757-9-5 (paperback) | ISBN 979-8-9995738-0-3 (ebook) | ISBN 979-8-9995738-1-0 (audiobook)
Subjects: LCSH: Young adult fiction. | Drug addiction--Juvenile fiction. | CYAC: Murder--Young adult fiction. | Teenagers--Fiction. | Autism--Fiction. | BISAC: YOUNG ADULT FICTION / Mysteries & Detective Stories. | YOUNG ADULT FICTION / Coming of Age. | YOUNG ADULT FICTION / Social Themes / Drugs, Alcohol, Substance Abuse. | YOUNG ADULT FICTION Neurodiversity.
Classification: LCC PZ7.1.B76 2025 (print) | LCC PZ7.1.B76 (ebook) | DDC [Fic]--dc23.

BROTHER ISLAND

a novel

CHAD ALAN GIBBS

For Tricia,
duh.

"What strange creatures brothers are!"
—Jane Austen

BROTHER ISLAND

PROLOGUE

Mustang Jones should have known this day would come.

He'd stepped on too many toes and made too many enemies. He'd given too many people a reason to take a long, sharp blade and stab it into his chest. Still, when Mustang pictured the end, he was in bed on his hundredth birthday with a beautiful woman beside him—or maybe two.

But not here.

Not like this.

Anything but this.

As his life flashed before his eyes, Mustang Jones traveled back to Pensacola. To the dilapidated shack in Brownsville on one of the alphabet streets. To the tiny bedroom he shared with three brothers and two sisters. He was Terrance then, and he was always in trouble.

Expelled for bringing a dirty magazine to school.

Arrested for lifting a pair of Adidas from Sears.

Sent away for knocking out his eighth-grade math teacher with a blindside punch.

Football saved Mustang Jones by providing a constructive outlet for his destructive tendencies. Though fast and agile enough to run untouched to the end zone on every carry, Mustang still sought out contact. He'd charge the backpedaling linebackers and defensive backs, trampling them like a wild horse, leaving cleat prints on their chests, and earning himself a nickname. Bardo Academy soon came calling, then Florida State. A Heisman Trophy followed, then a six-year NFL career cut short by a broken leg and obliterated knee ligaments.

Six months and a hundred pounds later, Mustang Jones's luck had run out. Without defenses to destroy, he seemed intent on destroying himself. Doctors warned that type 2 diabetes was only a Twinkie away, and his crooked leg hadn't healed correctly thanks to Mustang's near fanatical avoidance of anything resembling physical therapy. Twice during this downward spiral, he was arrested for driving under the influence, leaving two unfortunately hilarious mugshots that would later become internet memes. But then Mattesserie called with the offer of a lifetime. Get back into shape, attribute his healthy new lifestyle to their fat-burning grill, and pitch the contraption on late-night television for the rest of his life.

"I don't want to get back into shape," Mustang had said.

"We'll pay you three million dollars a month."

"Where do I sign?"

Selling grills, not scoring touchdowns, made Mustang Jones one of the wealthiest athletes of all time, but there are itches money cannot scratch. The thrill of victory. The agony of defeat. The sound of 80,000 fanatics chanting your name after scoring the go-ahead touchdown late in the fourth quarter. Sure, mornings on the golf course and afternoons by the pool are nice, but ex-athletes will chase the adrenaline rush of top-level competition for the rest of their lives.

Like so many before him, Mustang first trod the well-worn trail of washed-up jock turned degenerate gambler. Want to feel your heart pounding through your chest the way it did when the game was on the line? A $100,000 hand of blackjack will do the trick. But where so many athletes' borderline insane self-confidence led them to financial ruin, Mustang realized the game was rigged. To the benefit of his net worth, he understood those men in the desert didn't build those giant casinos by losing money. He quit cold turkey and looked for something else.

There was fleeting excitement in driving too fast and sleeping with other men's wives. He earned his pilot's license but nearly killed himself crash-landing on a golf course. Later, he paid a small fortune to shoot a five-hundred-pound lion in Zimbabwe, only to spark online outrage when news broke he'd killed Clarence, the most beloved mammal on the continent. Like so many dads, he would have gladly relived his gridiron glories through his son, but Mustang knew by preschool that sports were not in his son Elton's future. Defeated, he conceded that his life would always be missing that special some-thing, and then he found it.

Ever since his rookie year, investment offers had poured in. Men hoping to tie Mustang's name, money, or both to their latest project.

An airline with topless flight attendants.

A restaurant chain called Soft Rock Cafe.

A cable news network aimed at angering viewers on both ends of the political spectrum.

The offers piled up faster than Mustang could reject them, but eventually, one caught his eye. An offer that promised more than money—although he'd make enough to buy the NFL team he once played for. An offer that would scratch that itch and give him that rush he'd been desperately seeking for years.

But when something looks too good to be true, it usually is, and when it all went to hell a decade later, Mustang was in too deep. Still, he'd once broken five tackles in the backfield on what became the crowning jewel of his Heisman highlight reel. If he could escape those defenders' grasps, he could escape this. If he could get out of that rundown shack in Pensacola, he could get out of this mess. Like most famous athletes, spoiled and coddled since the day he scored his first touchdown, Mustang Jones hadn't faced the consequences of his actions in so long that he forgot they existed. He thought money was a game. Like football. Like women. Money was a game, and Mustang was a winner.

Only money isn't a game.

Money is life or death.

And stumbling through the woods, clutching the knife buried in his chest, Mustang Jones finally understood that his game was over.

CHAPTER ONE

It was a cold December night in Orlando, and my mother was crying like a baby. We'd spent that morning at Walt's magical kingdom, blowing money we didn't have, but that wasn't the reason for her tears. She was crying because her son, Axl Rose Brown, had just taken a knee on the final snap of the 4A State Championship Game and raised the ball to the heavens while his teammates mobbed him in celebration.

"We did it," Mom said, squeezing the breath out of me. "We did it, baby girl."

I hugged her back, conceding now wasn't the time to tell her we hadn't done anything, and all a state championship guaranteed was that Axl would never have to pay for a beer in Dandridge, Florida, for the rest of his life. She wouldn't have listened anyway. Mom believed, with the conviction of a zealot, that Axl was destined for the NFL. Preordained by God almighty to make millions and rescue us from the poverty we'd wallowed in for most of our existence. For Mom, financial planning consisted of clipping photographs of mansions from magazines and showing them to my brother, a practice I mocked relentlessly. But now, even we skeptics had to admit her prophecies were coming to pass.

Axl was the top-ranked pro-style quarterback prospect for the class of 2011, and he had football scholarship offers to every college in the country that fielded a team and some that didn't. Famous coaches stopped by Dandridge High all the time to chat him up, and recruiting services called our house so often I began answering to screw with them.

"Sorry, Axl isn't home right now. He moved to Nepal to study Buddhism in a Himalayan monastery and play football at the University of Kathmandu."

I'm Izzy, by the way. Izzy Rose Brown, seventeen years old of Dandridge, Florida, and Axl's twin sister. Older by five minutes, shorter by a foot, and at least a hundred pounds lighter. Unlike my brother, I hadn't received the first scholarship offer, and I wasn't the top-ranked anything for the class of 2011, though I was voted most likely to return to juvie by a couple of bitches in my study hall who didn't think I could hear them whispering.

Axl's teammates carried him off the Citrus Bowl field like a conquering general, while men in the press box—relieved to write about something other than Tiger Woods's wife beating him with a pitching wedge—banged out stories calling my brother the second coming of Tim Tebow. Once they set him down, Axl jumped into the stands, looking for Mom and me. When he found us, he flashed that smile—the one that always makes Mom melt and makes me want to punch him in the mouth. Then the three of us hugged, and fine, I'll admit it, I shed a tear or two, finally overcome by the emotion of it all.

We'd been here before. Two years ago, when Axl was a freshman, the whole town of Dandridge drove east to watch their Manatees get destroyed 42-7 in this stadium. There'd been tears then, too—different tears.

So much had happened in those two years. A wealthy booster from Bardo came calling with scholarships to a fancy private school by the sea. I met a boy there named Elton Jones-Davies, who became my best friend in the world, and I met another boy named Blaine, who gave me OxyContin and set me on the path to self-destruction. Elton and I solved a murder in Bardo, a good deed that didn't go unpunished. Expelled, arrested, and banished from the Garden with my newfound knowledge of good and evil.

Next came London with Elton and his mother. A luxury flat and a posh private school. Another murder solved, and another trail of destruction left in my wake.

And finally, a summer in the North Carolina mountains. A summer spent solving yet another murder and exposing the horrendous secrets of a sleepy resort town while almost getting myself killed, something I'd done far too often of late.

Since returning to Dandridge in August, life had become routine. Not a good routine, but a quiet one that didn't involve chasing murderers or nearly dying on a regular basis. I worked twenty-five hours a week at the Piggly Wiggly in Chipley, running a cash register and bagging groceries. Most of my paycheck went to the Panhandle Pain Clinic next door. Pain consultations, which were required for a prescription, cost $150 and consisted of describing your pain to a creepy doctor who licked his lips while assuring you if you didn't have the cash, he and you could work out a special payment plan on his office couch.

"I've got money," I mumbled the first time, and the asshole pointed me down the hall to the onsite pharmacy that sold 20 mg OxyContin tablets for ten bucks each, but not before adding, "Well, if you're ever short, I'm just letting you know you don't have to go without."

But at one pill a day, and I only took one a day, except when I took two, I'd be fine. Sure, most of what I made at the Pig should have gone toward clothes, food, and normal teenage stuff, but the pills came first. The pills were the reason I was doing okay. I hadn't missed school for a headache all year, and my anxiety, while still hiding in the deep recesses of my mind, was more of a nuisance than the all-encompassing dread of days past. My grades were good, and I scored a personal best on my latest ACT. Not scholarship-worthy yet, but I was getting there.

Families got to walk onto the field for the trophy presentation, and while Mom snapped pictures and continued to cry, I checked my phone for a text from Elton. Throughout the playoffs, he'd requested score updates, but tonight, he'd yet to reply to a single text, even one with a photograph of Axl holding me in one arm and the state championship trophy in the other. Elton still hadn't responded by the time I fell asleep next to Mom at 4 a.m. in our room at the Best Western Orlando West, where the whole of Dandridge celebrated late into the night at an impromptu pool party. But even in my dreams, something felt off, and when I finally woke up the next day and checked the news alert on my phone, I knew why.

Hall of Fame Running Back Mustang Jones Stabbed in the Bronx.

CHAPTER TWO

The news was a mess—half the articles swore Mustang Jones had been stabbed in his apartment, a few claimed he'd been shot, and Twitter was already blaming everything from the mob to a jealous supermodel. I turned on the television in our hotel room and flipped the channel to ESPN. A bright red ticker at the bottom of the screen flashed the breaking news, and two men in expensive suits spoke solemnly with a black and white photograph of Mustang Jones on the screen behind them. I recognized the bald white guy from the countless hours Axl made me watch SportsCenter. Still, I couldn't place the ridiculously handsome black man he was talking to until a graphic on the screen identified him as Rev. Denzel Davis, Hall of Fame linebacker and Mustang Jones's childhood friend.

"Since kindergarten," Denzel said when the host asked how long he'd known Mustang. "John A. Gibson School on North C Street. We were in Mrs. Templeton's class. That poor woman," he added with a laugh, "I know Terrance and I drove her to an early grave."

The host smiled and said, "Again, if you're just joining us, former Heisman Trophy winner Terrance 'Mustang' Jones was found stabbed last night in the Bronx. He is out of surgery at Mount Sinai Hospital, and a hospital spokesperson said Jones remains in critical but stable condition. We will continue to provide updates throughout …"

He was alive. Elton's dad was still alive. This was … good, I guess.

Look, I'll admit it. I was a little conflicted by the news. While Mustang Jones was my best friend's father, he was also a world-class asshat. He'd cheated on Holly Jones-Davies for most of their marriage, and he'd ignored his son since realizing the boy didn't care for sports. Once, during an argument, Mustang told Holly that Elton's autism was proof he wasn't his son. This was in the early stages of their divorce when Mustang wanted to leave Holly and Elton with nothing. Now, it seemed he'd accepted Elton as his flesh and blood and was fighting for full custody. I couldn't fathom why he'd want full custody of a boy he couldn't care less about until I realized that with full custody, he could still leave Holly with nothing and only be on the hook for Elton until he turned eighteen in a couple of years. Like I said, a world-class asshat. If Mustang had died, it would have solved a lot of problems. But it looked like he might pull through, so yay, or whatever.

I was annoyed at Mustang Jones for not dying, but I was also annoyed at him for getting stabbed in the first place. Holly Jones-Davies had invited Mom, Axl, and me to spend two weeks of Christmas break with her and Elton in New York. We were supposed to fly out of Pensacola on Monday and stay through January 3rd, but that seemed unlikely after the morning's news. I texted Elton again, and he finally replied.

ME – Hey, Big E, I just woke up and saw the news. Sorry about your dad.

ELTON – According to some neurobehavioral scientists, persons with near-death experiences often become more compassionate, caring, and altruistic, three traits my father, as you know, sorely lacks.

I shook my head at Elton's scientific detachment, though, as usual, it was hard to argue with his unshakable logic. Besides, if near-death experiences made you compassionate, maybe Mustang Jones would finally turn into a human being.

ME – Way to find the bright side. But I'm guessing your Mom doesn't still want us flying up on Monday?

ELTON – Incorrect. We had no intentions of celebrating the holidays with my father, so his hospitalization is of no consequence to your plans.

Since social cues weren't always Elton's strong suit, Mom called Holly to make sure our visit was still on. To my delight, it was, and on Monday morning, we boarded an American Airlines flight to New York's LaGuardia Airport.

"Didn't Elton's mom fly you first class to London?" Axl asked through a mouthful of complimentary cookies.

"Nope. Private jet," I said. "We flew home first class."

"After you pissed off that mobster?" my brother asked.

"After we saved thousands of lives," I corrected. "And pissed off a mobster."

We'd had a good fall, Axl and me. Now that he'd retaken his throne as king of Dandridge High, and our mailbox was flooded with scholarship offers, he'd seemingly forgiven me for getting us kicked out of Bardo and Ashes.

"Well, not to sound ungrateful for the free trip, but these seats are a little cramped."

"Hush your mouth," our mother said without turning her head. She was in the aisle seat, Axl at the window with me between, and she hadn't turned her head since takeoff. Her only movement I could tell was to grab my hand during our ascent and squeeze it until I whimpered in pain. Seems she believed her stillness was the only thing keeping our jet aloft, and one turn of her head would send us plummeting to the ground. I considered giving her one of the pills in my bag to take the edge off but thought better of it.

"If you say one ungrateful thing to Holly while we're there, I'll take you outside and whip your butt. I'm sure they have hickory switches in Central Park."

I wagged a scolding finger in Axl's face, and he shot me a bird.

"I'm not ungrateful," Axl said. "But I am big, and these seats are small, and—"

"Hush," Mom said again, and my brother huffed but obliged, though not before muttering, "When I'm in the NFL, we won't fly coach."

I couldn't see much of the famed NYC skyline on approach because Axl stuck his giant head in the window and wouldn't move, but after disembarking the plane, I got more than an eyeful of LaGuardia. At our gate, we were greeted by a garbage can catching water from a leaking pipe in the low ceiling. Temporary walls made the narrow hallway even narrower, and a cacophony of power tools from what Holly warned us was eternal airport construction gave me an instant headache. "What a dump," Axl noted as we fought through a sea of ornery holiday travelers.

"Says you," Mom said. "I ain't never been happier to be on the ground."

After baggage claim, where I almost had to cut a man who tried to walk off with my suitcase, we made our way to the arrivals hall, and I saw a familiar face smiling high above the crowd.

"Elton!" I shouted, running across the room to give him a hug he'd tolerate for nearly ten seconds, a new record.

"Monday greetings," Elton said when I finally let him go.

"Monday greetings, you donkey," I said, then hugged him again for good measure.

CHAPTER THREE

Elton and his mother lived in the penthouse of a thirty-five-story condominium on Jay Street in Brooklyn, where graffiti-tagged industrial buildings were giving way to upscale high-rises with twenty-four-hour doormen and heated lap pools.

"Why Brooklyn?" I'd asked Holly Jones-Davies when we returned from London in the spring.

"Because I refuse to live on the same tiny island as Terrance Jones," Holly had replied with a wink.

Their place looked worth every penny of the nine million dollars Elton matter-of-factly told us his mother paid for it. Holly gave us a quick tour, pointing out Agloceppo honed stone floors and Antolini marble countertops to a family whose only frame of reference was linoleum and vinyl. The space-aged furniture, which looked stolen from the Museum of Modern Art, was similar to the furnishings in Holly's London flat, and a panorama of floor-to-ceiling windows offered postcard-worthy views of the Manhattan skyline across the East River, which she told us, we fortunately couldn't smell from this distance.

"That is the Brooklyn Bridge, that is the Manhattan Bridge, and that one in the distance is the Williamsburg Bridge," Elton said to Axl and me as the three of us stood shivering on the giant wrap-around balcony off the penthouse living room, watching a cargo freighter glide silently out to sea.

"That's great, Elton," Axl said through chattering teeth, "but can we go back inside, or at least get in that jacuzzi? It's freezing."

My winter in London hadn't exactly acclimated me to subfreezing temperatures. Still, I was doing better than Axl, whose one summer in North Carolina had done little to toughen up his thin Florida blood.

A winter storm had dumped nine inches of snow on New York City two days earlier, and Elton took Axl's comment on the weather as an opportunity to opine on where this most recent blizzard ranked in Manhattan's meteorological history. But when a gust of wind tried to blow the three of us into the river, even Elton conceded, "Perhaps we would find the indoors more comfortable."

"So, school is going well?" I asked Elton as the three of us sat thawing out in the living room, sipping hot chocolate Holly made for us and watching the city sparkle in the setting sun.

"Affirmative," Elton said. "I have excelled academically and made several friends."

"Lady friends?" I teased.

"Six of my eleven friends are female," Elton said, then added, "which aligns with national demographics."

Axl squinted at me, but I could only shrug and smile.

"Many of my classmates are traveling for the holidays, but I hope you will meet some of them during your stay."

"I hope so," I said, happy that Elton appeared to be thriving at his new school, Kanner Academy.

Kanner Academy was a private high school in Tribeca attended primarily by autistic students. From what I'd read online, the kids at Kanner were all over the spectrum, from brilliant yet slightly awkward types like Elton to severely autistic children with significant communication and social challenges. Scholarships made the school accessible to all, though from talking to Elton, I got the impression plenty of super wealthy kids were there with him.

"You on the football team?" Axl teased, well aware of Elton's aversion to sweating.

"Kanner Academy does not field a tackle football team," Elton said, his height not keeping Axl's joke from going over his head. "I am, however, on the robotics team."

"The robotics team?" I asked.

"Affirmative. We construct robots that fight robots from other schools to death in a steel cage."

"Why does this sound like a supervillain's origin story?" Axl asked.

"Speaking of origin stories," Elton said, his eyes lighting up, "are the two of you watching *Star Wars: The Clone Wars*? I have all thirty episodes recorded on our television." Elton grabbed the remote and turned on the giant television, intending, I suspect, to make us watch fifteen hours of cartoons. "If we begin watching tonight, you should be caught up by the time—"

Elton stopped short at the sight of his father on the TV screen. The volume was down, but a scrolling ticker at the bottom informed us that police had no new leads in the case. Then, the news went live to a reporter standing across the river from a construction site on something called Brother Island.

"What is Brother Island?" I asked. We'd all skillfully avoided talk of Mustang until then, but this seemed like as good an opportunity as any to broach the subject.

"It is an uninhabited island in the East River," Elton said. "Between Rikers Island and the Bronx."

"And that's where your dad was stabbed?"

"Affirmative," Elton replied.

"Wait, what the hell was your dad doing on an uninhabited island in the East River?" I asked, just the thought of it giving me creepy vibes.

"Apart from getting stabbed," Axl added, not being helpful in the least.

"To understand my father's connection to Brother Island, I must first explain the history of Brother Island."

"Or you could just tell us what your dad was—"

"In the late nineteenth century, Riverside Hospital moved to North Brother Island from what is now known as Roosevelt Island. The hospital treated and isolated victims of quarantinable diseases like smallpox, typhoid, and tuberculosis."

"That sounds horrible," Axl said.

"It was," Elton agreed. "Typhoid Mary was confined to Brother Island for over two decades."

"Okay," I said, "but what does that have—"

"Public health advances eliminated the need to quarantine people in large numbers, so following World War II, the island housed war veterans attending local colleges, and in the late 1950s, the hospital was used as a center to treat teenage drug addicts."

A hot flash ran up my spine at the mention of teenage drug addicts, and I shivered at the thought of being held on some creepy island in an old and undoubtedly haunted smallpox hospital.

"Brother Island was abandoned in the sixties," Elton continued, "and though several New York mayors have proposed uses for it, the island has been off-limits to the public for half a century and until recently served as a sanctuary for herons and other wading shorebirds."

"So … your dad was birdwatching?" Axl guessed, and this time I couldn't help but laugh.

"Negative," Elton huffed. "Two years ago, a wealthy developer named Sachin Patel persuaded the city to let him build several high-rise condominiums on North Brother Island."

"Persuaded how?" Axl asked.

"With money, I suspect," Elton said.

"But what about the birds?" I asked.

Elton shrugged. "There is always South Brother Island. It is too small to develop."

"Okay," I said, "so this Patel guy bribed the city to build condos on Bird Island—"

"Brother Island," Elton corrected.

"Whatever. And your father was out there, why?" That money and bribes and powerful developers were involved had raised my antennae, and I had to fight back the intrusive thoughts that Elton too might somehow be in danger.

"Father and Sachin Patel are business associates," Elton said, just as the news program cut to an interview with the developer, a handsome, brown-skinned man with the slightest British accent. He looked nice enough, but nice-looking men had tried to kill me several times of late. "It's a setback, for sure," Sachin said to the reporter. "And we're all wishing Mustang a quick recovery. But construction continues, and the Blades of Brother Island will open as scheduled, their iconic silhouettes adding to the city's—"

"The Blades of Brother Island?" I asked Elton.

"Affirmative," Elton said. "The three high-rise towers will be shaped like gigantic, fifty-story curved blades. Hence the name."

"And your father literally got stabbed there?"

"That is only a coincidence," Elton said.

"Probably," I agreed, though I'd long stopped believing in coincidences.

CHAPTER FOUR

"Tuesday greetings," Elton said, stomping into my bedroom. It was 7 a.m., and I groaned and threw pillows at him.

"Mother serves breakfast in half an hour," Elton announced, lifting the window shades, oblivious to my drowsy protests. "And breakfast," he added, "is the most important meal of the day."

"You told me breakfast is no more important than any other meal," I groaned, covering my head with my comforter and hiding like a vampire from the sunshine Elton let in.

"Scholarship differs," Elton said, leaving the room but not before flipping on the lights.

"Second shower," Axl shouted from the neighboring bedroom, and I didn't have the energy to argue, so I shot a bird in his general direction and stumbled into the bathroom.

Taking a pill every morning was now such a part of my daily routine I did it instinctively. That warm, everything's gonna be alright feeling I got when the drug hit my bloodstream was as much a part of waking up as brushing my teeth or washing my face. I expected it. Anticipated it. Needed it. And I got a little freaked out when I thought about life without it. But that wasn't an issue, thanks to my steady stream of income and the not-so-good people at the Panhandle Pain Clinic.

OxyContin was developed to give relief to patients with severe pain, which, technically, I did not have. Sure, my headaches were awful and debilitating when they came, but I'm talking about non-stop chronic pain. Like shattered both legs in a car accident pain or wrenched your back operating heavy machinery at the factory pain. OxyContin works by targeting opioid receptors in the brain to block the feeling of pain for twelve hours. Twelve glorious hours. And when the pain returns, patients take their next pill. But since I often had no underlying pain to reemerge when my morning pill wore off, I just felt exhausted in the evenings. Hollowed out and spent. A little anxious. A little depressed. Some nights, I'd take a second pill to feel like myself again. Some nights, I'd crash and fall asleep.

I'd kept this routine for four months now, since we moved back to Dandridge. It was twice as long as I'd taken the pills in Bardo, and if I tried to stop now, I'd feel worse than shit. Just the thought of quitting gave me heart palpitations. But why would I stop? My prescription was legal, and I was thriving. I didn't know the 20 mg pill I took every morning soon wouldn't do its job quite so well. I didn't know a lot of things. But I did know a little dry mouth and constipation (sorry, it's true) were a small price to pay to feel the way I did. To finally feel like life was something you could live, not just survive.

"So, what's on the agenda today?" I asked Elton as we sat around the breakfast table, watching Lower Manhattan come to life in the morning sun.

"Something indoors, I hope," Axl said. Temperatures would climb above freezing that afternoon, but only for about an hour.

"We are visiting Kanner Academy," Elton announced.

"You're taking us to school during Christmas break?" Axl asked, incredulous at the thought of going anywhere near a school when you didn't have to.

"Elton, love, I'm afraid your school is closed for the holidays," Holly said.

"Negative. Kanner Academy is open 365 days a year for students wishing to access the laboratories, library, and study rooms." Elton raised a hand to silence Axl's pending protest. "However, we are not going to study. Kanner is a convenient location to meet my friends and introduce them to Izzy and Axl."

"Well, remember," Holly said, winking at me, "Izzy and Axl are your guests, and they didn't come all this way to watch you and your schoolmates play Pokémon."

When Elton expressed his intentions to let us participate in all card games, Axl shot me a look, but all I could do was shrug.

The walk from Elton's apartment to High Street station took only six minutes, but it felt much longer, with Axl complaining about the temperature every step of the way. But if my brother was out of his element on the cold Brooklyn streets, he was on a different planet altogether once we boarded the A train for Manhattan. Not that I was an expert, but three months of taking the Tube in London left me somewhat prepared for the sights, sounds, and smells of the New York City Subway.

"Are you sure this is safe?" Axl whispered a dozen times on our ten-minute trip under the river and into the city.

"No," I teased, guiltily enjoying watching the big baby flinch every time the train clattered so loud he thought it might fall apart.

The truth was, I felt perfectly safe on the train, even if a man in a Knicks jersey and pink tutu spent the duration of our trip meowing at us. I felt safe because I was with Elton Jones-Davies, my best friend in the world and the boy who'd saved my life with such frequency of late it was like having a superhero on retainer. Watching him purchase our MetroCards and guide us through the underground maze to our train, I marveled at how much he'd changed since summer. Elton was growing up. Maturing. And for the first time, I could envision him going off to college. Living on his own one day without Holly. Meeting someone and getting married. It made me happy ... and sad. One of the two devils on my shoulders (apparently I didn't get an angel) reminded me another pill would take that sadness away, but I told him to pipe down, something I had to do a lot of these days.

Kanner Academy occupied the top four floors of a hundred-year-old six-story building on Franklin Street near the Ghostbusters Headquarters in Tribeca. We entered with Elton's keycard and took an elevator to the top floor, stepping out into a brightly lit corridor of glass-walled classrooms and laboratories. Having attended St. Beckham's in London, I was used to schools not looking exactly like schools. But this place, as Axl put it, "looked like where James Bond goes to get all his new gadgets."

"The meeting is in Conference Room A," Elton announced, stomping down the hallway while we struggled to keep pace.

"What meeting?" I called after him.

"You will see," he said, and after typing a six-digit code into the door, we entered to find two kids already seated at a long glass table. Elton took a seat, motioned for us to join him, then called the meeting to order by saying, "Introductions."

"Milo Klink," said a small, freckled boy with thick glasses and a 9x9 Rubik's Cube in his hand. "I specialize in computers and numbers, both concrete and abstract."

"Nice to meet you," I said to Milo, who was wearing a T-shirt featuring his own face.

"Please hold your pleasantries until after introductions," Elton scolded me.

"Kadambari Patel," said a beautiful dark-skinned girl while staring daggers through me. "Most Americans butcher my name, so you can call me Kari. I play four instruments, speak ten languages, and scored 1600 on the SAT with minimal preparation."

All that and humility to spare, I thought. "Nice to meet you," I said, extending my hand.

Kari ignored it, and added, "I am also Elton Jones-Davies's girlfriend."

"Girlfriend," I repeated, then shoved Elton so hard he almost fell out of his chair. "You didn't tell me you had a girlfriend?"

"We do not talk often enough for me to share such intimate details of my personal life," Elton said, which was a total lie, but then I realized he'd said this to Kari, who'd crossed her arms after I shoved him. Holy shit, she was totally jealous of me, and Elton was scared of her. I prayed after this morning I would never have to see this girl again.

"Milo, Kari," Elton said, nervously returning to his introductions, "these are my friends Izzy and Axl from Florida. Their mother named them after members of Guns N' Roses."

Axl and I waved uncertainly as Elton pulled several folders and a MacBook from his backpack and said, "Time to work."

"Hold on, Elton," Axl said, "remember, your mom said no Pokémon."

"We are not playing Pokémon," Elton said in his most serious tone. "We are investigating my father's attempted murder."

DENZEL DAVIS

Mrs. Templeton didn't know any better when she sat Denzel Davis and Terrance Jones at the same table on their first day of kindergarten at John A. Gibson School in 1969. But sixty seconds later, after the boys had broken into their markers and written every swear word they knew on their classmates' arms, legs, and faces, she knew she was in for nine months of hell.

School administrators wisely separated the boys in first grade, meaning only the PE teacher had to deal with them simultaneously. However, Terrance and Denzel still found ways to make mischief, and after school, they tore through the alphabet streets like two miniature tornadoes. The boys grew so close they even failed fourth grade together, Denzel later claimed on purpose, so they could have an extra year of beating the hell out of a third-grade boy who made fun of Terrance's shoes.

Both boys credited football with saving their lives. At Pensacola High School, Terrance played running back and linebacker. Denzel, the larger of the two by thirty pounds, played fullback and wrought havoc at defensive end. Dalton Wolfe, a wealthy Florida developer, wanted both boys to play for Bardo Academy, the ultra-exclusive private school he'd built in Walton County. But Dalton knew parents would raise hell if he brought in one black kid to play football. If he brought in two, they'd revolt and leave in droves. Terrance got the scholarship, and Denzel stayed at Pensacola High.

There were hurt feelings.

Resentment.

Envy.

The boys had always dreamed about playing college football together. However, when Terrance committed to Florida State, Denzel called Jimmy Johnson and committed to rival Miami. In Tallahassee, Terrance won the 1987 Heisman Trophy, but in Miami, Denzel won three of his four matchups against his old friend and a National Championship.

As fate would have it, the Houston Oilers had two first-round draft picks in April. With their first pick, they selected Denzel, and with their second pick, Mustang Jones. The two stood nose to nose backstage that night in New York, bystanders scrambling to either run from or break up the inevitable brawl. But to everyone's surprise, both men burst into laughter that turned into tears. They'd made it. Out of the alphabet streets. Out of poverty.

Hatchets were buried.

Olive branches were extended.

Bygones were bygones.

When Mustang married Holly Davies in London, Denzel was the best man. Terrance returned the favor when Denzel married Stacey, an Oilers cheerleader Mustang had set him up with. Denzel played ten seasons with the Oilers, retiring as the franchise's sacks leader and a first-ballot hall-of-famer. Mustang's career was cut short by injury after six seasons, but fortune smiled on him again, and he made more money in retirement than he ever made carrying a football.

Over the next decade, the two men saw less of each other. Family life kept them busy, as did their second careers—Mustang selling grills and Denzel pastoring the East Village church he started after finding religion during the Y2K scare. But Mustang still made time to see Stacey, Denzel's wife. He'd been seeing her on and off for twenty years.

Since Houston.

Before introducing her to Denzel.

And after.

Denzel wouldn't find out Stacey and Mustang were seeing each other on the side until 2008. Divorce was out of the question. It would destroy his ministry; besides, he'd had his flings too. Before finding God, and after. But still, what Mustang did was unforgivable, and it erupted a volcano of resentment that had lain dormant for decades.

Denzel wanted payback.

He wanted Old Testament vengeance.

He wanted Karma to do her thing.

And now, with Mustang Jones comatose in a hospital bed, Denzel Davis just had to hide his smile.

CHAPTER FIVE

"Dammit, Izzy, not again," Axl said, letting his head fall onto the conference room table with a thud.

"This wasn't my idea. I swear. Elton, tell him this wasn't my idea."

"This was not Izzy's idea," Elton said.

"It was mine," Kari Patel said, but Axl wouldn't look up. He kept his head on the table, pulling at his hair in frustration.

"Elton," I said, putting a hand on my friend's shoulder, which he tolerated for two seconds, "the police will figure out who hurt your dad."

"I beg to differ," Kari said. "The police did not solve Ricky Lee's murder. Elton did."

"Well, I did, and Elton helped," I said. "But this is the freaking NYPD. They have their own hats and T-shirts and everything."

"Scotland Yard did not solve the Red Lion Bombing," Kari said. "Elton did."

"Again, Elton helped, but I did most of the—"

"Elton solved Vance Fuller's murder as well," Kari said, ignoring me completely, "and with his help, I will solve this one."

I turned to Elton, but he wouldn't look at me.

"Look," I said, turning back to Kari, "this isn't fun and games. Sure, we solved three murders, but we almost got killed all three times."

"I laugh in the face of danger," said Milo Klink, though the crack in his voice said he'd be more likely to wet his pants in the face of danger. "Besides, Kari told us solving a murder will set our college applications apart."

"Okay, first off," I said, "Mustang Jones is still alive, so you're not solving a murder. And second, aren't you all like super geniuses? You won't have a problem getting into college."

"My older sister, Lakshmi, finished high school with a 4.82 weighted GPA," Kari said.

"Good lord, how is that even possible?" I asked.

"She scored a perfect 1600 on her SAT," Elton's new girlfriend continued, ignoring me again, "finished sixth at the International Science and Engineering Fair, was the seventeenth-ranked female chess player in the United States, interned with New York City's most prestigious law firm, captained her varsity volleyball team, and was voted homecoming queen ... twice."

"Wait, why aren't male and female chess players ranked together?" I asked.

"That is not the point," Kari snapped. "The point is, Lakshmi's first choice school was Harvard, and she was waitlisted."

"The horror," Axl said, raising his head momentarily before dropping it back on the table.

"Waitlisted!" Kari shouted, and we all flinched.

"Okay," I said, raising my hands to show Kari I came in peace, "that's crazy about your sister, but I'm sure she still got into a good college, right?"

"She graduated from Princeton with a degree in molecular biology and now attends The Johns Hopkins University School of Medicine. But again, that is not the point. I will not be waitlisted by Harvard or anyone else."

"Right," I said, because Kari didn't seem like the sort of girl I wanted to argue with.

"Listen, guys," Axl said, lifting his head again and letting out a long sigh. "Izzy and I are here for Christmas break. We just want to see the Rockettes, maybe try ice skating, and avoid any and all interactions with attempted murderers." My brother turned to me for confirmation and added, "Right?"

The others looked at me, waiting for a response; however, that Kari's sister had compiled perhaps the greatest academic record of all time and still didn't get into her school of choice momentarily paralyzed me with panic. Sure, my grades were up this year, and I'd improved my ACT score a couple of points, but I wasn't even in the same universe as this girl. As for the rest of my résumé, I could intern with Tanner Cobb, the most prestigious shirtless lawyer in Cowden, Florida. But I'd never captain a varsity sport, didn't even know the rules of chess, and would definitely never be voted homecoming queen. Dammit to hell. I was never getting into college.

"Huh?" I asked.

"I said we didn't come to New York to solve a crime," Axl repeated, his face pleading with me.

"Right," I said, mainly to Milo, because eye contact with Kari made my heart race. "We've got lots of touristy shit planned. The Empire State Building. The Golden Gate Bridge. All that stuff."

"The Golden Gate Bridge is in San Francisco," Milo corrected.

"Then whatever bridge you guys are famous for," I said.

"I told you she wouldn't help," Kari barked at Elton. "But we don't need her. You solved those three murders, and we can solve this case."

My annoyance with this girl finally outgrew my fear of her, and I snapped. "No, Kari, Elton, and I solved those three cases together, and neither of us could have done it alone. But we were lucky every time. Lucky the cops were crooked or the killers were dumb, and lucky we didn't die. Have you ever had a gun pointed at you? I have. I've been held at gunpoint twice in the past twelve months. Once by my boyfriend's mom and once by a crazy, rich stoner."

"Four times," Elton said, speaking up for the first time in a while. "Buster McClellan held us at gunpoint."

"True," I said, snapping my fingers and pointing at him. "But I don't count that one since he's our friend now. Who's the fourth one?"

"Ethan Taylor."

"Oh yeah," I said with a laugh. "I forgot Ethan had a gun since he planned to kill us with a bomb."

Milo, who laughs in the face of danger, whimpered and sank into his seat, but Kari was unmoved.

"And don't forget you fell off the side of Twilight Rock and nearly died," I said, the memory of Elton tumbling off the mountain tightening my chest and sending a cold shiver down my spine. It was no wonder it took a few more pills these days to make me feel normal. I'd experienced a lifetime of trauma in the last twelve months. If I had a therapist, they'd likely frown on my going down this road again.

"And don't forget my life was absolutely perfect in Bardo until you two kicked a hornet's nest and got us thrown out of town," Axl said, and I realized there was some actual anger behind his feigned exasperation.

"You're currently quarterback of the state championship team with a dozen cheerleaders lined up outside your bedroom," I said. "It's turned out okay for you."

"But I'm not living in a beach house," Axl said, which I couldn't argue with.

"Don't worry," I said to Axl. "We're not going to spend our Christmas vacation solving crimes."

"I told you we don't need her," Kari repeated through gritted teeth.

Elton turned back to me, his eyes pleading for help. It was apparent his new girlfriend would make him investigate his father's attempted murder whether I helped or not. But if I did help them, I could at least keep Elton safe. Maybe. Either way, I owed it to him for all he'd done for me. Besides, I missed him, and if this is what I had to do to spend time with him, so be it.

"Never mind, I'll help," I said, and Axl's head fell to the table again. The slightest smile flashed across Elton's face, and I asked, "But do you even have any suspects?"

"We have one," Kari said, and the room grew quiet like it was expecting a drumroll. "My father."

CHAPTER SIX

"Elton, can we, uh, have a word? Outside."

Elton looked to Kari for permission, and after she nodded, we left the conference room to talk in the hallway.

"Okay, a couple of things," I said, trying to wrap my brain around everything I'd just heard. "First of all, you—"

"Always accuse you of looking for dirt on your significant others' parents," Elton said, "and now my significant other's father is our prime suspect?"

"Actually, no, I hadn't even thought of that yet. But now that you mention it, yeah, you do always accuse me of—"

"Because you do," Elton interrupted. "Blaine Park, Marco Lane, Sterling Masters."

"And one of their parents was a murderer," I said, counting on my fingers. "That's 33 percent."

"I am aware of how percentages work, Izzy. What I am trying to tell you is I did not suggest my girlfriend's father tried to murder my father. Kari suggested it."

"Wait, really? Why?"

"Because our fathers are business associates."

"Your father has a thousand business associates. That doesn't mean anything. But more importantly, why didn't you tell me you had a girlfriend?"

"I wanted to surprise you," Elton said, smiling broadly. "Do you like her?"

No, not at all, I thought. "No, not at all," I said before I could stop myself.

Elton's face dropped, and I felt shitty, so I lied, "I'm just kidding, Elton. She's lovely. But you're not letting her boss you around too much, right?"

"I am not," Elton said. "We occasionally disagree, but Kari is brilliant and always helps me see the error in my thinking."

"Oh, I'm sure she does," I mumbled, but Elton didn't hear me. "Okay, well, I hadn't planned on spending my Christmas vacation helping you solve a crime, but I suspect I won't see much of you if I don't, right?"

"Mother will insist I come home in the evenings," Elton said, "but this case is turning cold, and the A-Team needs to—"

"The A-Team?" I asked.

"Affirmative. *The A-Team* was an action-adventure television series on NBC from 1983 to 1987 about former members of a fictitious special forces unit. Kari, Milo, and I have adopted their moniker. However, in our case, the *A* stands for autism."

I smiled because how could I not?

"Fine," I said, "I'll help you guys. Besides, scouring New York City for clues is probably as good a way to experience the sights and sounds as one of those tour buses. But listen, I don't think busting into your girlfriend's dad's house and accusing him of stabbing your father is such a great idea."

"It sounds exactly like something you would do," Elton replied.

"True," I conceded with a laugh. "And it may come to that, but let's wait until we have more proof than Kari said so."

"Okay," Elton huffed, though I could tell he was angry I'd already disagreed with his girlfriend's theory on whodunit. "Where do you think we should start then?"

"I don't know," I said, trying to think of somewhere we could go that would provide the illusion of investigating, while also keeping us out of any danger. "Could we get into your dad's apartment? Snoop around his office? Maybe there's a note on his desk reminding him to meet Tessio and Clemenza on Brother Island the night he was stabbed."

"Tessio and Clemenza were fictional characters from *The Godfather*, Izzy. However, with over two million Italian-Americans living in the greater New York metro area, it is possible he—"

"Elton, I was joking. But we should start at your dad's place. Do you have a key to his apartment?"

"Negative," Elton said, holding up a key. "But I have a key to his elevator."

Kari paid for a cab, and we all went downstairs and piled in. Well, all of us except Milo, whose parents wouldn't allow him to go anywhere besides Kanner Academy unaccompanied. On the drive we passed through trendy SoHo and the tree-lined avenues of Greenwich Village before heading north along the West Side Highway where the skyline towered over the Hudson River. I realized this city was actually dozens of cities smashed together in some sort of fascinating urban collage, and I tried to envision my life if I lived here, but intrusive thoughts about how agreeing to another investigation would likely soon find me staring down the barrel of another gun kept getting in the way. As the bustling city eventually gave way to the quieter, residential streets of the Upper West Side, I cracked my window, hoping cold semi-fresh air would ward off the rising panic.

Mustang Jones lived on the upper floor of the Majestic, a nearly hundred-year-old apartment building on Central Park West. A doorman recognized Elton outside, chatting him up under the awning about his famous father, offering well wishes and cursing whoever stabbed the former football star.

"We intend to apprehend the suspect," Elton told the doorman, because of course he did. "We are here to look for clues."

"Well, Ms. Martin is home, but I'm sure she won't mind you looking for clues," the doorman said with a chuckle before letting us in from the cold.

We passed through the Art Deco doors and into the swanky lobby, and after another doorman ushered us onto an elevator, I asked Elton, "Who is Ms. Martin?"

"Father's girlfriend," Elton said, and I could tell by his tone he didn't really care to talk about her.

"So, uh, any celebrities live around here?" I asked, trying to change the subject.

"This building was once home to several heads of the Luciano crime family," Elton said after using his key to unlock his father's floor on the elevator. "Lucky Luciano, Frank Costello, and Meyer Lansky, among others."

"All of them less sketchy than your father," I said, and Elton considered this for several seconds before realizing it was a joke and laughing too loud.

"In 1957, Vincent 'The Chin' Gigante shot Frank Costello in the lobby of this building," Kari said, adding with some disappointment, "but he survived."

"Have any non-mafia-related celebrities lived here?" Axl asked.

"Conan O'Brien lives here now," Elton said, "And Yoko Ono lives across the street."

"No shit? Have you met her?" I asked.

"Twice," Elton said but didn't elaborate.

The elevator door opened, and we entered a massive corner living room with a panorama of Central Park views. For a poor girl from the Florida panhandle, I'd stepped into my share of swanky homes in the past eighteen months, but this one was on another level. Granted, I knew next to nothing about home decor not available at Big Lots, but everything in this place, from the rugs to the furniture to the paintings on the walls, looked like Mustang Jones told his interior decorator, "I'd like whatever costs the most."

"Holy hell, Elton," I said, as the four of us spread out into the room.

"My father's home is nicer," Kari said.

"Affirmative," Elton agreed. "Kari's father's home is nicer."

"No, not that," I said. "Your dad really likes nude paintings."

There were six or seven in the living room alone, all gigantic, all of the same gorgeous blonde woman, and all so lifelike I wasn't sure where to look. On the other hand, Axl knew precisely where to look, and after examining one of the paintings like he was the curator of the Louvre, my brother asked, "Hold on, Elton—is your dad's girlfriend Jade Martin, the *Sports Illustrated* swimsuit model?"

"Yes, she is," said the gorgeous blonde from the paintings, walking into the room wearing leggings and a shirt so sheer she might as well have not been wearing one at all. "And Elton, dear, you know you're supposed to call before visiting."

"I am supposed to call my father before visiting," Elton said. "However, he is currently in Mount Sinai Hospital in a medically induced coma."

"Hi, I'm Axl," Axl said, offering Jade Martin a hand she ignored.

"Well, you can call me now because I can't have a bunch of weird kids showing up here all hours of the day." At this, she and Kari seemed to exchange a look I couldn't quite read.

"I will do no such thing," Elton said with more force than I'd ever seen him talk back to an adult. "This is my father's apartment, not yours, and I will come and go as I please. And now, my friends and I are going to—"

"Elton," I started, "no need to tell her—"

"Going to search his office for clues so we can bring his attacker to justice."

And now Jade knew why we were here, which wasn't great, because as Mustang's girlfriend, she'd typically be high on my suspect list. I didn't have a good reason for her sticking a knife in Mustang's chest, but I had little doubt Mustang was capable of providing several. Still, I'd rather my suspects not know they are suspects because I don't want them going on the defensive before I ever asked a question. Now all I could do was read Jade's face as she digested Elton's words, looking for any sign of panic. But she literally yawned in our faces before rolling her eyes and saying, "Well, make it quick. My masseuse will be here at noon, and I want you all gone."

CHAPTER SEVEN

Jade Martin led us into Mustang's office off the living room behind a bookcase that slid away at the push of a button.

"Bitching," Axl said as we entered a room that looked like an annex of the NFL Hall of Fame in Canton, Ohio. Framed jerseys, programs, and magazines covered every inch of the walls, footballs and helmets lined the bookshelves, and a cardboard cutout of the former running back holding one of his famous fat-burning grills stood watch over us from the corner.

Jade went straight to Mustang's cluttered desk while the rest of us stood around and gawked, and after shuffling through some papers, she slid something into a manila folder and turned for the door.

"Something you don't want us to see?" I asked before Jade made her escape.

The swimsuit model's eyes narrowed, but then she forced a laugh and said, "Just some Polaroids I took for Mustang. I thought it would be awkward for Elton to find nude photographs of his future mother."

Axl, who was standing in silent awe before Mustang's Heisman

Trophy, spun around at the mention of nude photographs, and Jade winked at him, turning my stupid brother to a stuttering heap of testosterone.

"Even if my father marries you," Elton said, "which is unlikely considering I have heard him tell you on four separate occasions he'd rather eat a subway rat than marry again, you would be my step-mother, not my mother."

"So you do want to see these?" Jade teased, waving the folder at Elton. I lunged for it, but Jade snatched it away at the last second and snapped, "Ten minutes, and I want you all out of here."

With Jade gone, the four of us got to work sorting through the mess of unopened mail, contracts, and sundry legal documents that might as well have been written in Mandarin Chinese.

"Okay, y'all are the detectives," Axl said, showing us a brochure for erectile dysfunction pills before tossing it on the floor, "what exactly am I looking for?"

"Incriminating evidence on my father," Kari said, tearing into Mustang's mail.

I squinted at her and said, "Look, Kari, I know you're like, lit-erally the smartest kid in America or whatever, but I can say from more experience than I wish I had that settling on a suspect first, then looking for evidence against them, isn't the best way to go about solving a crime."

"I can attest," Elton said. "Izzy has tried that method several times, and it always sets us back." Kari glared at Elton, so he added, "Though, I suppose, past performance does not guarantee future results."

I opened Mustang's American Express bill and marveled at

$67,431 in charges over the past thirty days. But before I could look for anything suspicious, Kari took the bill from me and said, "Izzy, I know Elton's mother invited you to New York for Christmas, and he was too kind to tell you not to come. But we do not want you here, and we do not need your help implicating my father in this crime."

I glanced at Elton, who wouldn't dare meet my eyes, before turning back to Kari and asking, "So, are you, like, mad at your father?"

"I am not," Kari said matter-of-factly. "Father is loving and kind. He has provided a stable home and rarely interferes with my social life."

"But you want him convicted of attempted murder?" I asked.

"It's not a matter of what I want," Kari said, not hiding her annoyance with me. "Father and Mustang Jones were business associates, but their deal soured, and on the night in question, I heard my father express his desire for Mustang Jones to die a gruesome and most painful death."

"Izzy wishes that on me every other day," Axl said, giving up on the investigation and trying on Mustang's Houston Oilers helmet.

"That's true," I said to Kari with a shrug. "Doesn't mean I'd stab him."

"My father stabbed Mustang Jones," Kari said, jabbing a finger into my chest and pushing me backward. "And when I write about solving this crime for my Harvard essay, they will have no choice but to accept me."

Jade Martin wanted us out in ten minutes, so I didn't have time to stop and process all this, but I couldn't help myself. I'd been around plenty of Type A personalities; I even had some of those traits myself, but this girl was on a whole other level and willing to throw her own flesh and blood under the bus to get what she wanted. Then again, maybe I was no better. I would never willingly implicate my family in a crime. Well, maybe my father back before he got in my good graces, but not anymore. Still, my investigations had cost my family plenty. I'd hurt Axl and Mom over and over, yet here I was, at it again. Someone who learned from their mistakes would have grabbed Elton and Axl and gone back to Brooklyn and enjoyed the rest of their Christmas vacation without a second thought to solving an attempted murder. But I'm apparently not someone who learns from their mistakes, and the devils on my shoulders whispered in both ears that the only thing better than solving this crime would be solving it and proving Kari wrong at the same time.

"So let me get this straight. You're okay sending your father to prison for life if it gets you into Harvard."

"Yes, Izzy, please try and keep up," Kari said, rolling her eyes at me. Then, perhaps noticing the horror on my face, she added, "I would not like to see my father, or anyone, convicted of a crime they did not commit. However, my father did commit this crime, and if I can benefit personally from implicating him, I will not hesitate to do so."

I turned to Axl to see if he'd heard this shit, but he was now throwing imaginary passes with one of Mustang's game balls. Looking back at Kari, who was halfheartedly shuffling through some of Mustang's papers, I wondered if she was lying. If she wanted something so badly that she'd eagerly send her father to prison, setting him up to look guilty wasn't much of a leap. Under normal circumstances I'd mention this hunch to Elton, but I already knew he wouldn't like it one bit.

I got back to work sorting through Mustang's mail, noticing several letters were from the same place. "Looks like your dad has done a

lot of business with something called Spencer Investment Securities,"
I said, holding up an envelope for Elton to see.

"That's Arnie Spencer's company," Kari said. "Everyone in the
city invests with him. Those aren't important."

I ignored Kari and opened the envelope, which Elton quickly
reminded me was a violation of U.S. Code 1702—Obstruction of
correspondence, and punishable by up to five years in federal prison.
"Tanner Cobb would get me off," I said, taking a look at Mustang's
statement.

"Unlikely," Elton said.

Even though Dandridge High School dropped personal finance
in lieu of a bass fishing class, I could see Mustang's investment returns
were astronomical. "Holy hell, your dad is rich," I said.

"Affirmative," Elton said.

"But who is Anders Larsson?" I asked, pointing to the in-care-of
name at the top of the statement.

"Anders is my father's assistant," Elton said. "He is from Sweden,
hence the name."

"Okay, he's definitely someone we need to talk to."

Kari huffed, annoyed I'd suggested something that didn't involve
her father's immediate arrest and imprisonment.

"And can you log into your father's computer?" I asked Elton,
pointing at the MacBook on his desk.

"He does not trust me with his password," Elton said.

"Well, could we take his laptop to Kanner Academy and see if
Milo could hack into it?"

Elton wasn't thrilled with this plan but didn't argue when I
stuffed the computer into my bag.

"Okay, children, Javier is here, so it's time to leave," Jade Martin said, standing in the doorway as an obscenely hot man stood behind her, rubbing her shoulders and kissing her neck. "You can show yourselves out," she added as the four of us shuffled past.

As Jade and Javier went to the bedroom for her massage, Axl and I followed Kari and Elton through the living room toward the private elevator. Axl first noticed the manila folder Jade had taken from Mustang's office lying atop the grand piano. I watched as he peeked back down the hallway to ensure Jade hadn't followed us, then he slowly opened the folder, eyes wide in anticipation.

"Naked Polaroids, my ass," he mumbled, tossing the folder back on the piano and moping past me toward the door.

I laughed and turned to follow but realized if Jade wasn't hiding dirty pictures, I needed to know what was in the folder. Walking back to the piano and checking over my shoulder, I quickly opened the folder. Inside was a single piece of fancy stationery with "From the desk of Sachin Patel" printed across the top. There was a series of numbers scribbled on the top of the page, but it was the message at the bottom that made my jaw drop.

Pay up, asshole, or your life is over.

CHAPTER EIGHT

It's hard to say precisely why I didn't share with the others what I found in the folder at Mustang's apartment. I like to think it's because Kari had already zeroed in on her father as the culprit. Like Old Man Fuller back in Ashes, she'd started with the suspect in mind, then looked for clues to prove she was right. I knew any evidence, no matter how circumstantial, pointing toward Sachin Patel would only push Kari further in that direction, possibly to the case's detriment. I was also, I'll admit, a little jealous of her. Jealous of her relationship with Elton. Jealous she'd seemingly replaced me in his life. So as sure as Kari was her father stabbed Mustang Jones, I decided to be equally sure he did not, if for no other reason than to be contrarian. Perhaps not the most effective way to run an investigation, but I was on vacation and didn't want to investigate anything anyway, so shut up.

We got back to Elton's Brooklyn apartment around dusk, and Axl and I had to lie and tell our mother a bunch of touristy shit we'd done, pretending we hadn't spent most of the day investigating an attempted murder. I hated lying to Mom, but I did it so much now the guilt was short-lived.

"So, first impressions of Kari?" Holly asked over dinner—pizza from Di Fara that a concierge picked up because none of us felt like venturing into the cold evening.

"She's hot," Axl said through a mouthful of pepperoni, and Mom and I hit him simultaneously.

"Well, she is," my brother said with a shrug, and Holly laughed.

"Izzy, your thoughts?" Holly asked.

"She is very pretty," I said, which was no better than Axl's answer, but telling Holly I already hated her guts seemed inappropriate.

"I wouldn't know," Holly said. "Elton refuses to bring her round."

"Kari keeps a busy after-school schedule," Elton said. "Between test prep—"

"Test prep? Doesn't she already have a perfect SAT score?"

"Affirmative," Elton said. "However, most students with a perfect score stop there. Kari intends to submit several perfect SAT scores on her college application." I shook my head in both admiration and horror, and Elton continued, "Between test prep, lacrosse and cello practice, her internship at NYU, and her popular hair and makeup vlog, Kari has little time for socializing outside of school."

"Okay," I said, shaking my head at this girl's insane schedule, "but if you only see her in class, how is that even a relationship?"

"She is my girlfriend," Elton said, growing agitated. "She asked me to be her boyfriend, and I accepted. We enjoy each other's company and share several common interests."

"They're also up texting half the night," Holly added, and I felt a lump rise in my throat, because Elton hardly texted me at all these days.

"But no movie night snogfests like you had with Zadie Carrick?" I asked Elton, and he blushed.

I took comfort in the fact Elton and Kari weren't spending all their time making out, then felt shitty because it wasn't any of my business. Besides, it's not like I wanted to make out with Elton. If there was a worldwide ranking of teenage boys I wanted to kiss, he was just one spot above Axl. But Elton was my friend, and I worried about him, and, if I'm being honest, I didn't want to share him with Kari on this trip.

"Speaking of Zadie Carrick," I said with a grin, "what does she think about your new fling?"

Elton huffed in frustration, his love life not his favorite dinner topic, and said, "Zadie and I both believe we will end up together in the end, but seeing other people will only make us appreciate each other more in the future."

"They don't know about each other, do they?" I guessed.

"No," Elton said after a moment's hesitation, "and I would appreciate it if you helped me keep it that way."

That night, I lay in bed, staring at my phone, wondering how to respond to a series of texts from River Lewis, the boy I now begrudgingly referred to as my boyfriend. The texts began with a declaration of unconditional love followed by several apologies for making things awkward. River did this about once a week. I let out a heavy sigh and typed out my reply, then silenced my phone so I wouldn't see his reply until morning.

Me—Fun day in NYC. So much to see! I don't think two weeks will be long enough. Luv you.

Recently, I'd started signing off this way, mostly out of guilt. River had been proclaiming his love via text for weeks, and when I didn't reply in kind, I could imagine the soul-crushing disappointment on his face. And I did love him, I guess. He was sweet and funny and cute in a non-threatening way. His you-look-lovely-today-Mrs.-Brown schtick annoyed my mother. Otherwise, she'd likely let River sleep over without any worry about what we'd get up to. River didn't annoy me, but I sometimes found him exhausting. I mean, seriously, look at this text …

River—Every time I see you smile, I think my heart will explode. You're like oxygen, and without you, I can't breathe. You're perfect.

I got these all the time, and most of our arguments consisted of me trying to convince him I didn't deserve his adoration. The boy was mad about me, though, and the most I could offer in return was an affectionate misspelling of love.

I took a pill and a steaming hot shower, the new nightly ritual I sometimes began anticipating mid-afternoon. Two was my daily limit, though sometimes the devils on my shoulders whispered that a third would be understandable after a particularly shitty day. I suppose, on some level, I knew I was hooked again, but I justified it by telling myself people with diabetes were hooked on insulin. I needed these pills to survive. To function as a productive member of society. And like insulin, my pills were legal, and I took them roughly every twelve hours as prescribed. Some days, I even took less than prescribed, though those days were fewer and further between.

After showering, I turned on the television and began drowsily flipping through the channels. I was almost in dreamland when something on TMZ made me sit up straight in bed. Shaky video footage showed Denzel Davis leaving a New York City nightclub. He was intoxicated, and a couple of paparazzi snapped photographs and shouted questions.

"Rev. Davis, have you visited Mustang Jones in the hospital?"

"Next time I see Mustang Jones," Denzel said, striking a wobbly Heisman pose, "I hope he's in an open casket."

Holy hell, and this guy was supposedly a preacher? Of course I'd seen the Dandridge Church of God and Prophecy's associate pastor taking upskirt photos of cheerleaders at one of Axl's football games. Still, this was a much different tune than Denzel struck earlier that day when he tearfully spoke about how he and Mustang had been friends since kindergarten. I wasn't sure if Denzel had anything to do with the stabbing, but he definitely wanted Mustang dead, which made him a suspect in my book.

Now wide awake, I got up to tell Axl. His door wasn't closed, so I gently pushed it open in case he was asleep, and I saw my brother hunched over the writing desk in his room. I couldn't see exactly what he was doing, but when he lowered his head, snorted loudly, then looked to the heavens and shook his head violently, I had a good idea.

This wasn't good.

This wasn't good at all.

JADE MARTIN

You should have seen me in high school.

Jade Martin couldn't recall how many times she'd uttered those words. Strolling the red carpet at some fashion gala, movie premiere, or whatever else people roll out red carpets for these days. Photographers blinding her with flashbulbs, Jade blinding them in return with her radiant smile.

Who are you wearing tonight?

Versace.

And the necklace?

Vintage Cartier.

Then, inevitably, a comment on Jade's beauty. Her otherworldly, can't-look-away beauty. And Jade, who still couldn't believe this was her real life and not a dream, would say, "You should have seen me in high school."

She was tall then. Seemingly taller than she was now. Much taller than the other girls and half of the boys. Lanky was the kinder way of saying it. Gangly is what her mother called her. She had braces, of course. Wore glasses, of course. And her frizzy blonde hair was styled by the only hairdresser in her small Georgia town, a barber named Lester.

The talking heads on E! will sometimes look at Jade's sophomore yearbook photograph and pretend they can see the supermodel to come. Hints of her otherworldly beauty hiding beneath the teenage awkwardness. But they're lying. You can see no such thing; otherwise, at least one boy at Robert E. Lee High School would have taken a chance on Jade. Hedged their bets, as it were, and invited her to prom. But the boys avoided her, and now they rue the day.

Jade's freshman roommate at Georgia Southern made her over. Did her makeup. Tossed the glasses. Styled her hair.

Stop hunching.

But I'm too tall.

There's no such thing. Now, stand up straight.

Jade listened and then glimpsed herself in the mirror. My God, she was pretty. No, something more. Jade was stunning.

Next came modeling auditions at some big convention center in Atlanta. Jade's roommate drove her. Held her hand. Reminded her to stand tall and be confident. Every girl there was pretty, but Jade stood out. High cheekbones, aqua-blue eyes, and the precise measurements needed to meet the modern era's impossible standards of beauty. Six months later, Jade was walking a runway in Milan. Four years later, she was on the cover of the *Sports Illustrated* swimsuit issue. A week after that, she was in Mustang Jones's bed.

Mustang was old—well, forty, which seemed ancient to a girl in her early twenties. Still, he was handsome, treated Jade well, and most of all, made her feel secure.

Security meant everything to Jade because her fame felt so

random and fleeting. She feared it could disappear as quickly as it arrived. The guys she dated before Mustang—a couple of rock stars and an NBA rookie—spent their money like it would never stop rolling in, and this terrified Jade. Nothing scared her more than the prospect of returning to Georgia, no better off than she left. But with Mustang, she didn't have to worry, so when he asked her to give up her lucrative modeling career to be at his beck and call, she didn't hesitate.

Mustang was smart.

Mustang invested his millions.

Mustang was the answer. Until he wasn't.

When they met, Mustang was already talking about leaving his wife. But now it was happening. Lawyers were involved, and soon, Jade would be the next Mrs. Jones. Or so she thought until one drunken night when Mustang told her there was no way in hell he'd ever marry again. She was his girl, sure, but there was no need to sign any papers and make things more complicated than they had to be. He'd tried that once, he said, and it wasn't worth the hassle.

That night, Jade stood in the mirror, wiped off the tear-streaked mascara, and studied the lines on her face. Lines that weren't there the last time she strutted down a runway. She was twenty-eight now. Ancient. The peak of her beauty wasted. Forfeited. Which would have been a reasonable tradeoff for a big fat diamond. But now Jade's future was at the whims of something worse than fate and fortune. Her future was at the whims of a rich old man who liked chasing ass.

She needed a plan, an escape. But more than that, she had to prove she was still Jade Martin. Not the scared little girl from Georgia, but the badass bitch in the bikini and stilettos. And when she was finished with him, Mustang Jones would pay for every single second he'd stolen from her.

CHAPTER NINE

"Izzy, it is ten in the morning. You cannot spend the entire day in bed."

I sat up and blinked Elton into focus, then groaned as the day's headache slapped me upside the face.

"Wednesday greetings," Elton added with an awkward bow.

"Good morning," I mumbled in return, shaking my head and trying to remember why I felt so shitty. I'd only been hungover once in my life, back in Bardo, after drinking too many cups of home-made punch and making out with Blaine Park. This felt similar but worse, though I couldn't for the life of me remember what had made me—wait. Axl. Before going to bed last night, I'd seen Axl snorting something off the desk in his room, and I'd stayed up most of the night debating whether I should barge in and demand an explanation or run and tell Mom. I was too tired then, too scared maybe he'd have turned the tables back on me. Now, in the glaring light of day, I still wasn't sure if doing nothing was the coward's choice or the smart one. Dammit to hell.

I still did not share my mother's faith in Axl Rose Brown as our family's savior. There are hundreds of hotshot high school quarterbacks around the country, and only the tiniest fraction of them ever play in the NFL. But I couldn't deny my stupid brother seemed destined to play big-time college football on scholarship. At worst, he'd get a degree, and even if he missed the NFL, he'd find a job, and half our mother's problems would be solved. But not if he snorted shit off his desk every night. Not if my cowardice let him slide down the path to ruin. After falling asleep, my nightmares featured several versions of his arrest and dismissal from the Dandridge football team.

I stumbled into the bathroom, took a pill and a shower, and found my breakfast waiting on the counter, ready to nuke in the microwave. Mom and Holly were last-minute Christmas shopping that morning, so Axl, Elton, and I were free until the evening, when the five of us had tickets to see the Rockettes at Radio City Music Hall.

Axl and Elton were on the living room couch watching *SportsCenter*, dressed and ready for the day. I took the recliner beside them and picked at my toast and eggs. Axl looked … normal. Same as always, really. Maybe he snorted drugs all the time? Maybe he'd been shooting heroin since third grade? His normal appearance was both comforting and alarming.

SportsCenter transitioned from NBA highlights to a photograph of Denzel Davis, and the anchor, using his most serious news tone, said, "ESPN has suspended part-time NFL analyst, Rev. Denzel Davis, for inflammatory remarks Davis gave to paparazzi last night while leaving a holiday party in New York. In a written statement posted on Village Tabernacle's website, Davis said, in part, 'While I will not attempt to justify my remarks, Terrance and I have been friends since kindergarten, and we've always joked in ways some people might find offensive. If my words caused anyone harm or offense, I apologize. However, Terrance knows we are brothers for life, and he remains in my prayers.' Attempts to reach Rev. Davis for comment were unsuccessful."

"What did he say?" Axl asked.

"That the next time he saw Mustang, he hoped it was in an open casket," I said, and my brother nearly spit out his orange juice. I'd forgotten this was why I'd gone to see Axl last night in the first place.

"That's beyond messed up," my brother said. "What preacher would say something like that?"

"The sort who would ask his congregation to purchase him a Gulfstream jet for personal use," Elton said.

"Wait, for real?" I asked, and Elton nodded. "Okay, then we've got to talk to Rev. Davis."

"Denzel Davis did not stab my father," Elton said. "They are friends."

"Friends don't say shit like that about each other," I said. "I don't even think I have enemies I'd say that about."

"Blaine Park?" Axl offered.

I hesitated long enough for Axl to know he was right, then said, "You're not helping. If you're going to be a part of this investigation, you need to agree with everything I say."

Elton's phone rang, and he answered it with, "Wednesday greet— yes, my sincerest apologies. No, I am very sorry. No, you are correct. It is unforgivable, but Izzy overslept. We will leave now."

Half an hour later, we were back in Conference Room A at Kanner Academy with Kari and Milo, which I suppose was better than sitting around worrying about Axl spiraling out of control, but it still wasn't my idea of a vacation.

"Don't mind us, just get here when you can," Kari said, side-eyeing me. "Now, let's get to business."

"Okay, I'm not sure if you saw TMZ last night," I began, "but Denzel Davis—"

"We do not have time for celebrity gossip," Kari snapped, cutting me off mid-sentence. "Milo, please."

Milo Klink began passing out financial spreadsheets that I blinked at for several seconds.   "Milo, tell us what you see here," Kari said.

Milo cleared his throat and began. "Down this lefthand column, you will see a list of Kari's father's—"

"The suspect," Kari corrected, and Axl and I shot each other a look.

"Sorry, the suspect's investments," Milo said. "Most, as you can see, have done quite well, apart from the large red number two-thirds of the way down the page labeled 'SIS,' which stands for Spencer Investment Securities."

"Seven hundred and eighty million dollars," I said, coughing out the number.

"Cut the chatter, Izzy," Kari barked, then turned to Milo and said, "The calendar please."

Milo handed out another sheet, this one showing several months of Sachin Patel's daily schedule.

"As you can see," Milo began, "over these months, Mustang Jones persuaded Kari's father, excuse me, the suspect, to invest nearly eight hundred million dollars in Spencer Investment Securities."

"We see no such thing," I said. "All this shows is Sachin had lunch several times with someone named M. Jones. There's no mention of Spencer Investments, or eight hundred million dollars."

"Thank you, Milo," Kari said, ignoring all the holes I'd just poked in her case. "Now, please roll clip one."

Milo pressed a button on his laptop, and Sachin Patel appeared on the projector at the front of the room. The video was from a recent interview, and he looked exhausted. "No," Sachin says to the reporter, "unfortunately, construction has fallen behind again. There was another issue relocating the birds to South Brother Island, so we'll miss our targeted completion date of July 2010."

"As you can see," Kari said, "over the course of several weeks, Mustang Jones conned my father out of eight hundred million dollars, jeopardizing his latest business venture. This is undeniable proof my father stabbed Mustang Jones."

"Okay, first," I said, "Michael Jordan would be impressed at how far you jumped to this conclusion." Kari clenched her fists, and I pushed my chair back from the table a couple of feet to be safe. "And second, why is Mustang's account with Spencer Investments flush with cash if your dad lost everything?"

"Because Elton's father stole money from my father," Kari said.

I turned to Elton for a reaction, but he was unmoved. I guess we both knew his father was capable of any and all manner of crime.

"And my father stabbed him in retaliation," Kari continued. "Now please, Izzy, try and keep up."

Kari's condescension and overconfidence in her conclusions

flustered me to the point of silence. It wasn't that her logic made sense—quite the opposite—but arguing with someone so convinced of their own truth felt pointless. Sure, it appeared her father had lost a lot of money with Spencer Investments, and we knew Mustang had made a lot with the same firm, but that didn't constitute proof of theft. Besides, we knew Mustang's numbers were legit; we had authentic statements. Kari could have made her father's numbers up just to implicate him.

"Assuming your father's numbers are real—" I began, but Kari's fists clenched, ready for a brawl.

"Of course they're real," Kari snapped. "All the financial statements I provided Milo came directly from Father's laptop. I was able to access them because I've stolen all his passwords."

"Of course you have," I mumbled, shaking my head in disbelief. "But does Milo even understand those statements? He's not a tax attorney."

"My father owns a multinational pharmaceutical conglomerate," Milo said, "and I have prepared his taxes the last two years."

Good lord, I'd forgotten the caliber of kids I was dealing with here. "Fine, but—"

"It's settled," Kari said, apparently finished listening to me talk. "Let's go confront my father."

The others stood to leave, while I sat and stared at the ceiling. I didn't want to solve this stupid case to begin with, and now we were about to confront Sachin Patel, one of the wealthiest men in Manhattan, with almost no real evidence. This was going to be a shit show.

CHAPTER TEN

"You know this is a terrible idea, right?" I whispered to Elton on the cab ride to Patel Industries, which occupied an upper floor of the shiny new Bank of America Tower on Sixth Avenue.

"I know no such thing," Elton replied in something much louder than a whisper. "The evidence against Sachin Patel is damning."

Kari glanced over at the mention of her father, but she was too busy telling Axl about chronic traumatic encephalopathy and what repeated blows to the head were doing to his brain to ask us what we were talking about.

"He's worth investigating further, sure," I said, "but we've accused people of murder with more evidence than this and been dead wrong."

"Negative," Elton said. "You have falsely accused people of murder. I only stood by your side and winced."

I laughed because he wasn't wrong, and I spent several seconds trying to recall everyone I'd falsely accused. Dalton Wolfe, Junior Wolfe, Mason Driscoll, Tanner Cobb. And those were just the Bardo folks. My history of unfounded allegations stretched from the mountains of North Carolina all the way to London. "Okay, fine, I've accused people of murder with more evidence than this and been dead wrong, but you should have at least learned the same lessons as me due to your proximity."

Elton huffed, which was his way of conceding a point, and we sat quietly for a moment, listening to Axl and Kari.

"But I don't take repeated blows to the head. I was only sacked once last season, and even then, they got me by the ankle."

"You're not taking repeated blows now because you're a grown man playing against children," Kari said after patting him on the hand, and Axl frowned at the implication his accomplishments to date were achieved against toddlers. "But if you play professional football against four-hundred-pound behemoths, you will undoubtedly suffer repeated head trauma."

Maybe Kari's warning scared my brother, but I knew Axl would never show it, and after considering things for a moment, he said with a shrug, "But I'll be rich."

"True," Kari agreed. "You can afford one of the nicer assisted living facilities."

Not one to lose an argument with anyone, especially a football jock, Kari continued describing the symptoms of CTE, which occurred in stages and typically appeared decades after a person experienced repetitive mild traumatic brain injuries. "Confusion, disorientation, memory loss, dementia, speech impediments, vertigo, depression, and suicide."

That what I'd now begrudgingly admit was our family's most likely escape from poverty would cost my brother his health and shorten his life was very on brand for us. But what if Axl was already feeling the effects of too many shots to the head? What if snorting drugs was his way of dealing with all the symptoms Kari had spent the better part of a minute listing? I didn't think of my brother as a winning lotto ticket like Mom did, but we'd never make it without him. A familiar panic rose in my chest for the first time since I'd begun my steady regimen of self-medicating back in the summer, and I asked Elton if he'd mind cracking the window because I was suffocating.

Sweet Elton cracked the window and let in some arctic air. It helped a little, but I still couldn't shake the image of Axl drooling in a nursing home and Mom and me living out back behind the dumpster. Sensing I was upset, Elton said, "Out of over one million high school players, just 2.6 percent play NCAA Division I football, and only 1.5 percent of those players make it to the NFL."

"Thanks, Big E," I whispered, giving him a hug that Kari saw and disapproved of. "But we're still making a mistake accusing Sachin Patel of stabbing your dad. You're just too scared of your girlfriend to say anything."

The cab dropped us off outside the BofA Tower, and after Kari paid the driver, she took me by the wrist and led me toward the entrance.

"It's funny," she said, squeezing my arm too tight, "to have so much in common, Elton and I have some major differences. For instance, so long as you don't specifically address him, you can have a conversation right in front of him, and he won't hear a single word. But not me."

Shit.

"I am always listening. Always observing. And now, I have some observations for you."

Double shit.

"Elton is not scared of me. He respects me. He respects my intelligence, as should you. He's not going along with my plan to confront my father because he's my boyfriend. He's going along with my plan because he knows it's right."

I opened my mouth to argue, but Kari silenced me by raising a finger too close to my face.

"I know all about the cases you and Elton solved before he met me. I know how you bumbled through each investigation, falsely accusing innocent people, following dead-end leads, and making wrong turns until you accidentally went in the right direction. Elton likes you, Izzy, so I will try to tolerate you. But I will not let you compromise my investigation. This will be clean and professional. Something Harvard admissions will take note of. Not just a bunch of kids causing mischief. Understood?"

It took me a moment to let out a stunned, "Uh, yeah," but by then, Kari had already turned on her heel and marched into the building.

Inside, Elton, Axl, and I followed Kari through the cavernous lobby to a security checkpoint guarding a bank of elevators. Waiting in line, I mentally prepared myself to lie our way through this barricade of stern-looking men in dark suits. But Kari flashed a badge, and one of the men smiled and asked, "Here to see your father, Miss Patel?"

"I am here to confront him," Kari said.

The guard squinted at this but regained his composure and said with a smile, "Very well."

The offices of Patel Industries were sleek and modern, with a sea of cubicles surrounded by glass-walled offices featuring stunning

Manhattan skyline views and flooding the entire space with bright winter sunlight. The news was always going on about the Great Recession and the 10 percent unemployment rate, but there wasn't an empty cubicle in sight, and the cacophony of raised voices, ringing phones, and buzzing printers and fax machines led me to believe Patel Industries was still thriving. The reception desk looked like something from the Death Star, and unlike the guards downstairs, the receptionist frowned when she saw us. "Kari," she said with a long sigh, "your father is very busy today, and this isn't—"

"I'll scream again," Kari said, and the receptionist shook her head violently.

"No, dear, please. There's no need to cause another scene. Let me call back, and—"

While we waited, I wondered how many times Kari had walked into her father's place of business and begun screaming until she got her way. Judging by the panicked look on the receptionist's face, I'd guess more than once.

"Okay, your father will see you now," the receptionist said, motioning us toward the corner office. "But remember, Kari, he's a very busy man and—"

"Shut up, Tracy," Kari barked, and the three of us followed her through a row of cubicles to her father's office, the only one on the floor with mirrored privacy glass.

We walked in to see Sachin Patel standing behind his desk, talking on the phone. He held up a finger to let us know he'd be a second, and Axl and I walked over to marvel at the view from his floor-to-ceiling window. Below, people were ice skating in Bryant Park. I wanted to be down there with them, busting my butt and feeling the cold air on my face. Not up here with Kari, doing whatever it was we were about to do.

Finally, Sachin finished his call and flashed an exhausted smile. "Alright, Love, what couldn't wait? Come to accuse me of attempted murder again?"

CHAPTER ELEVEN

"Come to accuse me of attempted murder again?" Sachin Patel asked his daughter, who huffed in reply.

"Wait, again?" I asked.

"Yes, she's already accused me several times," he replied. "Most recently this morning over breakfast." The business mogul then squinted at me and asked, "And who might you be? You look a bit young for the NYPD."

"I'm Izzy Brown, and this is my brother, Axl. We're friends of Elton's, visiting from Florida."

"Ah, Elton's famous friend from Florida," Sachin said with a smile. "Kadambari mentioned you were in town. Are you here to accuse me of murder as well?"

"Not really," I said. "I'd like to be ice skating, but I got roped into—"

"We're not accusing you of murder, Daddy. It's attempted murder," Kari interrupted.

"That's right," he said, feigning an exaggerated sigh and lightly smacking his forehead. "Mustang Jones survived my vicious attack, so it's only attempted murder. With good behavior, I'll be out of prison in what—twenty years? I'll likely miss your wedding but should be out in time to see my grandchildren graduate high school."

Axl and I exchanged a wide-eyed glance, and Sachin laughed. "Izzy, Axl, judging by your bewildered expressions, I gather you've not spent much time around my youngest daughter. She's driven. Highly motivated, with intelligence to spare. She … perhaps doesn't exhibit the loyalty a father might hope for," he added with a wry smile in my direction, "however, she's mine, and I love her dearly."

Kari started to speak again, but her father silenced her with a raised palm and a patient smile. He then turned to me and continued, "I suppose it all began when Lakshmi, my eldest, who despite being accepted to two dozen of the finest universities in the world, was waitlisted by Harvard. A small thing for her, but a world-shattering offense to Kadambari. From that day forward, she's barely thought of anything else but Harvard admissions. By now, I suspect she even dreams of it. And while I admire her tenacity, I find myself exhausted by the never-ending accusations. Which brings us back to your latest accusation," he said, raising his eyebrows at Kari with a wry smile.

"Elton's father convinced you to invest seven hundred and eighty million dollars with Spencer Investment Securities," Kari said, going back on the offensive.

Sachin started to reply but then seemed to register his daughter's words. "Wait—how do you know that?"

"I know your passwords," Kari said. "And I had Milo go over your financials."

"I … see. And where is Milo now?" he asked, rubbing his temples.

"At Kanner Academy," Kari said. "His parents use an ankle monitor to confine him to a five-block radius."

"Not the worst idea," Sachin mumbled before pressing a button on his desk phone. "Tracy, remind me to call Bob Klink this afternoon and let him know what his son has been up to."

"Hang on," I said, trying to keep up with all the accusations Kari was tossing out, "so Elton's dad really talked you into investing with Arnie Spencer?"

"No," Sachin said kindly. "We have lunch quite often, as Kari undoubtedly knows if she's reading my emails. But no one, particularly not Mustang Jones, talks me into doing anything I don't want to do. I invested with Arnie Spencer because he's a financial wizard."

"A wizard who made eight hundred million dollars disappear," Kari said. "And now, after fighting the city for a decade to build on Brother Island, your signature project is dead in the water."

"You know the delays on Brother Island are due to those nesting herons that wacko environmental group discovered," he replied. "Besides, this isn't my signature project. The Infinity Tower in Mumbai. Chaos Spire in Singapore. Those buildings are iconic." Sachin shook his head, clearly frustrated by yet another round of accusations. "But that is not the point. Tell Milo I have not lost a dime with Spencer Investments. In fact, I've made a nice profit—close to sixty million this year. The document you discovered by hacking into my laptop was a financial stress test. We do them for all our investments to see what would happen if any one of them went to zero."

I turned to give Elton my best "I told you so" grin, but he was watching Kari, who was now in her father's face.

"Then explain to me, Father, why on the night Mustang Jones

was stabbed, you came home, smashed the television in your bedroom, and shouted that Mustang Jones could, and I quote, 'go fuck one of his stupid fat-burning grills.'"

Sachin's eyes widened. "How did you—"

"You thought I was at the library studying, but I had a headache and came home," Kari said. "I was in my bedroom, and I heard everything."

I glared at Kari, irritated she hadn't told me this before. Sure, she didn't want my help—but still, if she was right about her father, this was huge. And to think, she hadn't even seen the note he wrote Mustang that said, *"Pay up, asshole, or your life is over."*

The room felt warmer, and Sachin tried several times to reply but faltered, then finally he said, "That night—what you heard—we had a bet. Mustang and I. We had a rather large and stupid bet on the Jets game, and I lost more money than I'd like to admit."

Even Elton, whose bullshit detector is nonexistent, knew this was a lie, and when none of us replied, Sachin reached into his desk drawer. I froze, a chill creeping down my spine. In my experience, this was the "all is lost" moment, when the bad guy pulls out a gun with zero intent to negotiate. My mind raced looking for an exit, though the privacy glass and a locked door meant this would end with our bodies buried somewhere in Jersey. But before I could signal the others to run, Sachin Patel pulled out his day planner and tossed it on his desk.

"Look," he said, flipping through to December 15th. "I left the apartment at 9:30 and went straight to Teterboro for my flight. If you'd like to see the flight manifest, I can get that for you too."

"Manifests can be forged," Kari shot back.

"They cannot, Kari," he replied, his voice growing tight. "I was in Boston when Mustang Jones was stabbed, and that is final."

"Then surely someone in Boston can vouch for you," Kari pressed.

Sachin began to reply but stopped himself. He was hiding something; I didn't need to be a detective to see that.

"That's what I thought," Kari said. She turned to leave, and hesitantly, the rest of us followed.

"Kadambari, I'm begging you," Sachin said. "Don't take this nonsense to the police. With Brother Island in limbo, the last thing I need is bad publicity. And besides, when you're proven wrong, even Dartmouth will waitlist you."

That last part gave Kari pause, but it was clear she'd already made up her mind. She straightened, her jaw set, and turned to stride confidently out of the office. We had no choice but to follow.

CHAPTER TWELVE

Downstairs in the BofA Tower lobby, Axl ran to the bathroom, leaving me with Elton and Kari. He'd been fidgety upstairs in Sachin Patel's office, though perhaps that could be attributed to the awkwardness of listening to a girl accuse her father of attempted murder. But something was off. Hadn't his face looked red and sweaty on the elevator ride down? Now, I couldn't remember and feared I'd always be paranoid whenever he had to pee. I would have asked Elton to follow my brother to the bathroom to make sure he wasn't snorting drugs, but that would have taken several hours of explanation and required levels of discretion Elton did not possess.

"Do you believe me now that my father is the culprit?" Kari asked, louder than you'd think someone would want to talk about such things in a crowded lobby.

"It's not a matter of my believing you or not," I said to Kari in a low voice. "It's about the facts. And one rather important fact you seem to be disregarding is that your father was not even in New York the night Mustang was stabbed."

"He's lying," Kari said. "Just like he lied about that stupid football bet with Elton's father. Just like he lied to my mother when he promised to love and cherish her until death do us part but instead had sex with all three of my nannies."

I started to reply, but the nanny revelation overheated my brain. Was the sex all at once? Staggered over the years? Was there a rotating schedule? A draft system? Were they aware of each other? Did they unionize?

"If he was truly in Boston," Kari said when I hesitated, "why doesn't he provide the names of anyone who could verify it?"

"Because ..." I began to say, but Axl had rejoined us in the lobby, and I got distracted when he rubbed his nose several times. Shit. Had he really just snorted OxyContin in a freaking public bathroom? Or was his nose just runny because it was thirty degrees outside and everyone's nose was runny? I frowned, knowing I was barely holding it together before adding this to my list of things to constantly worry about. How did anyone make it through a day without pills?

"What?" My brother asked after he noticed me staring.

I shook my head back to the present and said, "Nothing. I just forgot how ugly you are."

"Why will my father not provide an alibi?" Kari demanded.

Because that would involve talking to you more, I thought. "Because it's probably embarrassing," I said, turning back to her.

Kari laughed bitterly and rolled her eyes.

"Look," I said, trying to keep my voice down, "you don't have to believe me. I've only solved three more cold-case murders than you. But in my experience, and Elton can vouch for this, when someone hesitates to provide their alibi, it's usually out of embarrassment.

They're doing something shady, like having an affair, but not something illegal, like stabbing a man in the chest. If your father were worried about going to jail for attempted murder, he'd provide his alibi, but he's not because he's innocent."

Kari turned to Elton, who said, "This is true. Buster McClellan, in particular, comes to mind."

"My father has had so many affairs even the *New York Post* is tired of covering them," Kari said. "But even if he was in Boston, he could have hired a hitman. That's just as bad, and he will still face several years in prison."

"Your father didn't hire a hitman," I said.

"And how could you know that?"

"Because a hitman would have killed him," I said, "not stabbed him once and gone on their merry way."

"Like you know anything about hitmen," Kari snapped.

"I know your father is too rich to hire a shitty one," I snapped back, drawing strange looks from a passerby. "But I could almost imagine you doing it in some lame attempt to frame your father."

Elton, who'd been gazing up at the impressive lobby ceiling and seemingly not paying attention, took a giant step and cut Kari off before she could get her hands around my throat. "An accusation like that could ruin my chances of attending Harvard," Kari snarled.

"I guess you know how your father feels," I said with a shrug.

"Izzy," Elton said, still holding Kari back.

"What?"

"Izzy," he repeated, "please."

"Fine, Kari, I know you didn't hire a hitman to kill Elton's dad." This was enough of an apology to stop her from wanting to strangle me, but the rage hadn't left her eyes, so I added, "And look, I think you're on to something with your dad. He's fishy as hell. And you should circle back to him, but only after looking at the big picture because there are other people you need to question if you want to do this right."

"Like who?" she asked, her hatred of me less intense than her desire to get into Harvard.

"I'd start with the pastor who got drunk and said the next time he saw Mustang Jones, he hoped it was in an open casket."

After humble beginnings in Denzel Davis's apartment, Village Tabernacle now owned a 500-seat theater on Avenue A near Tompkins Square Park in the East Village. Standing-room-only crowds attended seven weekend services, and their simulcast reached an estimated 1.3 million people online. Outside, on the marquee, Rev. Denzel Davis loomed large over passing traffic—both arms raised in triumph like he'd just won the Super Bowl, only he wore a choir robe and held Bibles in each hand. Inside, an ornery receptionist told us we didn't have an appointment and needed to vacate the premises before she called the cops. So much for Christian hospitality.

"But we need prayer," I lied.

"Izzy, Mother says I no longer have to—" I elbowed Elton, and he whimpered.

The receptionist eyed us before saying, "If you really need prayer, you can fill out a form and drop it in that box by the wall. Someone on staff will lift up your needs to the Lord."

"But we need prayer from Denzel Davis," I said. "Can't we pay extra for that?"

The receptionist didn't like this at all, and as she stood to tell us where we could go—hell, I'm guessing—a man with shoulders wider than the Red Sea walked into the room and did a double take.

"Elton?" Denzel Davis asked, blinking in bewilderment. "Elton Jones-Davies?"

"Affirmative," Elton said, and Denzel smiled broadly, crossed the room, and tried to hug Elton, which didn't go well.

Denzel, assuming Elton's aversion to his hug was because he was angry and not because he was, well, just Elton, launched into a stumbling apology.

"Listen, Elton, you know your old man and I go back a long way, right? You've been there when we joke around, and you know we don't hold back. Nothing's off-limits, right? Still, there's a time and place, and last night, I ... Look, I had a bit too much to drink at our Christmas gathering last night, and ... I mean, we're not teetotalers. The apostle Paul says we're free in Christ to eat and drink whatever we ... But still, last night I—"

"We're not here to talk about your drunken rant," I said, stepping up next to Elton.

Denzel looked down at me and forced a smile. "I'm sorry, Elton," he said, "these must be your friends. Please, introduce me."

"This is my girlfriend, Kari," Elton said, and Kari ignored Denzel's outstretched hand, only adding to the awkwardness.

"This is Axl. He plays football like you and my father."

Axl, who was now acting normal so far as I could tell, made up for Kari's slight by going all fanboy and shaking Denzel's hand for far

too long while saying what an honor it was to meet the money-grub-
bing preacher.

"And I'm Izzy," I said, bringing Denzel's attention back to me.
"And we're here to talk about why you stabbed Mustang Jones."

ANDERS LARSON

Anders Larson was too brilliant to be this poor.

He had bachelor's and master's degrees in finance from Stockholm University and an MBA from Stanford to boot. Anders was fluent in six languages. Swedish and English, of course, but he also spoke French, German, Spanish, and Mandarin and could order dinner in five or six more. He looked the part too. Six-foot-four, blonder than blond, with a chiseled face straight out of a cologne ad and the body of an Olympic swimmer, Anders caught your eye. People on the street assumed he was famous because how could someone look like that and not be?

But Anders wasn't famous.

And he wasn't rich.

And he had only one person to blame.

Anders could have had any Wall Street job he wanted. Funny, personable, and brilliant, he smashed every interview he ever sat for. Firms had to have Anders on their team, but more than that, they couldn't afford to see him go to the competition. Often, Anders left interviews with offers for even better jobs than he'd applied for, so desperate was everyone to land him.

Spencer Investment Securities was one of the smaller firms Anders spoke to. Although it occupied only two floors of a Manhattan high-rise, it had a reputation for making its clients rich—and Anders wanted to be rich.

He sat for an interview with Arnie Spencer, president and founder of the firm, and typing on his BlackBerry, Arnie ignored the tall Swede for several minutes before finally saying, "We're not looking to hire anyone right now."

Anders's confident facade melted in the face of Arnie's disinterest. Every other potential employer had fawned over Anders like a college football coach trying to land his next five-star recruit. But not Arnie. Arnie could obviously not have cared less about the highly coveted young man sitting across his desk, and Anders stumbled over his reply.

"I'm not … I, uh … why did you ask me to come in?"

"Mustang Jones needs an assistant," Arnie said, still not bothering to give Anders his full attention, "so I told him I'd find one."

Anders wasn't familiar with American football, but Mustang Jones was unavoidable. Anyone who watched a minute of television after 10 p.m. had seen his smiling face hocking fat-burning grills. Whenever a magazine ranked the world's wealthiest athletes, Mustang Jones always cracked the top ten.

"Mustang makes more money than he can keep track of," Arnie said, "but he'd make a lot more if someone bright like you kept him focused. Wake him up every morning and point him in the right direction. If you can do that, I promise you'll make more money than you could ever imagine."

The job was below him, but the deal was sweet. Perhaps too sweet, looking back. A town car and driver. A penthouse. A private jet whenever he needed it. Anders technically didn't own any of these things, but his access was unlimited, so it was like he did. He was paid, too, albeit modestly, considering all his job entailed. The real money went straight into Anders's account with Spencer Investment Securities. Two million dollars a year plus performance bonuses, invested with a man whose touch turned everything into gold. If Arnie Spencer's returns stayed consistent, and they always stayed consistent, Anders would turn forty-six with a quarter of a billion dollars in the bank. Sure, there was a flicker of doubt now and then. A small, unsettling voice asking why this had been so easy. But Anders silenced it. He was brilliant and hard-working and deserved everything coming his way.

Anders was rich.

On paper.

But paper burns so quickly.

CHAPTER THIRTEEN

In 1988, during his rookie season with the Houston Oilers, Denzel Davis was arrested and briefly detained on charges of battery against a woman he met at a local nightclub. The story went, Denzel and the woman left the club together, but before they reached his apartment, a verbal altercation led to a physical one in which Davis pulled the woman from his car by her hair and threw her against a lamppost, shattering her collar bone in the process. Charges were pressed and suspensions handed down, but the woman, likely after cashing a fat check, changed her story. Charges were dropped and suspensions lifted, and when Denzel entered the NFL Hall of Fame fifteen years later, not a single news story mentioned the incident.

Denzel, however, mentions the story quite often these days as a sermon illustration of human depravity. He'd used it just three weeks ago in the video I found on his church's website after googling "Denzel Davis + arrested" while searching for dirt on the lineman-turned-televangelist. And while accusing powerful men of heinous crimes always got my heart racing, I usually felt my slight stature shielded me from physical retaliation. I mean, who would beat up a hundred-pound girl? Denzel Davis, apparently. He'd thrown one against a lamppost, and when I told him we were there to find out why he stabbed Mustang Jones, he looked ready to do the same thing to me.

"But, you're a busy man," I added, as Denzel's eyes burned holes through me, "so we can come back later when—"

"Follow me," Denzel said, stomping past the ornery receptionist and down a long hallway. A minute later, we found ourselves sitting on a couch in his office, surrounded by dozens of framed photographs of Denzel with every politician and celebrity that worshiped in his church.

"Okay, I have some explaining to do," Denzel said.

"Told you," I whispered to Kari, who snarled in reply.

"But not about stabbing Mustang," Denzel snapped. Then, after calming himself with some deep breaths, he said, "Look, I shouldn't have opened my mouth last night. Ministries are built on trust, which is earned in drops but lost in buckets. The Lord has given me so many sheep to tend, but I've let them down. I let Him down. I … I just … I just hope I can—"

"Please stop crying," I said, "you're not on TV now."

"Fine," Denzel growled, turning off the faucet as quickly as he turned it on. "I shouldn't have said the next time I see Mustang I hope he's in an open casket. I shouldn't have said it because it's a lie. The truth is, I hate that son of a bitch so much I wouldn't go to his funeral if you paid me."

By now, Elton and I were used to shocking confessions, but judging by the look we exchanged, neither of us expected this one.

"But I didn't stab him," Denzel said, reacting to our expressions. "Elton, you remember my wife, Stacey?"

"Affirmative," Elton said.

"Well, your daddy introduced us. They'd actually been seeing each other before. The problem was, they kept seeing each other after, and for the next twenty years."

"Oh, shit," I said.

"Yeah, shit," Denzel said. "So, while I should have known better than to speak my heart in such a public forum, can you now understand why I said what I said?"

"Absolutely," I said, "and why you tried to kill him."

"I didn't try to kill him," Denzel said, more annoyed than angry.

"But you do have a violent past," I said. "I read about that woman in Houston."

"A drunken mistake I paid dearly for," Denzel said, "but no one should be defined by their worst moment. I am not a violent person."

"Your nickname was Gravedigger," I countered, and Denzel only shook his head and shrugged.

"Listen, there was a time twenty years ago when I was jealous as hell of Mustang. Elton, I doubt you ever saw where your daddy and I grew up in Pensacola, but it wasn't the Upper West Side, I can promise you that. We were poor and didn't think we'd ever get out, but your daddy did when Dalton Wolfe called. Mustang went to Bardo, and I stayed behind. Now, he always swore he knew I'd make it out of there just fine, but he knew no such thing. He took that scholarship and ran and never looked back. He didn't call to congratulate me when I signed with Miami, and he hardly spoke to me after our games in college when we kicked their ass. Every time I tackled your daddy in college, I tried to kill him. Every damn time. And then, wouldn't you know it, we ended up in Houston together. On draft night, when I saw him cry and hug his mama and tell those reporters he didn't think he'd ever make it out, I realized he'd been just as scared as me. And I was finally honest enough to admit if given the chance, I'd have left him behind in Pensacola too. So we buried the hatchet, and we were close until a few months ago when I found out about him and Stacey. And sure, I know what the Bible says about forgiveness. I preach it every week. But ask yourself, what's the worst someone ever wronged you? Have you forgiven them? Or can you still make your blood boil just by thinking about it?"

"My ex-boyfriend sold me out to Dalton Wolfe and got me arrested for drug possession," I said. "You could power lower Manhattan on my hate."

"See, you get it," Denzel said.

"Sure," I said. "And if I had the chance, I'd gleefully kick him in the nuts. But I wouldn't stab him."

"Kids, I'm a preacher," Denzel said, standing up to show our meeting was over. "I can assure you, I didn't stab anyone."

"Oh sure," I said, "everyone knows preachers never do anything wrong."

"Not what I meant, young lady," Denzel said as his BlackBerry buzzed on his desk. I caught the caller's name, Anders Larsson, just before Denzel silenced the call and pocketed his phone, and I literally gasped. Why the hell was Mustang's personal assistant calling this preacher who obviously wanted Mustang dead?

Before I could ask, Denzel rubbed his chin and asked, "Do you believe in hell?"

I grew up there, I thought. "No," I said, mostly because if I believed in hell, I'd also have to concede I'd likely spend my retirement there.

Denzel smiled, and I swear the room grew slightly darker. "Well, I do," the preacher said, his voice dropping a few octaves into demon-possessed range. "And that's precisely where Mustang Jones will go when he dies. And you know what he'll do there for eternity?"

"Burn?" I guessed.

"Burn," Denzel said, then he literally cackled. If Kari couldn't see that this was the bad guy, maybe her book smart/street smart ratio was way off. Then again, she likely wasn't even paying attention since her mind was already made up about the culprit.

"Now eternity," Denzel continued, grinning way more than you'd think a pastor would when talking about damnation, "that's a mighty long time. Thirty years here or there makes no difference to it. So why would I risk spending the rest of my life in jail just to send Mustang Jones to hell a little quicker?"

"Good lord," I said, taken aback by how quickly Preacher Denzel turned Psycho Denzel.

"His logic is sound," Elton said.

"Only if you presuppose the existence of hell," Kari added.

"Okay, fine," I said, "just tell us where you were the night Mustang was stabbed, and we'll be on our way."

"I don't have to tell you anything."

"Because ..." Axl said, thinking out loud. We all turned and watched him think, and after a moment he snapped his fingers and said, "Because you're embarrassed by the truth." I raised an eyebrow at my brother to show that I was impressed he'd been listening to me, and he said, "What? Like this is hard?"

"Elton," Denzel said, standing again, "do you know I've been talking to your mama?"

"Oh shit, I was right," Axl said. "You're having an affair with Elton's mom." He paused, brow furrowed. "Right?" He added, with considerably less confidence.

"Wrong, you dumbass," Denzel growled, before turning to Elton. "I've been talking to your mama because she offered me a way to hurt Mustang—legally. I'm testifying at the divorce hearing. Gonna tell that judge everything I know about your daddy. And trust me, it goes way beyond sleeping with Stacey. That's just the tip of the asshole iceberg. I'm going to cost Mustang Jones half his fortune. Or, at least, I planned to, until y'all came here accusing me of nonsense."

Elton turned to me in panic, and I began apologizing as fast as possible. "Please, Rev. Davis, I'm so sorry. We thought it would be fun to pretend we were investigators, and we didn't even consider whose feelings we'd hurt, and I'm so, so sorry. Please, Elton had nothing to do with this, don't punish him by—"

"It's okay," Denzel said, smiling without a hint of kindness. "You're just a stupid kid, so I forgive you." Then he leaned toward me and said in his devil voice, "But if you ever come back around here asking this shit again, you'll find out why they called me Gravedigger."

CHAPTER FOURTEEN

We left Village Tabernacle and stood shivering on the icy sidewalk, the noise of taxis and buses honking adding to the chaos already in my brain. Steam billowed from grates beneath our feet, and I pulled my jacket tighter as the cold bit at my cheeks. I could feel the others staring at me, but I kept my head down, trying to think. If Denzel planned to testify against Mustang, if he truly was Holly's ace in the hole, I didn't want to screw that up. But I couldn't get past my sneaking suspicion he hadn't said one honest word to us the entire time we were in his office.

"I told you this was a waste of time," Kari said to Elton. When I glanced up, she said, "Do you have any other bad ideas?"

I hadn't planned to argue with Kari, but her smirking face got the better of me.

"Oh right, we should take every word the shady pastor said as gospel."

"I believed him," Elton said.

"And your lie detector is virtually non-existent," I replied.

"I believed him too," Kari said, "and I know when people are lying."

"And you're a lovely person and lots of fun to be around," I dead-panned, and when Kari picked up on the sarcasm, she looked ready to strangle me. "Look, Kari," I said, raising my hands in peace, "I agree your dad is beyond suspicious, but he says he has an alibi, even though he won't share it. Same as Denzel Davis. They're dead ends, but only for now. Other suspects will shed light on your father or Denzel, and then we can turn the screws on them. It's like a tangle of fishing line. We've got to keep pulling on different strands until the whole thing starts to unravel."

Kari did not like this but must have agreed because she didn't argue. It was Elton who pushed back on what to do next.

"What other suspects?" Elton asked. "We have spoken to Sachin Patel, Jade Martin, and Denzel Davis. If we have no other suspects, circling back to Kari's father is our only option."

Dammit. I'd forgotten entirely about Jade Martin until Elton mentioned her. We hadn't questioned her. Not really. Partly because we were busy snooping through Mustang's office, but her yawning disinterest in our investigation had lowered my antennae. She'd tried to hide the note from Sachin to Mustang, but why? And why hadn't I even thought about it until now? What the hell was wrong with me? Were the pills doing weird things to my brain? I shook off the thought and tried to recall what I'd left Denzel's office curious about. The phone call. The phone call from Anders Larsson.

"We have to talk to Anders Larsson," I said.

"You think Elton's father's assistant stabbed him?" Kari asked.

"No, but I saw Denzel's caller ID when his phone rang. Anders Larsson was calling, and I'd like to know why."

We stood silent for a moment, and then Kari said, "I can think of no valid reason for Anders to call Denzel Davis. Elton, how can we reach Anders? Do you have his phone number?"

"Affirmative," Elton said, holding up his phone.

I snatched his phone from his hand and typed in his passcode.

"How does she know your passcode?" Kari demanded.

"Because it's my birth date," I said, then glanced up to see Kari's face, which was even angrier than I'd hoped it would be.

I scrolled through Elton's contacts until I found Anders. I was about to hit call when Axl said, "Izzy, it's freezing. Can't we please go somewhere for lunch and call inside?"

"Actually," I said, remembering we were on vacation, "yeah, we can. Elton, call us a cab."

Twenty-five minutes later, I was standing in Times Square. Cold air stung my face, but I barely noticed. Neon billboards flashed in broad daylight, towering over Broadway marquees promising the best night of my life. Taxi horns blared. Bike messengers sliced through traffic like they had a death wish. Steam rose from subway grates. Tourists clogged the sidewalks, staring up, mouths open. The smell of hot dogs and roasted peanuts mixed with exhaust. It was loud. It was fast. It was too much, and I loved it, until Elton and Kari made us eat at McDonald's.

"Why the hell did we pick McDonald's?" Axl complained from our booth on the second floor. "This is literally the only restaurant Dandridge and New York have in common. Couldn't we have gone anywhere else?"

"All the restaurants in Times Square are tourist traps," Kari said matter-of-factly.

"But we're tourists," Axl argued. "We want to be trapped."

"This McDonald's does have two stories," Elton pointed out, and motioning toward the window at the madness below added, "and better people watching than the one in Dandridge."

I wanted to remind Elton I once saw a man walking an alligator on a leash outside the Dandridge McDonald's, but I popped a McNugget in my mouth and called Anders instead.

"You have reached the voicemail of Anders Larsson …"

"Not much of an accent," I whispered across the table to Elton.

"He is Swedish," Elton said, "not the Swedish Chef."

I laughed and waited for the voicemail to beep. "Mr. Larsson, this is Detective Izzy Brown with the Police Department of New York City. We have some questions for you regarding the stabbing of your employer, Terrance Jones. Please return my call at your earliest convenience, or you will be held in contempt of court."

"Holy hell, Izzy," Axl said when I hung up. "I'm barely a C student, and I know it's illegal to impersonate the police."

"I wasn't really impersonating the police," I said, "because there isn't a Police Department of New York City." I had actually thought through the semantics part of this plan, but not the rest of it, and Axl calling me out made my heart race. Jumping in headfirst without looking was kind of my specialty, and it explained most of my troubles in life.

"While technically there isn't a PDNYC," Elton said, "I am not sure this would exonerate you, and in New York, criminal impersonation is a Class E felony, punishable by up to four years in prison."

"No one will throw me in jail," I said. "We'll say it was a joke. Besides, we need Anders to call us back and—"

Elton's phone rang, and I glanced down to see Anders's name.

"And my plan worked like a charm," I said, answering the call. "Hello, this is Izzy Brown."

"Hello, Izzy. This is Anders Larsson. Why are you calling me from Elton's phone, pretending to be the police?"

I'd forgotten he'd see Elton's name on his caller ID, and Kari gave me a you're-an-idiot eye roll.

"We need to talk to you about Mustang Jones," I said, trying to retake control of the conversation.

"Yes, well, I am extraordinarily busy right now. Too busy to play investigation with you kids. So I'm afraid—"

"We think Denzel Davis had something to do with the assault," I blurted out.

There was a long pause. Too long. And I raised a knowing eyebrow at the rest of the table.

"As does every amateur crime blogger in American after seeing Denzel's drunken rant on TMZ," Anders said. "But speculation without proof? Just a story. And stories won't help you here."

"Well, we know you just got off the phone with Denzel Davis. We were in his office when you called."

This time, Anders muttered a swear under his breath before asking to speak to Elton.

"Fine," I said, and handed Elton the phone, but not before putting it on speaker.

"Elton," Anders said, "you're a good person. A much better person than your father. But good people can end up with a knife in their chest too, so you be careful and stay out of this."

CHAPTER FIFTEEN

"But good people can end up with a knife in their chest too."

"You listen to me, Anders," I snarled into the phone, "if you lay one finger on Elton, I'll—"

"I'm not going to hurt Elton," Anders said.

"You just threatened to stab him."

"I did not. I like Elton. I've always liked Elton and don't want him to get hurt. That's why I told him to be careful, or he'd end up like his father. I have to go now. I'm sorry I can't tell you more, but—"

"Don't you dare hang up on us, you Swedish Fish. Why did you call Denzel Davis? Are the two of you freaking out that Mustang will wake up from his coma and identify you as his attackers?"

"I didn't stab Mustang, and I doubt Denzel did either."

"You doubt it?"

"Well, I wasn't with him that night. Who can say what the reverend does in his spare time?"

"Then why did you call him?"

"Listen, I have to—"

"Why did you call him Anders?"

There was a long silence, and I thought Anders had hung up, but finally, he said, "To gloat."

"Wait, what?"

"That's right," Anders said, almost as if he was convincing himself, "I called Denzel to gloat. For ten years, I've been at Mustang Jones's beck and call, and for ten years, he has paid me peanuts while making tens of millions off my back. He led me to believe it would pay off in the end, like an associate working their way up at a law firm or a doctor slaving away during residency. But no, he was never going to pay me. He would work me to the bone until I got wise, then hire someone else and do the same thing. But I did get wise. I got wise to a lot of things. Things Mustang Jones will go to prison for, assuming he lives. So why did I call Denzel Davis today? I called so we could gloat. I called so we could celebrate the demise of a man whose guts we equally hate. It's not a crime to wish ill on someone. It's not illegal to throw a party when they get stabbed. Elton, please do not take this personally, but your father is the crowned prince of assholes. Now, please, I must—"

"Anders, wait, you said Mustang will go to prison if he lives. What did he do? If we knew about his shady business dealings, we could find who stabbed him."

"It was my father, wasn't it Anders?" Kari said.

"Who the hell was that?" Anders asked.

"Sachin Patel's daughter Kari. She thinks her dad stabbed Mustang."

"No," Anders said. "Well, maybe, I suppose. He'd certainly have a motive, but I don't think—"

In the background, we heard, "Final boarding for Scandinavian Airlines Flight 1903 to Stockholm Arland Airport."

"I must go. Elton, please lay low. Your father is paying the price for his crimes. There is no need for you to get hurt too. Goodbye."

"Oh my God, he's at the airport," I said. "He's leaving the country. Can we stop him?"

"How?" Kari asked.

"I don't know. Can we make it to the airport?"

Kari rolled her eyes. "He'll be airborne in twenty minutes. It would take us that long to hail a cab, and at least an hour to get to JFK this time of year."

"And his flight could originate from Newark," Elton said.

"Or LaGuardia," Kari added, "though that's unlikely, considering it's an international flight."

"We could call Homeland Security," I said, grasping at straws.

"And tell them what?" Elton asked.

"I don't know. That there's a bomb on the plane. Or a terrorist."

"Again," Axl said, "I'm no lawyer, but I suspect Homeland Security would frown on that."

"We've got to do something, Elton. He knows who stabbed your dad, or at least he knows a reason someone would want to stab your dad, and he's getting away."

Elton considered this, but when he left the table to order more McNuggets, I knew Anders Larsson was gone.

Kari wanted to return to her father's office and perform a citizen's arrest because, of course, she did, but I had a headache and told the others I wanted to go back to the apartment and lie down. I'd been looking forward to the Rockettes, but with my head pounding I couldn't imagine anything worse than dizzying high kicks and blinding Christmas lights.

Elton offered to send me home in a cab and spend the rest of the afternoon with Kari, which pissed me off. But she said she wanted to study for the SAT, a test she'd already aced.

Mom and Holly were still out shopping when we returned, so Axl and Elton cranked up the PlayStation 3, and I went to lie down. I was midway between my two daily pills and didn't need to take one now, so I tried a cold washcloth on my forehead and some Advil, but half an hour later, my headache was somehow worse. Vowing only to do it this once, I took my bottle from my suitcase and shook a pill into my hand just as Axl walked in to check on me. The sight of the bottle stopped him in his tracks.

"Oh shit, Izzy, I didn't know you still—"

"Have headaches? Yeah, I still have headaches."

"No, I didn't know you still took—"

"Not the same thing," I said, trying to sound breezy though my heart was about to beat out of my chest and bounce around the room. If Axl told Mom, she'd take away my pills, and then what? My headaches and anxiety would return full bore, but that would be the easy part. The withdrawals I had after quitting in Bardo were enough to make me wish I was dead. This time would be worse. Way worse. "I went to see a doctor back in August for my headaches and anxiety, and this is what he gave me," I said, which was mostly true. "This isn't Bardo again, I swear. I'm taking them as prescribed."

The lie sounded confident enough leaving my mouth, but the skepticism never left Axl's face.

"Does Mom know?" he asked.

"No," I said, "but only because I don't want her to feel shitty. Her insurance sucks, and she doesn't have the money to pay for these. That's why I take on some extra shifts at Piggly Wiggly. And honestly, you've been around me the last four months. Don't you think I'm fine? My grades are up, and I'm not an anxious wreck all the time. I know abusing pills is dangerous, but there is a reason they exist—to help people like me."

"I don't know, Izzy. It scares me. Those pills are crazy addictive. I know because—"

"Because you snort them?" I asked, and Axl's mouth fell open. Like a slot machine, his face cycled through several expressions before landing on one I couldn't read. Then my giant, football-star brother did something I hadn't seen him do since we were kids. His jaw started to quiver, then he burst into tears.

CHAPTER SIXTEEN

That evening, before the Rockettes, we had dinner at Ellen's Stardust Diner. It was awkward, and not just because Elton made a show of covering his ears during the waitstaff's performances. All the neon signs were trying to revive my headache, and Axl was so red-eyed and quiet that Mom asked him at least seventeen times what was wrong.

"Nothing," he finally snapped. "I'm just tired. Izzy and Elton had me running around the city all day in sub-zero temperatures."

"Elton," Holly admonished her son, "did you really keep your friends out in this cold all day?"

"Negative," Elton said. "Today's temperatures remained in the mid-thirties, and we spent most of our time indoors interrogating—"

I hit Elton with a sharp elbow to the ribs, but it was too late.

"Interrogating whom?" Holly Jones-Davies asked. When we didn't answer, she said, "Elton, I swear, if you and Izzy are up to your old tricks, I will put her on the next plane back to Florida, and I will send you to a boarding school somewhere hot without air-conditioning."

I laughed, though I don't think Holly was joking, then lied and said, "We were interrogating Kari. She was accused of war crimes in Model UN, and she wanted help prepping for her trial next week."

"Is she guilty?" Holly asked.

"She did recreate Agent Orange during chemistry lab, but since that class is unrelated, I believe the jury will acquit her on a technicality."

"Dear Lord," my mother said, "I think the most y'all ever did in science class was make a battery out of a potato."

"That was my project," I said, hoping we'd successfully changed the subject. "Axl grew mold in his jock strap."

This would usually be enough to start an insult war with my brother, but tonight, he didn't even look my way.

Later that night, after watching leggy women kick and dance in Santa suits for ninety minutes, I sat on Axl's bed and waited while he tried to break the world record for the longest shower. I'd fallen asleep when he got out and jumped when he barked, "Get out."

"How long were you in there?" I asked, blinking myself awake and trying to remember why I was in his room in the first place.

"I said get out."

"No, we need to talk."

"Nope," Axl said. "We do not."

"You're snorting pills, Axl."

"And you're still taking them," he shot back. "After going to juvie. After getting us kicked out of school and ruining everything over and over, you won't quit. So excuse me if I don't care to be lectured by a hypocrite."

He was almost yelling now, and I couldn't really blame him. I wasn't the best person to have this talk with him. "Listen," I said, in no more than a whisper, "I'm not here to lecture you. I'm worried, that's all."

"It's the same pills you take," Axl said. "If you're not worried about yourself, you shouldn't worry about me."

"*Take* being the operative word here. I take them as prescribed, not up my damn nose. I didn't even know people snorted OxyContin." Even after taking drugs for over a year, I was shockingly naive about it. "How can you even afford them?"

Axl shrugged, expression flat, and I thought about the boosters, the handshakes, the way those men slipped him twenties and hundreds like they were paying tribute to a king.

"Look, I don't do it all the time," Axl said softer. He dried his hair with a towel and tossed it on the ground. "Remember when I hurt my ankle back at Bardo? Well, it never really got better. Not one hundred percent. The team doctor in Ashes told me I probably needed surgery, but when? I'd be out of action for several weeks. I can't do it during the season, or during off-season workouts, or spring practice, or summer two-a-days. Someone would take my job if I miss eight weeks, and then the dream is over."

Axl's ankle seemed fine on the football field, but I'd seen him hobbling around the house in the morning when it was still stiff, and he looked like an old man. I wondered how much damage had already been done.

"Okay," I said, "but if you're in so much pain you have to snort that stuff, I don't think—"

"I told you I don't snort it all the time. I take them just like you do. One or two a day for the pain. I forget my ankle is even screwed up most of the time. And those pills, well, you know, they really do take the stress away."

"Oh, what stress do you have?" I teased, realizing I'd started to cry. "You're the king of school with a harem of cheerleaders."

"You ever tried keeping twelve girls happy?" Axl asked, then shook his head and smiled. "Seriously though, think about the opportunity I have. Think about what our lives would look like if I made the NFL. I don't hyperventilate and puke like you, but it's a pretty heavy weight on my shoulders."

I'd always viewed Axl as the happy-go-lucky twin. The golden child that life served on a silver platter. The boy who never worried about tomorrow because tomorrow would be awesome, just like today. I felt a twinge of guilt for never even considering that our shitty circumstances might occasionally be too much for him too.

"But snorting?" I asked. "That's like total drug addict shit."

Axl shrugged, not denying it. "A kid at Bardo taught me."

"Blaine?" I asked.

Axl shook his head. "One of his friends. You have to wet it to get the coating off. Lick it or whatever and wipe it on your shirt. Then crush it, and … you know that feeling, right? That warm, everything's gonna be alright feeling that lasts for hours?"

I nodded. Of course, I did.

Well, imagine it all at once and a thousand times more intense. And look, I've done that maybe ten times in the last two years. Only when I'm super stressed about something, like this trip to New York.

"Why would a New York vacation stress you out?"

"Because I've never been anywhere, Izzy. You're the one who lived in London. North Carolina is the farthest I've ever been from home. The airplane, this giant freaking city, even the cold weather." He sat on the bed beside me and added, "It's a lot for a poor panhandle boy to take in."

I smiled and patted him on the back. "Listen," I said, then hesitated. I wanted to tell Axl he needed to stop taking, but I was in no position to scold him on his pill use. Besides, he was probably right about his ankle and surgery. If he could put that off until after he cashed his first NFL check, it was worth the risk. Right?

"Please, Izzy, don't lecture me," Axl said, guessing my intention.

"I won't, but at least stop snorting, please," I said. "These things work. We both know it. But what you're doing can't be safe."

Axl nodded, and we hugged, having reached a fragile truce. And as I stood to go back to my room, he flipped on *SportsCenter*. I was almost out the door when he said, "What the hell?"

On the screen, men in uniform chased some chubby old guy onto the ice at a New York Rangers game. They caught him after much slipping and sliding, tackled him, then dragged him off the ice in handcuffs to thunderous applause.

"Again, if you're just joining us," the ESPN anchor said, "Federal agents arrested billionaire financier and longtime Rangers supporter Arnie Spencer during the second period of the Rangers' 4-1 win over the Florida Panthers tonight at Madison Square Garden. Spencer is charged with running a massive Ponzi scheme, and one source told ESPN the losses could amount to over seventy billion dollars." On the screen, photographs of Arnie Spencer and several famous athletes cycled by as the anchor continued, "A fixture at New York City sporting events, Spencer is often seen around town with current and former superstars, most notably Mustang Jones, who was stabbed last week in the Bronx. For more on this breaking story, we go live to—"

Axl and I turned to each, eyes wide, both of us thinking the same thing.

Holy shit.

ARNIE SPENCER

Arnie Spencer was amazed at the stupidity.

Well, stupidity wasn't exactly the right word. Maybe it was greed. A greed so blinding and all-consuming it turned people stupid. A greed so powerful it bum-rushed your brain, kidnapped your common sense, and held it for ransom.

Arnie was born in 1940 to immigrant parents in Washington Heights. He was the first in his family to finish high school and the first to go to college. A job on Wall Street followed, making money for the men with nice suits on the upper floors. Arnie liked the work. He understood the game.

Arnie was smart.

Arnie was intuitive.

Arnie was still broke.

Despite his proximity to millions, Arnie's quality of life wasn't much better than that of his parents, a maid, and a garbageman. Maybe the money would come with time, or maybe it wouldn't? Either way, Arnie wasn't patient enough to find out. In 1970, with his meager savings and a loan from his father-in-law, Arnie opened Spencer Investment Securities.

The next fifteen years were hard. Rewarding, sure, and lucrative, to a point, but hard. Spencer Investments was a one-man show, and that one man burnt the midnight oil, mostly to appease his wife, Ruby. Ruby Spencer came from money and expected always to have it. Arnie worked his fingers to the bone trying to keep Ruby happy. Sure, by the early eighties, he was rich, but he was also well on his way to an early grave. Then, he found the cheat code.

Arnie falsified his first statements in the spring of 1985. The numbers weren't crazy; they just weren't correct. All his account holders recorded a modest gain—nothing to get excited about. Arnie knew if he inflated the numbers too much, his investors would try to withdraw everything and move to the islands. No, Arnie's trick was convincing his clients their money was in the right hands and they should leave it there. The stock market crash of 1987 made Arnie a superstar. Investors called that morning in a panic, and Arnie talked them off the ledge one by one.

"We're hedged against this."

"You think I'd lose your money in this little crash?"

"I'm Arnie Spencer, trust me."

When statements hit mailboxes two weeks later, everyone breathed a sigh of relief. Modest gains. Arnie's investors made modest gains when so many had lost their shirts. They told their friends, and their friends called Arnie.

Still, things didn't get truly out of control until Arnie met Mustang Jones for dinner at Windows on the World one evening in 1995. By then, more people knew Mustang for selling grills than for running with a football, and he had more money than he knew what to do with. Still, he wanted more.

The two men talked about investing. Mustang wanted to grow his fortune, and Arnie said he could help, but he wanted the former running back to be his partner rather than an investor. "You know everyone," Arnie said, chewing on a cigar. "Athletes, movie stars, you know 'em all. And you know the stupid shit they do with their money. You bring them to me, and I'll show them the power of compound interest. I'll show them what generational wealth truly looks like. They'll make so much money their great-grandkids will never spend it all, and you and me, we'll make even more."

Arnie stretched out his hand.

Mustang shook it.

A match made in hell.

With Mustang's help, Arnie's client list grew to include Super Bowl MVPs, Grammy winners, NBA All-Stars, and supermodels. Arnie's fortune grew exponentially too. And with every new athlete or celebrity who handed over millions to invest, Arnie was amazed at the stupidity. Or was it greed? Greed so blinding no one bothered to ask how Arnie navigated the dot-com bubble without even a losing month. Greed so all-consuming no one questioned Arnie's unmatched consistency, even during the Great Recession. With Mustang's help, Arnie's house of cards reached the heavens.

Then someone brought it all crashing down.

CHAPTER SEVENTEEN

"Elton, you've got to see this!"

"Izzy!" Elton boomed as I barged into his bedroom unannounced. "How many times must I demand you respect my privacy?"

"I'll respect it next time," I said, grabbing him by the arm and trying to pull him out of bed with little success.

"I am on the phone with Kari," he said, as if that was something I cared about.

"Not anymore," I said, swiping his phone. "Hey, Kari, Elton has to go. It was great talking to you. K, bye."

I hung up before Kari could respond and tossed Elton's phone back onto his bed. He glared at me, but I could tell he was more curious about what was going on than angry I'd hung up on his horrible girlfriend, so I kept talking like the last thirty seconds hadn't taken place.

"Arnie Spencer," I said breathlessly, but Elton didn't react, so I added, "Arnie Spencer, the Founder and President of Spencer Investment Securities."

"Yes, Izzy, I know who Arnie Spencer is," Elton deadpanned.

"He was just arrested at the New York Rangers game."

"For stabbing my father?" Elton asked, jumping out of bed.

"What? No. For running a Fonzie scheme."

Elton laughed his big, awkward, Elton laugh and said, "I believe you intended to say Ponzi scheme. A Fonzie scheme would involve jumping sharks on waterskis."

"Whatever," I said because I had no idea what he was talking about. "Arnie Spencer was arrested."

"Okay," Elton said.

"He was arrested and charged with stealing seventy billion dollars."

At this, Elton's eyes lit up, and he followed me into Axl's room, where my brother was still watching the news about Arnie Spencer's arrest.

"Seventy billion dollars would be the largest financial fraud in human history," Elton said, just as the handsome news anchor said, "Analysts are calling this the largest financial fraud in history."

"I just said that," Elton said to the television, then turned to me and asked, "What do you think this has to do with my father?"

"I'm not sure," I said, pacing the room. "But it has to be some-thing, right?"

Elton shrugged. "*Possibiliter ergo probabiliter.*"

"What?" Axl and I said in unison.

"You're assuming probability just because something's possible. That is a fallacy."

"Your face is a fallacy," I muttered because I couldn't think of anything clever.

We rewatched footage of federal agents slipping and falling while trying to wrestle Arnie Spencer to the ice, which was hilarious. Then I sat at the desk where Axl had snorted OxyContin the day before and spun around in the chair while trying to think.

"Okay," I said, stopping the chair before I puked, "thanks to Milo hacking into Sachin Patel's laptop—"

"It's not hacking if you know the password," Elton interrupted.

"Fine, whatever. Milo found documents that showed Sachin Patel lost the seven hundred million dollars he invested with Arnie Spencer."

"Negative," Elton said. "Milo found a stress test that showed what would happen if Sachin lost that money."

"That's what Sachin told us, but he lied," I said, pointing at the television. "Every dime invested with Arnie Spencer is gone, including Sachin's seven hundred million." I thought for a moment, trying to recall our meeting with Sachin Patel the day before, just as the news showed another photograph of Arnie Spencer and Mustang Jones at a charity golf tournament. "We know your father and Sachin Patel had several lunch meetings, and Kari seemed to think your dad was trying to talk him into investing with Spencer. But why? Does your dad work for Arnie Spencer?"

"Father refers to Arnie Spencer as his business associate, but I do not believe he employs Father in any official capacity."

"Maybe …" Axl said, thinking out loud, "maybe Mustang recruits investors. Your dad is super famous, he's bound to know lots of rich people."

"Holy hell," I said, "that's it. Maybe Kari was right about her dad all along. So Sachin has this huge development on Brother Island, but he wouldn't just use his money, right? He'd have investors."

"Affirmative," Elton said. "Sachin Patel's equity in the Brother Island project is likely less than 20 percent of the total cost."

"So he raised hundreds of millions from investors. And I suspect when investors give you hundreds of millions to build a skyscraper, you're supposed to put that money somewhere safe, like a bank, not somewhere dangerous, like Arnie Spencer's Ponzi scheme."

"No one would purposely place money in a Ponzi scheme," Elton said. "Do you even know what a Ponzi scheme is?"

"No," I admitted, "and don't tell me because it doesn't—"

"A Ponzi scheme is a form of fraud based on payment of returns to early investors from money invested by later investors."

"So … as long as new money is always coming in, the scheme keeps going?" Axl asked.

"Precisely," Elton said.

"Then that's where your dad comes in," Axl said, surprising me with how into this he was getting. "He knows all the rich people, and he brings them to Arnie Spencer."

"But none richer than Sachin Patel," I said, thinking out loud. "Mustang talked Sachin into putting his investors' Brother Island money into Spencer Investments. Arnie has this reputation of never losing, right? So Sachin thinks, why not make myself a small fortune with other people's money while the Brother Island project is on hold? But the house of cards crashed, and Sachin lost it all. But he didn't just find out tonight when the Feds tackled Arnie at the Rangers game. He's known. Those files Milo found prove it. So what does Sachin do? He stabs the man who convinced him to put his investors' money into a Ponzi scheme."

"Negative," Elton said.

"What do you mean negative?" I yelled. "It makes perfect sense."

"Well, perhaps affirmative, but perhaps negative," Elton said. "There are variables."

"What variables?" I snapped, annoyed that Elton always tried to slow me down whenever I started racing toward a conclusion.

"Did my father know Arnie Spencer's returns were fraudulent?" Elton asked.

"Of course he knew," I said, though this was based less on evidence and more on Mustang being a dickslap.

"Wait," Axl said, "didn't y'all find Spencer Investment statements on Mustang's desk? Maybe he didn't know. Maybe he—"

Elton raised a finger, and we turned to the television to see an NBC News reporter interviewing an old woman outside a Manhattan high-rise. The woman had been crying and looked ready to cry some more. But she wasn't the only one. Dozens of people stood outside the building with her, some crying, some shouting and waving their fists at the upper floors. A graphic identified the building as the offices of Spencer Investment Securities, but no one was inside. Not this late at night and not two days before Christmas. Still, the people gathered outside looking for answers. "If my money is all gone," the old woman on TV asked through tears, "what will I do?"

Back in the studio, the handsome anchorman said, "A heartbreaking scene tonight in lower Manhattan. And while details at this hour are few, a source with the FBI's field office in New York tells NBC News the number of victims in the Spencer Investments fraud scheme exceeds forty thousand. A truly staggering number."

"Do you think your dad knew?" Axl asked Elton.

"I am not sure," Elton said. "If not, he likely lost most of his fortune."

"Shit, Elton, I'm sorry," I said.

"That would be the best outcome," Elton said without emotion. "Because if he did know, Father is a co-conspirator in the largest financial fraud the world has ever seen, and Sachin Patel is just one of forty thousand people with a reason to stab him."

CHAPTER EIGHTEEN

It's difficult to solve a crime on Christmas Eve. Well, it probably isn't difficult for real detectives, or at least no more difficult than on Halloween or some random day in April. But for amateur detectives, particularly teenage ones whose mothers expect them to spend the festive day in their company, it's damn near impossible.

The news about Arnie Spencer was on every channel. Talking heads now estimated over fifty thousand victims of his financial scheme, with total losses topping one hundred billion dollars. The estimates felt sensational but weren't off by much in the end.

Most of the tens of thousands who'd lost their life savings to Arnie Spencer were ordinary, everyday people. Retired teachers, bank tellers, and firefighters. Several were still gathered outside the offices of Spencer Investments, where reporters wearing serious frowns nodded solemnly as the victims burst into tears while wondering aloud how they'd ever find work again at their age.

These sob stories pulled at your heartstrings, but what Americans really care about is celebrities, and plenty of those lost their fortunes to Arnie Spencer as well. By now, pop stars, rappers, actors, politicians, and athletes from every major sport had come forward to say they, too, were victims of the greatest financial fraud the world has ever seen. We watched as a rapper called Master Menace, famous for penning some of the most violent lyrics of all time, told a CNN anchor he had little hope in recouping the thirty million dollars he invested with Arnie Spencer. Then Master Menace went on a tirade listing all the things he planned to do to Mustang "Motherfucking" Jones if he ever saw him again, causing CNN to quickly cut to commercial.

"What on Earth are you kids watching in there?" Holly said from the kitchen, where she was preparing our breakfast and playing Christmas music on her iPod dock.

"A man on television wants to kill Father," Elton said.

"Well, he'll have to join the queue like everyone else," Holly said, then laughed at her own joke.

I laughed too, then paused when a horrible thought crossed my mind. "Elton," I whispered, "where was your mom the night your dad was stabbed?"

"At home, with me," Elton said, "and our building's security cameras can verify. But I'm glad you finally asked. I was starting to worry that you were off your game if you had not even considered her."

I smiled and sighed in relief, happy this case wouldn't have the worst ending possible.

By now, enough celebrities had mentioned Mustang Jones when discussing Spencer Investments that we knew Elton's dad was in on the scam. Well, we knew he helped Arnie Spencer recruit investors; whether Mustang knew it was a Ponzi scheme was subject to debate.

Mustang had money invested with Arnie Spencer too, and surely he wouldn't be dumb enough to willingly invest in what he knew was a scam, right?

It was weird hearing person after person bash Mustang on television, because since he'd been stabbed, he'd achieved a level of public sympathy that's hard to find these days. Had pollsters run an opinion poll on former football stars who now sold kitchen appliances, Mustang would have achieved near-universal approval, the only dissenting voices coming from people in Holly's apartment. But now he was persona non grata, which is a Latin term that I think means asshole. Don't get me wrong, folks on TV still wanted Mustang to make it out of his coma, but only so they could put him into a new one.

I scribbled Master Menace onto my ever-growing list of people with a reason to stab Mustang Jones. Every hour or so, I'd text the names to Milo, and he'd already ruled out several of them based on their publicly visible travel schedules. Elton and I wanted to go to Kanner Academy that morning and talk over things with the rest of the A-Team, but his mother quickly shot this down.

"It's Christmas Eve," Holly said, "you're not going to your school today. And if you ask to go tomorrow, I'm taking you both to the doctor to have your heads examined."

Holly and Mom would make us turn the news off soon and participate in holiday festivities. Even Axl, who seemed mildly interested in the case, was annoyed I'd commandeered the television and wouldn't let him watch *SportsCenter* preview tomorrow's LeBron vs. Kobe matchup for the billionth time. But the pundits all seemed convinced Ruby Spencer would soon give a statement, and I wanted to hear it. Several reporters, bundled up in the biting cold, were camped outside the Spencer home, using the building as a backdrop for their live shots. Well, they camped outside one of the Spencers' homes, their Upper East Side penthouse, to be exact. Arnie and Ruby Spencer had at least a dozen more homes around the world, not including Arnie's current residence, the Metropolitan Correctional Center in Lower Manhattan.

A CNBC reporter was in the middle of a live shot, recapping everything we'd heard that morning a thousand times, when Ruby Spencer stepped out of her building, flanked by two serious men in dark suits. There was a dizzying moment where the cameramen jostled for position, and once the crowd settled, Ruby Spencer pulled a sheet of paper from her coat pocket. She took a deep breath to compose herself, blowing out mist in the freezing air.

"First and foremost," Ruby began in a quivering voice, "I want to reiterate my husband's complete and total innocence."

Ruby was a mousy woman who looked like she might soon retire after forty years of teaching ninth-grade English. Throughout her short speech, her voice cracked several times, and she seemed the exact opposite of her husband, whom several reporters had described as always being the loudest man in the room.

"The charges filed against him last night by the federal government are, in a word, ludicrous," Ruby continued.

"Isn't Ludacris one of the people who said they want to kill Mustang Jones?" Axl asked, and I shushed him.

"Spencer Investment Securities employs dozens of knowledgeable and trustworthy individuals," Ruby said. "Either they are all as evil as the government claims Arnie is, either they are all criminally complicit in stealing billions of dollars from elderly pensioners, or none of them are. A fraud this big, this sensational, could not be kept secret for twenty years. That no one was overcome with guilt and came forward to report any wrongdoing proves that there was no wrongdoing to report."

"There are so many logical fallacies in that statement I do not know where to begin," Elton said, and I shushed him too.

Ruby began crying, and I felt bad for her. Well, as bad as you can feel for a rich old woman whose husband was charged with scamming people out of billions of dollars. I kept picturing my mom and Axl in front of the cameras, trying to explain away my latest screwup to the bloodthirsty mob. Still, Ruby seemed blindsided by all of this, and the statement's unrehearsed quality gave the impression this was the last thing she ever thought she'd have to do. If it was all an act, she deserved an Oscar.

"Now, has Arnie's company lost money in the last two years? Possibly. Everyone else has. This current crisis is the worst since 1929, I'm told. Did investor statements reflect these losses? I'm told they may not have. But this could simply be a case of a low-level employee altering statements so investors wouldn't panic. I'm no financial whiz, but I've been with Arnie long enough to know if you panic when the markets are down, you'll miss the rebound. If this is the case, the employee will face disciplinary action, and Spencer Investments will pay whatever fine the government deems appropriate. But all this sensationalist talk of stolen billions, well, it's just not true."

Reporters began shouting questions at Ruby that were hard to hear on television, though you could deduce their questions from her answers.

"Yes," Ruby said, "we expect the judge to set bail this afternoon and Arnie to be home for dinner. My spaghetti and meatballs. His favorite."

Ruby looked left, smiled, and pointed to another reporter. "Of course," she said. "If the judge thinks Arnie is a threat to run, I'm sure he'll gladly wear an ankle bracelet." Ruby smiled and added, "That said, I've been trying to get Arnie to run for twenty years with no luck, so I doubt he'll take up the practice now."

The reporters laughed, and Ruby added, "And yes, he'll gladly turn in his passport if that's what they want. He's not running. He's not leaving the country. Arnie will prove his innocence and get back to work."

Ruby thanked the reporters for their time and began to retreat into her apartment building. Studio anchors began talking over the live shots, recapping everything we'd just heard, but fell silent as Ruby spun and stepped back up to the bank of waiting microphones.

"I'm not an angry person," Ruby said, with more force than before, "but it just burns me up that my husband, an innocent man, a pillar of this community and a philanthropic giant, is being persecuted this way, when a liar and a cheat and a fraudster like Sachin Patel walks the streets free."

The television strobed as cameras flashed like machine guns, and reporters shouted over each other as the two men in dark suits escorted Ruby back into her Upper East Side apartment building. I turned to Elton, a chill running down my spine. Sachin Patel, of all people.

CHAPTER NINETEEN

As predicted, we spent the rest of the day in forced holiday merriment. Elton and I built a gingerbread house, which collapsed within ten seconds of completion. I helped Mom and Holly bake and decorate Christmas tree-shaped cookies that Axl devoured. And I joined Elton and Holly on a glitchy ten-minute video call with Elton's grandparents, Alfie and Nadine Davies, in London. Then Axl and I called our dad, Rodney, and his wife, Destiny, in Nebraska to wish them a Merry Christmas. We made plans to visit over summer break, and Mom even got on the line to wish her ex-husband a happy holiday, which a year ago would have been about as likely as a peace treaty between dogs and mailmen. But here we were, in the season of miracles.

After dinner and a screening of *National Lampoon's Christmas Vacation*, we grabbed a cab to Dyker Heights, where the whole neighborhood tries to out–Clark-Griswold each other with Christmas light displays so bright, astronauts on the International Space Station are probably filing complaints. Hot chocolate made the freezing stroll bearable, and when it was over, I was ready to go back to the warm apartment and crawl into bed and wait for Santa. But instead, we went to Grace Church, Brooklyn Heights for their Christmas Eve service.

Grace Church was built before the Civil War, and while technically Florida had older buildings, I couldn't imagine anything back home looking this ancient and medieval. This church belonged in England, especially the interior, which could have doubled as Hogwarts' Great Hall. The five of us squeezed into an already-packed pew and sang carols with the congregation.

"Mother says I no longer have to attend religious ceremonies," Elton said loudly to Axl and me during a break between songs.

"I'm aware," I whispered back.

"But she appreciates my attendance on special occasions," Elton added, and Holly put an arm around her son and squeezed him.

This was my first Episcopal service, though I'd been to something similar with Blaine back in Bardo. It wasn't much different from the Catholic service I went to in London with Marco Lane and his family either. It was, however, a far cry from the Dandridge Church of God and Prophecy, where we occasionally attended back home, which met in a gymnastics studio and once featured a short-lived brawl after one parishioner accused another of stealing from the offering plate.

"Just stand when everyone else does and kneel when they kneel, and you'll be fine," I whispered to my mother, who eyed her program like it was written in Ancient Greek.

The service was quiet and beautiful, though I may have dozed off at one point during the homily. But kneeling next to Axl and my mother during Communion, I got emotional. I never prayed much.

Not since I was little, and Axl and I would pray for our dad to return when Mom tucked us into bed at night. Prayers she would tell God to disregard, then petition the Almighty to keep Rodney Brown as far away from us as possible. Since then, I've always felt hypocritical about prayer. We didn't go to church much, and I was never too excited to be there when we did. I wasn't even sure if I believed half the stuff the preacher said, particularly the stuff anyone who'd been alive for five minutes could tell you ain't possible, like talking snakes. Growing up in Pineview Villas, I saw more snakes than I care to recall, and not a single one of them offered me fruit, forbidden or not. So when I forgot to study for a math test, I was uncomfortable closing my eyes and asking God for the answer to number twelve.

Mom did not share this discomfort. If money was short or Axl had a big game coming up, we'd be at church the minute the doors opened so she could beg God for whatever she wanted without a hint of embarrassment. I guess we were just different that way. But that night, on my knees in that sacred place, I prayed. I prayed for Axl. I prayed for a doctor to fix his ankle so he could stop taking pills. I prayed he'd make it to the NFL, make millions of dollars, and get our mother out of Dandridge. I prayed so hard that by the time we stood to take Communion, tears streamed down my face.

"Baby girl, what's the matter?" Mom asked after she caught me wiping my cheeks with my sleeve.

Both of your kids are drug addicts, I thought. "Nothing," I said, momentarily shocked by my emotion. My pills, which got me through each day, kept me relatively numb from strong emotions. Feelings this raw scared me a little, to be honest, but then I remembered this is what being alive feels like sometimes. I wiped my eyes and said, "I'm just happy to be here with y'all."

Mom smiled and hugged me. "Me too. Love you, baby girl."

"I love you too."

Christmas was useless. Well, not useless, it was a lovely holiday. The nicest Christmas Axl and I have ever had. We woke Christmas morning to find dozens of presents under the giant tree in the den, courtesy of Santa Claus ... and Holly Jones-Davies, I suspected.

"Santa came," Holly announced as Axl, Elton, and I stumbled into the den, half asleep.

"Good grief, Elton," I said, taken aback by all the gifts, "You must have been a good boy this year."

"Negative," Elton said. "I have broken more laws in the last twelve months than in the previous sixteen years combined."

"I suppose that's true," Holly said, "but you did solve three murders and saved thousands of lives. Perhaps Santa grades on a curve. But not all those gifts are for you. Some are for Izzy and Axl."

"Then Santa definitely graded on a curve," our mother said while sipping her morning coffee and smiling ear to ear.

Holly and/or Santa gave us both MacBooks, Adidas sneakers (Mustang was a Nike guy), and designer jeans that cost more than Mom pays in rent. Axl also got a Miami Dolphins jersey autographed by Dan Marino, and I got a long green winter coat I'd only get to wear once a year in steamy Florida, but I planned to wear it every day while in New York.

We hugged Mom first because it would have been awkward not to, and then we hugged Holly knowing full well who had bought the gifts. Considering my mother's stubborn pride, I was shocked she even let Holly do this for us. So much so that I asked Holly about it later that morning when the two of us stepped out onto her balcony to admire the Manhattan skyline.

"I told your mother if the situation were reversed, and she'd married a deadbeat NFL star who made millions hawking grills, I know she'd want to do something nice for Elton on Christmas Day. I won't say she liked it, but she came around eventually."

As I said, Christmas was useless for crime-solving, but I'll always remember it as one of the happiest days of my life. So content was I that day, I didn't even remember to take my morning pill until sometime after lunch, and I didn't waste a moment's thought on Mustang, Denzel, Arnie Spencer, Kari, or any of them. Well, at least not until I got a text from an unknown number during dinner and looked down to see the following message:

—Izzy, this is Sachin Patel. I need to speak with you tomorrow at my office. Alone.

CHAPTER TWENTY

I told Sachin Patel I'd be at his office in the morning without considering how I'd get there. My first thought was to wake up early and go. I was a big girl. I'd taken the Tube alone in London and figured I could manage the New York Subway without much fuss. But when everyone woke up, and no one knew where I was, Mom would be pissed. So I told Elton we needed to go to Kanner Academy and work on the case with Kari and Milo. This would get me out of the house, and then I just had to figure out how to get away from Elton.

"You coming with us?" I asked Axl, sticking my head in his bedroom.

Axl made a noise that sounded like a cow dying, which I took as a no. At dinner the night before, I'd watched him go back for seconds, thirds, and fourths of Holly's Christmas feast, not to mention the two giant pieces of red velvet cake he later inhaled. So it was no wonder he felt like shit. Still, I couldn't help but worry about him and wonder if he'd done something even dumber than eating his weight in cranberry sauce the night before.

"I hope you feel better," I told Axl and left with Elton for Tribeca.

The others were waiting in the conference room at Kanner Academy when we arrived, and Kari started in immediately.

"Now that we know the staggering amount of money my father lost thanks to Mustang Jones, I suspect you now agree he is the culprit."

"Hi, Kari. Yes, I had a wonderful Christmas. Thanks for asking. How about you?"

Kari glared and said, "I understand how small talk and banal platitudes work, Izzy. I just refuse to participate because they are a waste of my time. I do not care how your Christmas was, so I did not ask. Now, about my father. He is—"

"One of over fifty thousand victims of Arnie Spencer's scam," I said, cutting her off. "Granted, Elton's father didn't talk all of them into investing, but your father is far from the only person with a reason to stick a knife in Mustang's chest. Hey, Milo?"

"Yes, Izzy," Milo said, jumping to his feet and saluting me.

"How was your Christmas?"

"I'm Jewish," Milo said, "but it was fine. How was yours?"

"Very nice. Thanks for asking," I said, with a side eye toward Kari. "Hundreds of celebrities have come forward in the past two days, claiming they are victims of Arnie Spencer's Ponzi scheme. We need to know who has a relationship with Mustang Jones and who was in New York the night of the crime. Then we'll have a more manageable list of suspects."

"I'm on it," Milo said, returning to his laptop and typing at the speed of light.

"We're wasting our time," Kari said, but I ignored her and headed toward the door.

"Izzy, where are you going?" Elton asked.

"Tiffany's," I lied. "I used some of my Piggly Wiggly money to buy Mom a pair of their cheapest earrings, but they didn't ship in time for Christmas. I'm just going to pick them up and come right back."

"Negative," Elton said. "Mother would not want you to—"

"Elton," I said, putting a hand on his shoulder he tried to ignore, "I grew up in a trailer park surrounded by snakes. I think I can handle Fifth Avenue."

He started to argue, but I was already out the door.

As I walked down to the street, my mind raced with possibilities. What did Sachin want to confess? If he didn't stab Mustang, why did he want to talk to me? I seriously doubted he had plans to build his next skyscraper in Dandridge. I tried to hail a cab, and several sped by, splashing black slush onto the curb. I was about to give up and walk when one finally took pity. The cab ride to Patel Industries was slow as New York returned to full speed the day after the holiday. I tried to think about what Sachin Patel could possibly want to see me about, but my driver spent most of the ride telling me the plot of *Avatar*. Sachin was on the phone when I entered his office, talking in a low tone so I couldn't hear the conversation. He held up a finger to let me know he'd be a moment, then kindly motioned for me to take a seat across from his desk. Instead, I walked to the window and watched the ice skaters in Bryant Park, wondering if I'd ever get to join them or if I'd spend the rest of my Christmas vacation trying to find out who stabbed a man I would have gladly stabbed myself if given the chance. Standing there, in another powerful man's high-rise office, I couldn't help but recall my ill-fated visit with Marley Craven in London. I hoped this meeting would turn out better, but knowing my luck …

"Izzy," Sachin said, hanging up the phone, "thank you for stopping by."

"Yeah, sure," I said, taking a seat. "But how did you even get my number?"

"It's in Kari's phone, and I know her passcode," Sachin said.

"Sneaky ass family," I mumbled, but I don't think he heard me.

"Izzy, I would like to confess to something," Sachin said.

"To stabbing Mustang Jones?" I asked, raising an eyebrow.

Sachin laughed. "No, not that. I could probably shoot a man if I had to, but stabbing, no, that's too intimate for my taste."

I hadn't thought of this, but Mr. Patel was right. Stabbing was a more intimate way to kill someone. Perhaps the suspect was a jilted lover and not someone Mustang ripped off. But then again, Ethan Taylor killed Davy Taylor with a bomb in a pub bathroom, which is about the least intimate way you could kill someone, and they were father and son.

"Okay, so what did you want to confess?" I asked.

"It's Kari," Sachin said. "I need her off my back."

"That's more of a request than a confession," I said.

"No, you're right," Sachin said. "But listen, Izzy, I did not stab Mustang Jones, but …" He hesitated, looking for the right words. "But I'm not perfect, and this Brother Island project has problems."

"O-kay," I said, not sure where this was going.

"Nothing illegal," Sachin said, trying to reassure me. "Well, nothing I'd go to prison for. There could be fines, civil suits, those sorts of things. But that's just the cost of doing business these days."

"Ruby Spencer sure seems to think you should be in jail," I said.

The media had mostly ignored Ruby's Christmas Eve statement, writing her off as an aggrieved spouse. Besides, celebrities had lost hundreds of millions, which was far more interesting. But I hadn't forgotten she called out Sachin Patel while defending her husband.

"Well, Ruby Spencer is a bird lover," Sachin said, and when I squinted in confusion, he added, "and she's given millions to Audubon New York. Needless to say, Ruby wasn't thrilled when the city permitted me to build on Brother Island. But now that I think about it, Ruby could help you."

"Help me?" I asked.

"Yes," Sachin said, nodding and smiling like he'd just figured out the answer to a crossword clue that had been giving him fits. "You, Kari, Elton, she could help you with your little investigation. I've long since given up telling my daughter what she can and cannot do. Kari is relentless, and she's going to dig and dig until she uncovers who stabbed Mustang Jones. But I need her off my back, okay."

"If Kari doesn't listen to you, she sure as shit isn't going to listen to me."

"No, she respects you, Izzy."

"Are you sure we're talking about the same Kari Patel? Tall girl, dark hair, all the charm of Voldemort."

Sachin smiled. "She talks about you all the time, Izzy. You're a hero of hers. And that's why I need you to help me get her off my back. Because my fear is if Kari keeps digging into my life, she'll find something she regrets ... something she'd never forgive me for."

There was no threat in Sachin's tone. No hint of malice. But he'd done something wrong. Something he didn't want Kari to know about. From experience, I knew it was either something embarrassing, like an affair, or he was a complete psychopath who could breezily talk about murder with a smile on his face. I'd met enough smooth-talking killers by now to know that charm could hide a lot of sins. Maybe Sachin wasn't so different from them after all.

"What did you do?" I asked. "Cheat on Kari's mom?"

"Several times," Sachin said. "But that was well-documented by the tabloids—she was a supermodel."

"Kari's mom is a supermodel?"

"Was," Sachin corrected. "Now she lounges around her Hamptons mansion all day, drinking rosé and popping Xanax. Kari spends every other weekend with her but thinks she's an idiot. Then again, Kari thinks most people are idiots. Either way, we've been separated for five years, and I don't have time for an affair these days."

"Then what is it?" I asked, now leaning toward the psychopath hypothesis.

"I ... I can't say," Sachin said with a sad smile, "but you have to believe me, Izzy, I did not stab Mustang Jones. And I can prove it if I have to, but that will cost Kari more than she knows."

As I tried to take all this in, Sachin handed me a slip of paper with a phone number scribbled on it. "Here," he said, "this is Ruby Spencer's number. She's desperate to save her husband. If you tell her you want to help Arnie, I bet she'll give you the name of every investor Mustang recruited. Then you'll have a suspect list so long, Kari will be a freshman at Harvard before you rule them all out."

SACHIN PATEL

Sachin Patel was born in Bombay, now Mumbai, in 1956. His parents immigrated to the United Kingdom before Sachin's second birthday, both taking jobs at a textile mill in Preston. A bright child, Sachin excelled in school, always a step ahead of his peers. His father called him a tiger, fierce and hungry for more, never satisfied. Sachin liked the sound of that—he always wanted more. After earning a bachelor's degree in engineering from Oxford, he moved to the States in the late seventies and earned a master's and PhD in computer engineering from MIT.

High-paying job offers came from the usual suspects.

But Sachin wanted more.

Sachin always wanted more.

The small tech company Sachin started in his Cambridge basement would go on to create breakthroughs in digital streaming, online signature verification, and targeted advertising. He built the kinds of things that people didn't yet know they needed. Sachin found his work hard to explain at parties, or at least hard to explain in a way people found interesting. However, the tech giants knew what Sachin was up to, and when AOL Time Warner acquired his start-up for $4.7 billion, they put Sachin on the Forbes list right between Michael Bloomberg and Phil Knight.

Now wealthy beyond his wildest dreams, Sachin was a little lost as to what to do next. He just knew he wanted more—Sachin always wanted more. And that hunger, that itch beneath his skin, wouldn't let him rest. Real estate wasn't an obvious next step, but Sachin had ideas—big ideas for the way people would one day live.

Retina-scanned entry.

Voice-controlled everything.

Green. Renewable. The future.

His first high-rise in Singapore was a hit, the second in Mumbai sold out its units in minutes. Now, he had his eye on New York City, but where? How does a new high-rise make a splash in a sea of high-rises? The answer came to him on a helicopter ride from Lower Manhattan to LaGuardia Airport. Brother Island.

He knew about the birds. Ruby Spencer had once talked him into a six-figure donation to help them mate or some other nonsense. He laughed every time he pictured old lady Spencer standing on the shore with a boombox blasting Marvin Gaye. But bribes could be made, and birds could be moved. Sachin knew the game, knew the rules, and knew how to break them. Hell, it only took a hundred million rupees for the Mumbai City Council to move an entire slum to make way for Sachin's skyscraper. New York officials might only ask for half that.

Investors were easy to find. People liked Sachin. Well, they liked that everything Sachin touched turned to gold. When Mustang Jones asked him to lunch, Sachin assumed the football star turned grill salesman wanted in on the action too, but he was wrong. Mustang didn't want to invest. He wanted an investor.

Over their $500 chef's tasting menu at Le Bernardin, Mustang told Sachin about his work with Arnie Spencer. While tens of thousands of ordinary Americans trusted Spencer Investments with their retirement savings, there was another investment vehicle not available to the public: an invitation-only fund for high-wealth individuals that boasted annual returns of over 20 percent.

"Even last year?" Sachin asked, blinking at the numbers Mustang showed him.

"What can I say? The man is a wizard," Mustang replied, before suggesting Sachin invest his Brother Island investors' money with Arnie Spencer while waiting on the birds to be relocated.

"No one would know," Mustang said with a wink, "and after a year, you could pocket tens of millions."

Sachin laughed and said he wished he could, but that Mustang Jones would even suggest something so illegal should have given him pause. It should have made him run from the restaurant, holding on tight to his wallet. But Sachin's unquenchable appetite for more got him into trouble. He wasn't reckless—gambling with investors' money was irresponsible, unethical. But Sachin saw the numbers with his own eyes. Twenty percent returns? That wasn't gambling. It was an opportunity.

But Sachin had another dinner with Mustang Jones less than a year later, and this time, he'd never wanted to reach across a table and strangle a man to death more.

The money was gone.

All of it.

Every. Fucking. Dime.

Sachin cursed so loudly that the entire restaurant went quiet. "This will ruin me," he hissed at Mustang.

Mustang didn't reply but did slide back from the table when he saw Sachin's knuckles turn white around his steak knife.

Sachin tried to think, but his mind went blank. The restaurant, the people, the noise—it all faded. All he could see was the end. The end of everything he'd built. His reputation, his empire, the image he'd carefully crafted for decades—it would all be rubble. He'd made it this far by being smarter than the rest, but now? Now, he felt trapped, like his ambition had led him into a cage with no way out. Doubt crept in, whispers that maybe, just maybe, he had finally reached too far. His chest tightened, and for the first time since he was a kid, Sachin was afraid.

But nothing is more dangerous than a cornered tiger.

CHAPTER TWENTY-ONE

"Where are the earrings?" Kari asked when I returned to the conference room at Kanner Academy two hours later.

"Huh?" I said, somewhat less than eloquently, before remembering my lie about going to Tiffany's. "Oh, right. They were way smaller than they looked online, and I got into an argument with the girl at the counter, and they kicked me out of the store."

"Izzy," Elton said with a huff, not doubting for a moment I was capable of causing a scene in Tiffany's.

"What?" I said. "She was a bitch, and she made fun of my accent. But I did find something on my way back that might help with the investigation." I held up the slip of paper Sachin Patel gave me and said, "Ruby Spencer's telephone number."

"How did you find Ruby Spencer's telephone number on your way back from Tiffany's?" Kari asked incredulously.

"Oh, you know," I said with a grin, "we investigators have our little tricks."

Kari didn't like this at all but held her tongue.

"Authorities are set to release Arnie Spencer today on ten million dollars bond," Milo said, his eyes glued to his laptop screen. "He will remain under house arrest until his trial begins and will wear an ankle monitor to prevent him from fleeing. He surrendered his passports as a condition of his release."

"Huh," I said, thinking aloud. "Should we call Ruby now or wait until Arnie gets home from jail?"

"Now," Elton said. "Ruby claims she knows nothing about Arnie's business dealings, but she may know more than she lets on or, perhaps, more than she realizes. We know she struggles to keep to a script from her statement two days ago. If we can talk to her alone, she may let something slip that could help us. However, if Arnie is present, he would likely prevent her from saying anything incriminating."

"Good call, Big E," I said, giving Elton a squeeze that earned me a glare from Kari.

"That's assuming Ruby Spencer will even talk to some random girl from Florida," Kari snapped.

"She'll talk," I said, with more confidence than I felt, then I took out my phone and dialed the number Sachin gave me. Ruby Spencer answered on the third ring.

"Ruby Spencer?" I asked.

"Yes, who is calling?"

"Ruby, my name is Izzy Brown, and I'm—"

"How did you get this number?" Ruby demanded. "I am not speaking to reporters."

"I'm not a reporter," I assured Ruby. "I'm a high school student from Florida."

"I … I don't … how did you get my number again?" Ruby asked, clearly confused.

"Sachin Patel gave it to me," I said, earning wide-eyed stares from the other three in the room.

"Why would Sachin Patel—"

"Ruby, I'm investigating the attempted murder of Mustang Jones."

"Well, I don't know the first thing about that."

"Of course not," I said. "We don't believe you had anything to do with Mustang's assault, but we do think—"

"Who is we?" Ruby demanded.

"Myself, Elton Jones-Davies, Mustang's son, and Kari Patel, Sachin Patel's youngest daughter." Milo cleared his throat, so I added, "And Milo Klink, whose parents I don't know, but apparently they're Jewish."

"Gretchen and Robert," Milo said, but I didn't relay this information to Ruby.

"I'm sorry, but I still don't understand why you called or how you even …" Ruby trailed off, pausing as realization hit. "Wait, you mentioned Mustang's son? Are you the young lady I read about in the *Times* who solved those murders?"

"Yes, ma'am, and now we're trying to find out who stabbed Mustang. We know he worked with your husband in some capacity, and it seems he convinced—"

"Oh, Izzy, I'm so glad you called."

"Wait, you are?"

"I need your help," Ruby said. "The FBI … the FBI took everything. They barged in and turned the house upside down and took everything, including my Arnie."

"I'm sorry," I said, wanting to kick myself for consoling the wife of the biggest fraudster in human history. Arnie Spencer deserved to spend the rest of his life behind bars and then be buried under the prison. Still, if Ruby thought we were on her side, she'd be more likely to help. "Well, that's why I called," I said, and Elton cocked his head in confusion. "We think your husband was set up. And whoever stabbed Mustang Jones is likely in on the setup. If we catch them, we can help Arnie."

"Oh, thank you, Izzy," Ruby breathed. "Thank you so much. It warms my heart to know there are people out there who believe in my Arnie—people who want to help. So many have already made up their minds about him," she said, her voice cracking as she choked back tears.

"You know," she said, after a deep steadying breath, "there is something of Arnie's the agents didn't take. It's not much, but he kept some scribbled notes in the Bible on his nightstand. I'm not sure you'll find anything," Ruby continued, her voice barely a whisper. "But ... if it could help clear my Arnie's name, I'm willing to risk it. Just ... please hurry. Arnie is due home in two hours, and it will be a madhouse. And knowing Arnie, he wouldn't want me talking to you about this anyway. But if you think you can help him, please come."

"We're on our way," I said, hanging up the phone. "Come on, let's—"

"When did my father give you Ruby Spencer's phone number?" Kari demanded, jabbing a finger into my chest and knocking me back into my chair.

"Elton, control your woman," I said, pushing myself away from her in the rolling chair.

"When did you speak to my father?"

"This afternoon," I admitted.

"And why did you speak to him without me?"

Because everything is better without you, I thought. "Because he texted me and said to come alone," I said.

"Of course," Kari snarled. "You're trying to solve this case without me. You want all the glory for yourself. You want … you want my spot at Harvard."

Kari's competitiveness was so consistently insane that I laughed out loud, which wasn't a great idea because she began visibly shaking with anger. So I raised my hands in surrender and said, "Kari, I have a 3.1 GPA at one of the worst public schools in Florida. After seven tries, I recently scraped out a 26 on my ACT. I'm no threat to take your spot at Harvard, just as you're no threat to take mine at Pensacola Junior College. Your father texted me last night and asked to speak alone. When you're in the room, it's difficult for him to get a word in because you're constantly accusing him of crimes. Maybe he did stab Mustang Jones. He still wouldn't provide his alibi. And if he did, we'll catch him eventually. But when a suspect calls and asks to speak to me alone, I'm going to listen to what they have to say. And sure, maybe it's all misdirection, but if so, we're clever enough to figure it out, right?" Kari nodded reluctantly, and I said, "Now, are you going with me to talk to Ruby Spencer or not?" I asked.

Kari didn't like a single word that came out of my mouth, but she knew I was right, so she followed me downstairs to hail a cab.

CHAPTER TWENTY-TWO

With Arnie due home from jail any moment, the media circus outside the Spencers' Upper East Side apartment building had reached Barnum and Bailey levels by the time Elton, Kari, and I arrived. Arnie, in his shiny new ankle monitor, was expected to give a statement regarding the charges that he'd stolen most of the planet's money, and it seemed every reporter with a pulse was there to witness it.

"We're here," I told Ruby on the phone, "but we can't get inside."

"Just push your way to the door," she said. "I'll send a man down to get you."

We fought through the crowded sidewalk, weaving around journalists and dodging delivery bikes until we reached the building's entrance, where a man in a dark suit pulled us inside as reporters shouted questions, wondering who the hell we were. By the time we squeezed into the foyer, I could still hear the hum of the city and shouts from the reporters through the glass doors.

We took the elevator and stepped out into the penthouse, which comprised the top two floors of the twelve-story building. There was lots of dark wood paneling and antiques on pedestals. The study, where we were told to wait, had floor-to-ceiling bookshelves with those fancy ladders that slide across the floor. And through the dark, dusty drapes, we caught glimpses of the wraparound terrace with Central Park views. It felt like we'd stumbled into a game of Clue—*It was Mrs. Peacock in the conservatory with a dagger*. And don't get me wrong, the place was nice. The media was already speculating that the feds could get over fifteen million when they sold it at auction. Still, it seemed a little understated for a man accused of stealing billions. But I suppose it's best to fly under the radar when you've been scamming your clients for decades.

We waited on an uncomfortable antique sofa until we all got bored. Elton and Kari began perusing the library while I played "Heart and Soul" on the grand piano. That's what we were doing when Ruby Spencer walked in, and we all mumbled apologies and returned to the couch.

"Thank you for talking to us, Mrs. Spencer. We just want to—"

"Please," Ruby said, waving off my pleasantries, "we don't have much time. Arnie will be home soon, and you have to be gone." I shut up, and Ruby continued, "You said you believed my Arnie was set up?"

I'd forgotten about my lie that got us in the door, and now I had to squirm. "Yes, well, maybe, I don't know. We're more concerned with finding out who stabbed Elton's father, but if in the process we learn that someone—"

"That's fine," Ruby said, cutting me off. "I believe he was set up, and once I tell you what I know, you'll believe it too."

"It was my father, wasn't it?" Kari said, and Ruby looked at her, puzzled.

"No, Miss Patel, your father is not the culprit here."

"You did call him a cheat and a fraudster on national television," I added, trying to keep my tone casual.

"Because he lied to me about Brother Island. At my prodding, he wrote a large check to the Audubon Society to help preserve the bird habitat there. Then he went behind my back and wrote a much larger check to bribe the city into letting him develop the island and remove the birds. He deserves to have his eyes pecked out by a murder of crows, but he did not set up Arnie."

"You keep saying Arnie was set up, but people gave him billions of dollars, and now it's all gone. Sounds more like he was busted than set up."

"It's not all gone," Ruby said, "not all of it. Not even close. The accounts are down, but show me an account that isn't after the last two years. Arnie loathed having bad months. He absolutely detested it. He is a genius, sure, but you can't beat the market forever, and the financial crash was as hard on him as everyone else. Still, Arnie messed up, and Elton, your father is partly to blame. Instead of showing the loss and trusting clients would ride out the storm, Mustang suggested altering the statements. Showing a small return instead of a large loss. Two, three, four years later, when the markets rebounded and accounts were back in the green, no one would be the wiser, and Arnie would maintain his reputation as a financial wizard."

Ruby kept saying it like Arnie was some innocent bystander. But if he'd cooked the books, it didn't matter if he'd meant to "protect" his clients or if Mustang Jones had pushed him—wrong is wrong. Illegal is illegal. And Arnie got caught red-handed. Still, Ruby had information we needed, so I had to play along.

"So you're saying someone found out Mustang convinced Arnie to alter the statements and went to the Feds?" I guessed.

"Denzel Davis," Ruby said.

"Wait, what?"

"I believe Denzel Davis went to the feds."

"How would Denzel Davis know about any of this?" I asked.

"He was a client of Arnie's. A client Mustang recruited."

"Okay. And Denzel figured out his account had lost money despite what his monthly statement said?"

"Yes."

"I don't know, Mrs. Spencer," I said. "I met Denzel Davis. I'm not sure numbers are his thing."

"No one who owns a private jet is as dumb as they seem," Ruby said. "Besides, it's common knowledge, at least in certain circles, that Mustang Jones was having an affair with Stacey Davis, Denzel's wife. In retaliation, it appears Denzel was sleeping with Mustang's latest girlfriend, Jade Martin. I suspect Denzel found some incriminating correspondence between Mustang and Arnie while visiting Jade."

"You're telling me all this stems from a booty call?" I asked.

Ruby frowned, but nodded. "Listen, I'm angry with Arnie," Ruby said, her voice tight. "But I still believe he did what he did out of loyalty to his clients. Nothing made him happier than making them wealthy. But Elton, your father's checkered love life has cost him everything."

Elton shrugged. He knew his father as well as anyone, and this was just another data point proving Mustang sucked.

"Hold on," I said, "Do you think Denzel stabbed Mustang?"

"Perhaps. Or perhaps it was Jade."

"Not my father?" Kari asked.

Again, Ruby shook her head in confusion. "No, dear, I wouldn't think so. Your father only kills birds."

Kari crossed her arms and huffed, not happy with anyone who had the nerve to suggest her father didn't stab Mustang Jones.

"Is that the Bible you mentioned?" I asked Ruby.

"Yes," she said, handing it to me. "It's about the only thing the investigators didn't think to take. As I told you, there are notes inside. See what you can make of them."

The leather-bound Bible was stiff, edges immaculate, as though it had spent more time collecting dust than saving souls. Yet, a few pages were dog-eared, as if marking secrets Arnie rarely revisited.

There was a roar from the street below, and Ruby stood and said, "Arnie is here. You have to go." She ushered us onto the elevator and said, "My husband isn't the monster they're making him out to be, and I know you'll help me prove it."

I held the elevator door and said, "Maybe, but we're trying to find who stabbed Elton's father, not exonerate your husband."

"No," Ruby said, her eyes unblinking. "You're searching for the truth. And if you find it, it will set us all free."

CHAPTER TWENTY-THREE

Outside the Spencers' building was pandemonium. Arnie stood at the door, flanked by attorneys and bodyguards, reading a prepared statement. A sea of reporters shouted questions, and the blinding strobe light of a thousand flashbulbs paralyzed me until Elton put an arm around my shoulder and pulled me through the crowd.

A couple of blocks from the commotion, I had to sit and catch my breath. My heart thudded like it did that day in London, when I'd faced another sea of journalists, gasping for air in an undertow of flashbulbs. This kind of fame—the flashbulb kind—might be something celebrities get used to, but I was just some girl from Florida, and I didn't need this nightmare on repeat. I was so upset I didn't respond when Kari, her voice dripping with condescension, asked Elton, "What's supposed to be wrong with her?"

"Izzy suffers from anxiety," Elton said, coming to my defense. "And though I am not a trained psychologist, I suspect the media crush we just experienced triggered flashbacks to a similar experience she had in London."

Kari snorted, clearly disapproving of my mental weakness, and said, "Well, we can't stand here all day while she has a breakdown. We have to—"

"I'm fine," I said, scrambling to my feet and heading toward Central Park.

"Where's she going?" Kari asked Elton.

"Mustang's apartment," I yelled back, not slowing down.

"A taxi would be quicker," Kari yelled, but I didn't look back. Truth was, I needed a brisk walk in the cold December air to calm myself. I would have tried the breathing techniques Dr. Carrick taught me in London, but every time I did, I remembered that Dr. Carrick had called me an ugly little pill-headed chav right before I punched her in the stomach. The irony stung. An effective way to stop panic attacks only reminded me of a woman who gave me panic attacks. So instead, I walked as fast as I could and tried not to think about anything.

Even with my short little legs going as fast as they could, it was a frigid thirty-minute walk across Central Park, but it did me a world of good. The trees were bare and ugly, like skeletal hands clawing at the white sky, but the cold air calmed me, and the peacefully gliding ice skaters at Wollman Rink were a stark contrast to the circus we'd just escaped. When we passed through Strawberry Fields on the west side of the park, I didn't even stop to pay tribute to John Lennon. But by the time I reached Mustang's apartment, I felt like myself again—tense but ready.

The doorman at the Majestic said hello to Elton, talked with him about Lego minifigures, and then let us inside, where we took the elevator up to Mustang's apartment.

"What the hell?" I said, stepping into the living room. It had only been four days since we last visited, but the place had been ransacked. Gone were the fancy couches, antique vases, and Jade's nude portraits. Gone was everything but some dust on the floor and the canned lights in the ceiling.

"Hello?" I said, and my voice echoed in the empty room just as Jade and two men carrying a giant wardrobe rounded the corner.

"And please, try not to scratch that piece. It's worth more than you'll make in—oh God, Elton, what do you want?"

"We know," I said, trying to sound tough.

"Know what?" Jade asked, exasperated. "That you're annoying the hell out of me?"

"We know you're having an affair with Denzel Davis," I said.

Jade rolled her eyes and sighed dramatically. "More like trying to have an affair. Denzel's performance in bed doesn't quite match his performance on the field. Hall of Fame, my ass."

This was not the response I'd expected; it set me back for several moments. "Well ... we know you told Denzel that Arnie Spencer's investment firm was a scam."

Jade snorted at this and said, "If I'd known Arnie Spencer's firm was a scam, there are several things I'd have done before I got around to telling Denzel Davis. Though I do feel sorry for the guy. Well, as sorry as you can feel for a crooked preacher. Can you imagine sacrificing your body for all those years? Ruining your knees and shoulders and getting so many concussions that your brain scans look like Jell-O. Doing all that to make a few million dollars, and then one day, it's all gone because a man you thought was your friend convinced you to invest with a fraudster."

"So … Denzel didn't know?" I asked.

Jade shrugged. "I suspect he found out a few days ago, like the rest of the world."

"I told you," Kari said, and I fought the urge to punch her.

"Although," Jade added, "he liked to snoop around Mustang's office while waiting for his little blue pill to kick in."

"That must be it," I said. "Denzel found something that tipped him off about the Spencer fraud in Mustang's office. Then I bet he left Mustang that note that said, '*Pay up, asshole, or your life is over.*'"

"Hold on," Kari said, all of us taking a step back because she looked like a volcano ready to blow, "you found a note to Mustang Jones that said, '*Pay up, asshole, or your life is over,*' and you kept it from me?"

"No, well, yeah," I said, "but only because I knew you'd jump to the wrong conclusion that your father wrote it … since it was on Sachin Patel letterhead."

Kari took a step toward me, her eyes bulging from their sockets, but stopped when Jade said, "You're both wrong. I wrote that note, and it has nothing to do with Arnie Spencer or Mustang's stabbing. And I tried to hide it from you the other day because Javier was coming, and I didn't want to talk to you snoopy kids a minute longer than I had to."

"Then what was that note about?" I asked.

"Oh, I'm sorry," Jade deadpanned, "I must not have made myself clear. I still do not want to talk to you snoopy kids a minute longer than I have to."

"Fine," I said, "we'll just—"

"Go to the cops and tell them about a mean note you read but don't even have in your possession?" Jade asked. "Fine, go tell them, I'm sure they'll be super interested."

"Whatever," I said. "Denzel found something in the office that tipped him off, and then he stabbed Mustang."

"Wrong," Jade said again.

"And then … you stabbed Mustang," I guessed.

"God, I wish," Jade said, her voice so nonchalant it could have been a weather report. "But no, wrong again. The truth is, I have no idea who stabbed Mustang, but if I did"—she smirked—"I'd send them an edible arrangement."

"Then you won't mind telling us where you were the night Mustang was stabbed." I said.

"Not at all. I was right there," Jade said, pointing toward a dusty spot where a couch used to sit, "having terrible sex with Denzel Davis under the watchful eye of Mustang's security camera."

"We're going to need a copy of that tape," I said.

"No, we don't," Kari said, "she is telling the truth."

"That's enough," Jade said, fed up with all of us. "I'm incredibly busy and—"

"Hold on," I said. "You were with Mustang for the money, right?"

Jade stared at me like I was an idiot. "No, it was his charming personality and the discounts on fat-burning grills."

"Then why would you risk throwing it away by sleeping with his best friend?"

Jade huffed and said, "Let's just say it became apparent in recent weeks that Mustang Jones had no intentions of ever making an honest woman out of me. So, I've tried to hurt him any way I could."

"That's why you're taking all of his stuff?"

Jade rolled her eyes. "No, I'm taking his stuff because Mustang—"

"Oh, shit," I cut in, the realization hitting me before she could even finish. "Mustang is broke, isn't he?"

"If he's not, he will be," Jade said with a shrug. "Mustang talked a lot of people into handing over their life savings to Arnie Spencer—including me. If that dumb fuck saw the scam up close and still invested with Arnie, then yeah, he's broke like the rest of us. But if he knew exactly what was happening the whole time? Then the feds are coming for every dime he's got, and he'll rot in prison for a long, long time."

I turned to Elton, my steady, rational-to-a-fault friend, who was now frozen in shock, his face a ghostly white. The realization had hit both of us in tandem: this wasn't just Mustang's failure—it was Elton's future, and Holly's, slipping through their fingers. In that moment, it didn't matter who stabbed Mustang Jones; everyone's lives had changed. Even mine.

"Now, if that's all—" Jade started.

"This isn't your stuff!" I yelled, suddenly realizing that Elton and Holly would need all the money they could get from selling Mustang's things. "You can't take it all."

"Stop me," Jade said, and I was about to claw her pretty face up when Elton's and my phones rang simultaneously. We glanced at each other before answering the calls to hear our mothers screaming in unison, "We just saw you on television. Get home now!"

CHAPTER TWENTY-FOUR

I don't know the Guinness World Record for the longest and loudest tirade by an angry mother, but I do know Holly and my mom both made serious runs at breaking it when Elton and I walked back into his Brooklyn apartment. For what felt like half an hour, neither of them paused even long enough to take a breath, and their blistering condemnation and threats of eternal punishment blurred into what became a soothing white noise until Holly punctuated their fire and brimstone sermon with a question.

"What do you have to say for yourselves?"

Elton hesitated, trying, I suppose, to process every word he'd just heard, so I pounced. "It was Elton's girlfriend's idea."

"Elton," Holly barked.

Again, Elton hesitated, this time stunned by my betrayal.

"She bosses him around like he's her henchman," I continued. "She's obsessed with getting into Harvard and thinks catching Mustang's attacker will impress the admissions board. I've already told her I've solved three murders, and every college in the country remains unimpressed, but she won't listen to anyone. The craziest part is she thinks her dad did it, and she'd gladly watch him go to prison if it got her into Harvard. After spending five minutes with her, I told Elton she was insane, but it was like she has a spell over him. I didn't want to spend two weeks in New York trying to solve some crime I couldn't care less about. I wanted to ice skate, watch Broadway shows, and go to the top of the Empire State Building. But I wanted to spend time with Elton too, and the only way I could see him was to go along with Kari on her harebrained investigation. I figured if I was with them, at least I could keep Elton out of trouble."

Every word of this rambling confession was true, which made it easier to say with conviction. Still, my mother eyed me with suspicion. However, Holly sat next to me on the couch, hugged me, and said, "Oh, Izzy, I knew I could always count on you to look out for Elton."

I glanced at Elton while hugging his mom, but he was so angry I quickly turned away.

"Elton," Holly said, returning to her feet, "I forbid you from seeing Kari outside school. I had no idea she held such a sway over you, or I'd have put an end to this weeks ago."

Elton began to cry, and I felt worse than shit. He turned to leave the room, but Holly said, "I'm not finished talking to you, young man." But Elton didn't stop, and his booming footsteps echoed through the apartment until he reached his bedroom and slammed the door.

I tried to slip back to my bedroom, but Mom said, "Hold on, little lady, you ain't completely innocent here."

"Oh, Brandi, don't be too hard on her. She does look out for Elton."

"Maybe," Mom said, "but all that trouble they've been in this past year was Izzy's fault, not this Kari girl's. I suspect Izzy is giving us an Izzy-friendly version of events."

I shrugged, only half paying attention because I worried Elton would never speak to me again.

"Well," Holly said, "either way, we'll keep a closer eye on the both of you for the remainder of Christmas break."

I nodded in defeat and stood to go to my room, but before I could leave, Holly asked, "That said, were the two of you able to learn anything about Terrance's assault? You have a knack for this stuff, even if I wished you didn't. I have a wager with one of my girlfriends that Terrance failed to reimburse a prostitute, and her pimp stabbed him."

My mom nearly spit out her tea at this comment, but I'd overheard Holly and Mustang talking on the phone once in London, and knew he deserved any nasty thing she could think to say about him.

I laughed, then lied and said, "We haven't had much luck."

"You were at Arnie Spencer's house," Holly said. "Please tell me Terrance didn't have something to do with the little Ponzi scheme they say he ran? That sounds like the sort of trouble he'd get in."

"We thought maybe he did," I lied again, "but he wasn't involved. Ruby Spencer told us Arnie just kept Mustang around because he was a big football fan."

Holly had a healthy disdain for the news, and it was clear she hadn't paid much attention that week if she was calling the biggest financial fraud in history "Arnie's little Ponzi scheme." A scam her soon-to-be ex-husband was at the center of. Not only that, but it was also a scam her soon-to-be ex-husband had possibly fallen for, losing every dime to his name. I didn't want to be the one to break the news. Holly would learn soon enough. But against all odds, Brandi Brown was now the most financially stable person in the room.

Axl was in his bed asleep when I barged into his room. I wondered if he had slept all day. He groaned when I turned on the lights, so I flipped them back off and asked, "What's wrong with you?"

"Headache," he mumbled, and outside a police siren wailed, only intensifying his groans. "I decided you were right about the pills. I was probably taking too many. So I didn't take one this morning, and now I'm pretty sure I'm dying."

I'd been through the same thing back in juvie in Florida. It only lasted a few days, but I'd only been taking five or six weeks. As far as withdrawals went, it wasn't anything to write home about. But like Axl, I remember being quite confident I was dying. But he'd taken for over two years now. He was even snorting pills from time to time. I couldn't even fathom how shitty he felt.

A girl I worked with at the Piggly Wiggly took OxyContin. I found out when we ran into each other at the Panhandle Pain Clinic one day after work. She knew more about them than I did. She even knew how to quit because she had once. She said you had to wean yourself like a puppy. If you quit cold turkey, you wouldn't die like you could from alcohol, but you'd wish you were dead. I told Axl this, and he sat up immediately.

"Really?" he asked.

"That's what Ava Grace said," I told him as if the teenage girl who bagged groceries next to me was the foremost expert on opioid withdrawal. Axl smiled, jumped out of bed, reached into his luggage, and popped two pills without a glass of water to wash them down.

I think about this moment a lot, because maybe he would have quit cold turkey that Christmas vacation in New York. Axl seemed lazy until he wanted something, and then he became the most determined person on the planet—a person who could seemingly make things happen by sheer force of will. But when the Oxy hit his bloodstream after a short twenty-four-hour hiatus, I don't think he ever wanted to go without it again.

Either way, we didn't discuss it further that night because moments later, Elton came in without a knock. He looked at me, then turned to Axl and said, "Excuse my intrusion." His voice was stiff, barely hiding the anger behind his usual calm tone when he said, "Will you please inform your sister that my father is out of his coma."

"Whoa, shit," Axl said. "For real?"

"Affirmative," Elton said. "And he wants to speak to me."

7:03 AM
DECEMBER 15, 2009
THE DAY OF THE STABBING

"Babe, are you going to answer that?"

Mustang Jones cursed, rolled over, and silenced the phone on his nightstand that had rung for the last five minutes, not even bothering to see who was calling.

"Who was it?" Stacey Davis asked, but Mustang only grunted in reply, already halfway back asleep.

The phone buzzed to let Mustang know he had a new voicemail, then began vibrating as another call came through. Mustang slapped the phone across the room, but it continued to buzz on the hardwood floors, and now he was awake whether he wanted to be or not. Dammit.

Mustang rolled over and kissed his best friend's wife good morning, then kissed her again until Stacey pulled away and said, "Did you hear that?"

"It's a telemarketer," Mustang said, kissing her again.

"No, not the phone. Someone is here."

"Probably the cleaning lady," Mustang said, even though he didn't know what day the cleaning lady came or if he even had one. His house was just always clean.

"Shhh," Stacey said, and the two listened.

Footsteps in the hallway.

A hand on the doorknob.

A Category 5 hurricane blowing through the room.

"Terrance!" Jade Martin shouted. "What in the literal fuck are you doing?"

Mustang Jones scrambled out of bed like a rattlesnake was in the sheets while Stacey Davis pulled up the comforter to cover herself.

"Jade, baby, I can explain," Mustang said, trying to untangle his foot from the comforter as he fell to the floor.

"Baby?" Stacey Davis said. "You're still with this whore?"

"He was until fifteen seconds ago, you skank," Jade yelled back.

"Listen, Stacey, if you'll let me explain," Mustang pleaded.

"Explain why you told me you and Jade broke up six weeks ago?" Stacey asked.

"Six weeks ago?" Jade yelled. "Six weeks ago, we were in Cabo, screwing on the beach like wild animals."

Stacey glared at Mustang, waiting for a denial, but all he could offer was a confirming shrug. So Stacey snatched the glass of water off her nightstand and threw it at him as hard as she could. Mustang ducked, avoiding the black eye he admittedly deserved.

"Listen, both of you," Mustang said, raising his hands and backing away from the two women who both looked intent on killing him.

"Jade, you've known from day one I'm not a monogamous man. For fuck's sake, I was still living with my wife when we met. You know about the other girls. You've been with some of them, too, and that's fine. I'm even cool with Javier, that stripper you call a masseuse. I'm cool with everything, and I thought you were too."

"And Stacey," Mustang said, turning to the woman in his bed, "we've been doing this for what? Twenty years? I've been married most of that time, and so have you, so let's not make a mountain out of a molehill here."

The room seemed to take a deep breath. Stacey and Jade had done a good job forgetting the other existed, and this sudden reminder was bound to elicit a violent reaction. But things had calmed now, and Mustang thought he was out of the storm. Turns out, it was only the eye passing over.

"You told me you were through with that slut," Stacey yelled.

"I'd rather catch you in bed with my mother than this bitch," Jade screamed.

"Bitch!"

"Slut!"

"Whore!"

The women were now screaming at each other, but Mustang preferred that to them screaming at him. Besides, they both knew what they signed up for—what did they expect? This shouting match had less to do with him, and more to do with them. At least that's what Mustang told himself as he grabbed his phone off the floor, ready to walk away from the mess like he'd done a thousand times before. He reached the door before Jade and Stacey stopped threatening each other and joined forces to tag team him. Stacey vowed to make

Mustang a eunuch by putting his balls in a fat-burning grill. Jade promised something similar, though she intended to use a blender. Mustang didn't hang around to hear the rest, and he was halfway down the hall before he glanced at his phone to see thirteen messages from Arnie Spencer. His jaw tightened as he read the last one ...

Arnie — Call me now. The shit hit the fan.

CHAPTER TWENTY-FIVE

I suspect Mom and Holly considered locking us in our rooms and not letting us back on the streets of New York for the remainder of the holiday, but the phone call from Mustang Jones changed their minds, albeit reluctantly. Elton hated his dad, and I wasn't a fan, but if Mustang remembered anything about the night he was stabbed, maybe we could crack the case.

Holly agreed I should accompany her and Elton to the hospital. He had a complicated relationship with his father, and she knew he'd want me there for support. However, picking up Kari and taking her with us was a non-starter, and when Elton suggested it, Holly's glare said more than words.

The ICU waiting room at Mount Sinai gave me airport vibes, full of anxious people with nothing to do but sit and worry, only this one had pretty views of Central Park, and there were a couple of New York City's finest guarding the entrance. I worried I couldn't go back to see Mustang with Elton since I wasn't family, but that wasn't an issue. The issue was visitors under eighteen had to be accompanied by an adult, and Holly Jones-Davies had no intention of seeing her soon-to-be ex-husband. But when Holly told the receptionist that Elton was eighteen, she took one glance at his six-foot-eight frame and accepted this with minimal consideration.

There were sixteen beds in this particular ICU—the hospital had several of them for all sorts of critical patients—and each bed sat tucked into its own little curtain-made enclave, offering a small degree of privacy. A nurse walked us back to the corner bed, where we found Mustang Jones waiting for us. He had one of those oxygen things up his nose and other tubes and wires on his hand and wrist, but compared to the rest of the patients in the room, he looked down-right healthy. Mustang smiled when he saw Elton and said, "Hello, son."

"Hello, Father," Elton replied. "I am thankful you are no longer comatose."

"You and me both," Mustang said with a laugh that made him wince in pain, followed by a short coughing fit. The monitors behind him beeped loudly for a few seconds, and Mustang growled, "Son of a bitch. Elton, don't ever get stabbed if you can help it."

Elton nodded, filing away this fatherly advice.

"And who are you?" Mustang asked, noticing me standing behind Elton.

"I'm Izzy," I said. "Izzy Brown."

"Izzy Brown," Mustang said. "Well, by God, it's a pleasure to finally meet the little lady who's been getting my boy into so much trouble."

It's a pleasure to finally meet Elton's asshole dad, I thought. "Nice to meet you too," I lied.

"Izzy is helping me solve your attempted murder," Elton said. "Unless you recall who stabbed you, in which case our efforts are unnecessary."

"No, the police already asked me about an hour ago," Mustang said.

I knew that Mustang was even better at lying than running with a football; still, I naively took him at his word that he didn't recall the attack.

"But that's not why I—"

"Sachin Patel's daughter thinks he stabbed you," I interrupted.

"Yeah, maybe," Mustang said, and Elton and I exchanged a quick glance.

"What about Jade?" I asked. "Could she have done it?"

"Oh, definitely," Mustang said.

"Stacey Davis?"

"No, not Stacey," Mustang said, then after a moment added, "Well, yeah, maybe."

"Denzel Davis told reporters the next time he saw you, he hoped it was in an open casket," Elton said.

Mustang only nodded and said, "Well, sure, I can see where he's coming from."

Elton and I exchanged another glance, and I said, "Okay, but what about—"

"Will you both just shut up and listen to me?" Mustang growled, growing agitated by our list of people who'd want to stab him. "It doesn't matter who stabbed me. There's something I've gotten mixed up in, and when word gets out, it'll be harder to find people without a reason to kill me."

"You mean talking Arnie Spencer into cooking the books so his clients wouldn't know they'd lost money?"

"What? No. Who told you that?"

"Ruby Spencer," I said, "but I didn't really believe her."

"Why the hell were y'all talking to Ruby Spencer?" Mustang asked, his eyes wide.

"Sachin Patel gave us her number to get his daughter off his back," I said, which did little to clear up Mustang's confusion.

"Okay, you two have to promise me you'll stay away from the Spencers. They're in trouble, and that makes them dangerous."

"Ruby Spencer is a bird-loving grandma," I said.

"Promise me," Mustang snapped, the effort causing him so much pain he had to grit his teeth.

"Fine," I said, "we'll stay away from the Spencers. But you really didn't talk Arnie into cooking his books?"

"No," Mustang said, "I recruited investors for—"

"His Ponzi scheme," I butted in.

"Wait, how the hell did you know it was a Ponzi scheme?" Mustang asked.

"Because Arnie was arrested while you were in a coma. He stole billions of dollars, and you helped him, didn't you?"

My question seemed to cause Mustang Jones physical pain, and it took him a moment to process everything I'd said. "Yes," Mustang said. "I brought him clients."

"And now all of those clients have lost everything they invested."

"Arnie called me that morning," Mustang said after a long silence. "He'd been tipped off about a complaint to the Securities and Exchange Commission. He knew the authorities were closing in, and he admitted everything. All the accounts were empty. Even mine."

"Wait, yours?" I said, my heart racing. "So you invested with Arnie Spencer too?"

"Not my own money," Mustang said. "He paid me a fortune to bring him high net-worth clients, but all the money went straight into an account at Spencer Investments. I thought I had a couple hundred million dollars piled up there, but apparently, he robbed me just like everyone else."

"So you didn't lose all our money?" Elton asked, visibly relieved.

"No, I never gave Arnie a dime. But only because he wouldn't let me. Said it was a conflict of interest for him to invest my money. I realize now he was doing me a favor, but it makes me look …"

"Guilty," I said.

"Guilty," Mustang repeated with a nod, "and that's why I need your help." He asked to see my notebook and scribbled an Upper East Side address and a five-digit code. "Now listen carefully," he said, "this is the other apartment I keep across town. I go there sometimes … to get away from Jade. There's a computer and BlackBerry there that I only use for Spencer business. If Arnie's been talking to the cops while I was out of commission, I know he's tried to shift the blame toward me. But if I can get that computer and phone to my lawyers before Arnie's people find them and destroy them, I can prove my innocence."

Of course Mustang had a secret apartment. And of course Elton was about to say this …

"I am currently grounded and unable to visit your secret apartment," Elton said.

"Well, I'm ungrounding you," Mustang replied, and Elton shook his head violently, not thrilled to have his father pitting him against his mother.

"Look, son," Mustang said, trying a different tack, "I'm in trouble here. And if y'all don't help me out—"

"You'll go to prison, where you belong," I snapped. "If not for stealing billions, then for treating Elton and his mother like shit as long as I've known them. I don't care who stabbed you, and I don't care if you go to jail and die there."

"Fair enough," Mustang said, "maybe I'm reaping what I've sown here. But if you don't help me, and I go down with Arnie for running this scheme, they'll take everything. My apartment, Holly's apartment, the London flat, the house in Bardo. They'll liquidate every asset to our name, including Elton's little Lego men, and give it all to Arnie's victims. So unless you want Elton and Holly moving into the trailer park next to you, you'll bring me my fucking computer, and you'll help me clear my name."

CHAPTER TWENTY-SIX

Half an hour after leaving the hospital, we were back in Holly's apartment, under lock and key. Mom even insisted on escorting me across the street for a pack of gum at the corner store; so firm was her conviction that I couldn't be alone for more than five minutes without adult supervision. Across town, Arnie Spencer could undoubtedly relate to my plight, though thankfully, Mom hadn't fitted me with an ankle monitor. Yet.

"We've got to get into Mustang's secret apartment," I told Axl as we sat on my bed watching the news for any mention of the Spencer scandal, but only learning that traffic was backed up in the Holland Tunnel and light snowfall was expected overnight. Elton was in his room, apparently still pissed off at me for throwing his stupid girlfriend under the bus.

"Good luck with that," Axl said. "You'll be lucky if Mom even lets you look out the window the rest of the trip."

I cursed under my breath because I knew he was right.

"But hey," Axl said, "Kari isn't grounded. Send her over there to look around."

"No," I snapped, louder than I'd meant to, and when Axl gave me a what-the-hell look, I lied and added, "I think she's in the Hamptons staying with her mom for a couple of nights."

The truth was, it made perfect sense to send Kari to Mustang's secret apartment, but I couldn't stomach the thought of her cracking the case while I sat here helpless. I know, I suck.

I fell back on the bed and sighed in defeat, but turning my head, I saw my backpack lying on the floor where I'd dropped it earlier that morning.

"Oh, shit, I totally forgot," I said, and unzipping my backpack, I pulled out Arnie Spencer's Bible.

"You forgot to read the Bible?" Axl asked.

"No, this is Arnie Spencer's," I said, quickly flipping through the pages, "Ruby said there's a—"

I pulled a slip of paper out of Deuteronomy and squinted at the handwritten note.

DnzDvs 16.7 Vil Tab 68.7

"What do you think this means?" I asked Axl, passing him the note.

"Beats me," he said, barely even looking at it. "Looks like a Bible verse."

I snatched the note back and read it out loud over and over until—

"Holy shit. I think Denzel Davis invested sixteen million dollars with Arnie Spencer."

"Jade already told us that," Axl said, not impressed with my detective work.

"But," I said, "it looks like he also invested seventy million of his church's money."

"Whoa," Axl said, taking the note back from me and looking it over. "That can't be good."

"Nope. Denzel's flock obviously doesn't mind him using their tithes to buy a private jet, but it might be different when they learn he lost it all in a Ponzi scheme."

"So what are you going to do?" Axl asked. "Call the IRS or something?"

"No," I said, picking up my phone, "I'm getting us out of this apartment."

"Peace and blessings," Denzel's voicemail said after the fifth ring, "You have reached the Reverend Denzel Davis. I cannot take your call at this time. However, if you …"

"Hey Denzel, this is Elton's friend Izzy. You remember, the teenage girl you threatened in your office a couple of days before Christmas. I was just calling to wish you a Happy New Year and say if you don't want the press to know you lost seventy million dollars of your church's money in a Ponzi scheme, you might want to put down your Bible and call me back."

I hung up and began counting, but there wasn't even time to get impatient. Denzel Davis called before I reached thirty.

"Okay, listen," Denzel said by way of hello, "I don't know what you think you know, but if you call the press—"

"Shut up, Denzel, I'm not calling the press, so long as you do what we want."

Axl laughed. He thought it was hilarious when I spoke to adults this way, so long as they weren't pointing a shotgun at us like Buster McClellan.

"What do you want?" Denzel asked. "I don't have the money right now to—"

"We don't want your money," I said. "We want you to invite us to church tomorrow."

"What? Why?"

"Listen, this is a little childish and embarrassing, but we're grounded, and we need out of the house so we can catch the person who stabbed Mustang. So, tomorrow morning, you're going to call Holly and tell her some celebrity is coming to your church, and you thought with everything that's been going on, Elton and his friends might like to meet them. Send a car to pick us up, and your little investment hiccup will be our secret."

"Okay," Denzel said, "but you've got to believe me, I never—"

I hung up before Denzel could finish because I didn't care.

The next morning at breakfast, Holly's phone rang, and she took the call to another room since she probably thought Denzel was calling to talk about testifying in her divorce hearing. But moments later, she returned and said, "I just got the nicest call from Terrance's old friend Denzel Davis. Apparently, Beyoncé is visiting his church today, and he thought with all Elton has been through lately, he and his friends might like to meet her.

"Oh my God, Beyoncé," I squealed while worrying Denzel had chosen way too big of a celebrity for Holly and Mom to buy it.

"I am not familiar with her work," Elton said, not looking up from his breakfast. "So please send Rev. Davis my regrets."

I stomped Elton's foot under the table, and he glared at me. "We can't turn down a chance to meet Beyoncé, you donkey," I said, winking at him.

"You should consult an optometrist about your eye twitch," Elton replied.

I gave up and turned to Holly. "We definitely want to meet Beyoncé. Can y'all drive us over there or ..."

"Denzel said he'd send a car," Holly said, "and if it's okay with Brandi, I'm fine with it."

"Please, please, please," I begged Mom while silently praying she wouldn't ask to meet Beyoncé too.

Mother locked eyes with me and I worried she'd figured me out. I found lying to adults almost too easy sometimes, but this was the one woman who could occasionally see through my bullshit. She opened her mouth, ready to say no. Ready to crush my plans and schemes. But I hadn't counted on the one thing she couldn't resist—Axl.

"Oh, come on, please, Mom," Axl said, putting his giant arm around our tiny mother. "It's not like we'll have another chance to meet Beyoncé at the Dandridge Dollar Store."

Mom sighed in defeat. "Fine," she said. "I don't reckon you can get into too much trouble if this preacher man is watching you. But promise me you'll go straight there and straight back."

"We promise," we lied.

CHAPTER TWENTY-SEVEN

Denzel sent a car to pick us up after breakfast. Well, it wasn't just any car. As Elton noted while climbing into the back seat, it was a Jaguar XJ Super V8 Sedan with an MSRP of $94,850. I'm not sure if the car belonged to Denzel or his church, or if there was a difference, but either way, it seemed an unnecessary extravagance. Then again, I guess you can't have the pastor of Village Tabernacle pulling up to his private jet in a Honda Civic.

"Axl," Elton said on the drive across the river, still not talking to me, "the last time we spoke to Denzel Davis, he was incredibly angry at us and threatened not to testify against Father in the divorce trial. It seems unlikely that just a few days later he would invite us to his church to meet Beyoncé."

"Axl, tell Elton he didn't invite us to his church," I said. "I blackmailed him into getting us out of the house so we could snoop around your dad's secret apartment."

Elton was not happy about this at all, but telling me would

involve talking to me, so he huffed and stared out the window. Then, defying his mother's edict not to see Kari outside school, Elton called his girlfriend, who was waiting outside the church when we arrived. Anytime Elton broke a rule, I felt a twinge of guilt, knowing it was my bad influence rubbing off, but I was also proud of him for finding some gray in his world of black and white. This time, however, I wish he'd listen to his mother.

Denzel greeted us at his office door, hugging Elton and shaking the rest of our hands like we were visiting diplomats. It was a far cry from our last meeting when he called me a stupid kid. We had the goods on him now, and he was scared.

"So," Denzel asked, sitting behind his desk, "what can I do for you?"

"Mustang Jones has a secret apartment on the Upper East Side," I said. "We need your Jesus Jaguar to take us there."

"Okay," Denzel said, visibly confused. "And that's all?" he asked, hopefully.

"Actually, no," I said. "Since you're more compliant this morning, why don't you answer some questions. Like, does your church know you lost seventy million dollars in a Ponzi scheme?"

"No," Denzel said after some thought. Most churches this large have deacons or elders—a group to oversee the pastor and hold him accountable. But here, I run the show, and my word is final. Only my accountant knows, and we're looking at liquidating some assets to cover our loss."

"You mean sell your private jet?" Kari asked.

"Lord no," Denzel said, scandalized by the suggestion.

"So," I asked, "how did you learn Spencer Investments was a giant scam?"

"A few days ago on the news, like everyone else," Denzel said.

"Not from Mustang Jones?" I asked.

"Mustang Jones didn't have the balls to call and tell me," Denzel snapped.

"But he was sleeping with your wife. That's reason enough to stick a knife in his chest," I said.

"I didn't stab Mustang," Denzel said, punctuating each word with a fist on his desk.

"Okay, fine," I said, raising my hands in peace. "Then you won't mind telling us where you were the night he was stabbed."

Denzel considered this momentarily before saying, "I was with Stacey."

"Not Jade Martin?" I asked.

"I was with my wife," Denzel snapped, banging his desk again. He seemed to think the louder he said something, the more likely we were to believe it, but Jade told us she was with Denzel the night Mustang was stabbed, so someone was lying. "We've both made mistakes, but we're working through them."

"And Stacey will corroborate your story?" I asked.

"She would, but there's no need when the entire night is on video. I'm talking four hours of Song of Solomon-type stuff."

I didn't know much about the Bible, but I knew this was the dirty book kids would read under the pew and giggle.

"We're going to need a copy of that tape," Axl said before I could.

"No we don't," Kari chimed in, closing off every road that didn't circle back to her father.

"Whatever," I said, knowing we could always come back to Denzel if we needed to. "Right now all we need is a ride across town, so tell Jeeves to fire up the limo."

Mustang's secret apartment was on the third floor of a non-descript brick building on East 78th Street between 2nd and 3rd Avenue. The codes he gave us got us into the building and into his apartment, which had all the charm of a frat house. There was a mattress, lamp, and television on the dusty living room floor, an old metal desk littered with papers in one of the bedrooms, and in the other bedroom stood a cardboard cutout of Mustang holding a fat-burning grill that scared the bejesus out of me when I stumbled upon it.

"Check the closets," I told the others so I could scope out the desk before Kari, but I would have needed weeks to sort through the pile of financial statements and junk mail.

We shoved everything into Kari's backpack as fast as we could and found the BlackBerry and laptop Mustang told us to retrieve buried under the pile of paper. The BlackBerry was dead, so I plugged it into an outlet on the wall. However, the laptop still had some battery, so we opened it, and Elton entered his dad's password.

"Check the web browser," Kari said, and Elton opened Google Chrome. The homepage was set to the *New York Times*, which currently featured a front-page story on Arnie Spencer's fall from grace, and when Elton clicked on the search history, it was mostly porn sites.

"Click on that one," Axl said, pointing at a website whose name alone made me blush. I slapped his wrist.

"Check his email," I said, and Elton clicked on the Gmail shortcut at the top of the browser. Mustang's password was already saved, so his account opened to reveal hundreds of unread messages, most, judging by the subject lines, from angry investors who wanted Mustang to die a most painful death.

"Lord, these will take a month to go through," I said, just as the phone lit up when its battery came back to life.

Elton grabbed the BlackBerry, entered his dad's passcode, and opened the messenger app to see the last message his father received from an unknown number at 10:37 p.m. on December 15th, the night he was stabbed. Elton's eyes widened, and he turned the screen around so we could see.

Unknown — Meet me on Brother Island in one hour.

CHAPTER TWENTY-EIGHT

"We should return to Kanner Academy," Kari said. "Milo can trace the unknown number back to my father, and we can have him arrested before dinner."

"Okay, first of all," I said, "you just broke the world record for the longest jump to a conclusion. And second—"

"We cannot return to Kanner Academy," Elton said, taking over because Kari looked ready to fight me. "Mother receives a text alert every time the school's retina scanners record my arrival or departure."

"Weird ass school," I mumbled.

"Our mothers have forbidden us from working on this case," Elton said, ignoring me, "and it took an elaborate lie just to leave the apartment because we seem to have eroded their trust."

"I wonder why," Axl said with a sigh.

"Whose side are you on?" I snapped back.

"Beyoncé's," Axl mumbled.

"Fine," Kari said, "we can work on this at Elton's apartment."

"Mother has forbidden you from visiting our apartment," Elton said.

"What? Why?" Kari demanded.

"Uh …" I said, scooting toward the door to put some space between Kari and myself.

"Mother knows of your high ambitions, and she fears if we spend too much time together out of class, you could lose focus and miss your goals," Elton lied, and Axl and I exchanged glances.

Kari thought for a moment and said, "I respect that. I will take the phone and laptop to Kanner Academy and instruct Milo to research this unknown number. You three can return to Elton's apartment and be useless."

I wanted to punch her, but instead, I slipped Mustang's BlackBerry into my pocket when she wasn't looking and said, "Fine. Whatever."

When we returned to the apartment, our mothers couldn't wait to see pictures of us and Beyoncé.

"She didn't show," I said, which wasn't a lie because Beyoncé didn't show up at Village Tabernacle.

Our moms were more disappointed than us and offered to take us to *The Lion King* at the Minskoff Theatre to make up for it. Elton had seen it, Axl could not have cared less, and I couldn't wait to go through Mustang's text messages, so we declined.

"Suit yourselves," Holly said with a shrug, "but we're going to lunch. I'm starting to feel claustrophobic cooped up in this apartment."

Lunch was awkward, as the three of us tried and only occasionally succeeded at making up consistent lies about our morning. When we finally returned to the apartment, I wanted nothing more than to lock myself in my room and snoop through Mustang's texts, but first, I had to call River. We'd exchanged a few texts that week, but I hadn't spoken to him since we left for New York, and I knew if the poor boy didn't hear my voice soon, he'd have a stroke.

By my estimation, River Lewis had loved me since first grade. We were in Mrs. Clayton's homeroom together, where alphabetical order serendipitously placed us next to each other in different rows. Twice that year, he got into trouble for telling me the answers to my math worksheet. I got into trouble, too, even though I never asked for his help, which led River to apologize ad nauseam. And by ad nauseam, I mean he felt so bad for getting me in trouble that he literally puked in class. Everyone exchanged cheap little cardboard cards their moms bought at Walmart for Valentine's Day that year. Well, not everyone. My mom took the cards I received the previous year and recycled them by scribbling out my name and replacing it with my classmates'. River ignored the rest of the class but gave me a box of chocolates so big it wouldn't fit into my backpack. He told me he used the money his grandmother gave him for Christmas to buy it.

River asked if I'd be his girlfriend in third grade, fourth grade, fifth grade, and twice in sixth. At Dandridge Middle School, this meant holding hands at recess and kissing behind the gym if you were forward. I told him no every time. My self-esteem wasn't great then.

That happens when one parent leaves you, and the one who stays always tells you you're pretty in all the wrong ways. I later learned what Mom meant. I was pretty, period, just like her. But she worried I'd inherited her looks and curse of attracting deadbeats. I figured all that out much later, but growing up, I was skeptical of anyone claiming to like me. River was sweet, but I didn't trust him.

Later, in high school, when dating was a thing, River still tried. Lord, did he try. But by then, I was embarrassed by our lot in life. The thought of having a boy drive out to Pineview Villas and see our ratty little trailer gave me heart palpitations. Not that River would have cared. He'd have still loved me if I'd told him I was the Zodiac Killer. Still, I couldn't risk it. If I said yes and things didn't work out, then what? River was one of the few constants in my life, and I couldn't stand the thought of losing him.

He cried the day I told him I was moving to Bardo and cried again when we moved back a few months later. He wept like a baby when I left for London and shed tears of joy when I returned. The summer I left for Ashes nearly did him in, as did the emotional whiplash of our homecoming. That September, he asked me out twice, and I told him no both times. I had a job. I worked on weekends. He didn't give up.

"Look, Izzy, it's homecoming," River said, walking me to class one random Tuesday. He walked me everywhere, worried that I'd take a wrong turn one day and he'd never see me again. "Everyone is going. It'll be fun."

"If everyone from school is there, how could it possibly be fun?" I teased.

"It's not prom," he continued. "You don't have to buy some fancy dress. You could wear a church dress or a bathing suit—it doesn't matter."

"Oh, wouldn't you like that," I said, and River blushed.

He took a deep breath to reset and tried one more time. "I like hanging out with you, Izzy, and I think you like hanging out with me, right?" I shrugged but didn't say no, which only encouraged him. "I swear, there's no commitment. I don't have an engagement ring or some big proposal planned. And if you want to go home after one dance, I'll take you home."

"Fine," I said.

River opened his mouth to convince me further before realizing I'd said yes, then he smiled and quickly walked away, lest I change my mind.

So, I went to the dance with River Lewis and had the time of my life. We danced, laughed, and plotted our violent coup to overthrow the homecoming queen and her court. We stayed until the end, then he drove me back to my apartment, and I kissed him in his car for half an hour. I figured it was the least I could do for the boy who'd waited on me his entire life. Besides, all it cost me was my heart.

I was shocked by the intensity of my feelings for River. It's like I'd opened the spigot of my affection to full blast after having it shut off for years, and I was not comfortable with it whatsoever. River worshiped me, and I knew I wasn't worthy of worship. Sure, he knew what happened in Bardo with the pills, but he didn't know I still took them. He didn't know so many things about me, and I feared I'd lose him forever if he found out. Every day, I had to fight the urge to break up with him and head off my heartache at the pass. I realized even then that this was not how healthy relationships worked.

"Are you still coming back to Florida?" River asked by way of hello when I called him after lunch. "You haven't joined the Rockettes, have you?"

"I tried," I said, "but I'm too short by six inches. They said I'd throw off the kick line."

"Well, you haven't missed much here," he said. "Actually, that's not true. That strip club out on Rattlesnake Road burnt to the ground on Christmas Eve."

"Shit, not the Hoochie Hut," I said. "Where will I work after graduation now?"

"Very funny," River said, then asked, "What's going on in New York?"

"Nothing much," I lied.

"Yeah, I guess there's a reason people call it the city that always sleeps."

I gave a pity laugh, then we sat there in silence for a moment, him probably worrying I was about to break up with him—he always did that whenever there was a pause in the conversation, and me wondering how I could end this call and dig into Mustang's BlackBerry.

"You okay?" he asked after a moment.

"I'm fine," I said, absentmindedly. "You know I just don't like talking on the phone."

This was true enough—even if River didn't always believe me. He, of course, was the polar opposite, and would be perfectly content to hold the phone to his ear and listen to me breathe for hours.

"That's fine," he said, "I can let you go if you—"

"Great," I said, jumping at the chance to end the call, "I'll be home soon and we can catch up then."

I was already powering on Mustang's BlackBerry when he said, "Sure. Sounds good. I love you, Izzy."

I didn't have time for this. Not now. "Bye, River, talk to you soon," I said, quickly ending the call, but not before I heard the poor boy's heart break a thousand miles away.

7:37 AM
DECEMBER 15, 2009
THE DAY OF THE STABBING

"Listen, Arnie, now isn't a great time."

There was never a good time to talk to Arnie Spencer. The man was known to wax poetic for hours on topics so wide-ranging you could never anticipate what was coming next. Once, Arnie spent the better part of brunch lecturing Mustang on the history of double-glazed glass windows, a subject the billionaire investor apparently had an intense fascination with. Mustang usually humored Arnie, nodding along like he cared. It was the least he could do for the man who'd made him as rich as the Vanderbilts. But with his mistress and girlfriend currently screaming at each other down the hall, now wasn't the best time.

"There's just a lot going on right now and—"

"Shut up and listen," Arnie barked. "We're in deep shit."

"We?"

"Well, mostly me."

"Arnie, what the hell are you talking about?"

"It's over, T. The game's over. You've met Percy, my oldest, right? He runs our real estate team."

"Yeah, I've met him," Mustang said, leaving out that he thought Percy was about as useful as a condom machine in a convent.

"The feds got to him," Arnie said, and Mustang's face was suddenly hot with sweat. He still didn't know what the hell Arnie was talking about, but the word *feds* set off alarm bells and filled his mind with images of men in blue windbreakers shoving him into the back of an unmarked van.

Federal trial.

Federal judge.

Federal prison.

"Someone tipped off the feds, and they leaned on Percy, so he flipped."

"Wait, so what did Percy do?" Mustang asked.

"Percy didn't do anything, T. But the feds must have scared the shit out of him, so he flipped on me."

Mustang huffed in frustration. It had already been a day, and it wasn't even 8 a.m. "Listen, Arnie, I'm going to need you to spell this out in the simplest terms you've got because I still don't know what the hell you're talking about."

"The feds know Spencer Investments is a scam," Arnie said. "The statements, the earnings, all of it. It's all a lie."

Mustang's knees buckled, and he sat down in his hallway. "Hold on, where is all the money people sent you?"

"Gone," Arnie said, and Mustang could hear him crying. "I blew through it as fast as it came in. I mean, sometimes new money would go to old donors, but the returns were so good, most people didn't want to touch their funds."

"What about my money, Arnie? What about the money you promised you were investing for me?"

Arnie didn't answer, so Mustang yelled, "What about my fucking money, Arnie?"

"It's all there, T.," Arnie said absently. "I kept it separate from the rest. Yours and Jade's."

Mustang's relief was fleeting as the enormity of Arnie's confession sank in.

He'd been used.

He'd been a pawn.

And pawns are sacrificed first.

"So all of my friends, all of the investors I sent to you, you've lost all their money?"

"Yeah, T. I'm sorry."

Mustang cursed under his breath. How in the hell did he not see this coming? Nothing in life was ever this easy. "What am I going to do?"

"Legally, I think you're okay. You didn't know what I was up to, and talking your friends into bad business decisions isn't a crime."

"I'm not worried about the Feds, Arnie," Mustang said, as furious faces of everyone he'd wronged flashed before his eyes. "People will want me dead. A lot of people."

"I know, T, but listen, if you—"

"You don't get it, man. Those NFL guys I brought you made their millions by sacrificing their bodies and taking years off their lives. These are dudes who gave and received concussions for a living, and a lot of them just lost every dime because of me. And don't even get me started on the rappers. If even 1 percent of Master Menace's lyrics are autobiographical, he's the most violent person since Genghis Khan."

"Come on, T., now isn't the time to panic, you—"

"No, Arnie, now is precisely the time to panic."

The line went quiet for a moment, then Arnie said, "Listen, T., we've got a few days. Percy was kind enough to tip me off about what's coming my way, the little shit. I figure I've got a week, maybe less, while the Feds get their ducks in a row. I've got the best lawyers money can buy, so I'll fight this thing. And like I said, you didn't do anything wrong, but you'll want to talk to your lawyers, too."

"Son of a bitch," Mustang mumbled.

"Come on, T., I'm trying to do right by you. I want to protect you."

"There's nothing you can do to protect me, Arnie. I'm a dead man."

CHAPTER TWENTY-NINE

After hanging up with River, I stared at my phone for five minutes, debating whether to call the poor boy back and tell him I loved him. Because I did love him, and I realized that after being away from him for a week. Or, at least, I loved the idea of someone loving me as much as River did, which maybe isn't love, but it's love adjacent. But I also wanted River to be happy, and dating me would only bring him pain in the long run. Helping him see that as quickly as possible would have been the humane thing to do. Put him out of his misery. Instead, I sent a text that said, "I love you," with correct spelling and all. Then, I took a pill because I didn't know how else to deal with everything I was feeling.

I felt better after the pill kicked in—I always did—so I plugged Mustang's BlackBerry into the charger, and while waiting for it to power on, I went to find Elton. He was in his bedroom, building the Temple of Doom Lego set Santa Claus brought him, but when I started to speak, he cut me off with a raised palm.

"Please know I am still furious with you for sabotaging my relationship with Kari," Elton said. "I only covered for you today in the car because I feared she would attack you, and were you to end up hospitalized, we would all be in more trouble."

"Elton, I'm sorry about—" I started, but he turned away and refused to discuss it any further, making me feel like shit.

I went back to my room, fighting back tears, and spent several minutes arguing with Elton in my head about Kari and how awful she was. Then I snatched Mustang's burner phone off the charger and began looking through it.

Mustang's phone was packed with contacts—hundreds of names—but nearly every conversation had been wiped clean. Only two threads were still standing. One was with someone saved as "A.S.," almost certainly Arnie Spencer. The texts were all Knicks scores and lunch plans, nothing more. If they ever talked business, they kept it old-school—face to face, no paper trail, no digital fingerprints. Either Mustang had been careful, or he'd cleaned house in a panic. The other conversation was with the unknown number—the one that lured him to Brother Island. I scrolled back to the beginning, hoping the ghost on the other end had left a few fingerprints.

Unknown — I know.

Mustang Jones — Who is this?

Unknown — A friend. Well, not a friend. But not an enemy.

Mustang Jones — Look, friend, I'm afraid you've got the wrong number.

Unknown — I don't think so, Terrance Jones. Terrance "Mustang" Jones. 1987 Heisman Trophy winner. World famous grill spokesman. Financial fraudster.

Mustang Jones — Seriously, who gave you this number, and what do you want?

Unknown — I want to help you, Terrance. Your colleague, Arnie Spencer, will go to prison for the rest of his natural life. You'll go with him, though I'd rather you not.

Mustang Jones — Arnie isn't going to prison. He's the most powerful man in New York.

Unknown — And Al Capone was the most powerful man in Chicago.

Mustang Jones — Yeah, but Arnie isn't a thief. His fund is down, but what fund isn't right now?

Unknown — Stop lying, Terrance. I know the fund isn't down, because I, like you, know there never was a fund.

Mustang Jones — I didn't know.

Unknown — STOP LYING. If you didn't know, you would have invested with Arnie too, but you didn't.

Mustang Jones — I swear I didn't know until this morning. And I didn't invest because Arnie wouldn't let me. He said it was a conflict of interest.

Unknown — And you think a jury would buy that?

Mustang Jones — What jury? I didn't do anything wrong.

Unknown — Would your friends agree? The friends you convinced to give their millions to a Ponzi scheme?

Mustang Jones — I told you I didn't know it was a scam. My friends invested because Arnie was a sure thing.

Unknown — Like you thought you had a sure thing when Arnie promised a percentage of all the new money you brought in. He'd even invest it for you. Too bad you didn't realize he was sending you doctored statements too, just like the rest of the suckers.

Mustang Jones — Wait, what are you saying?

Unknown—There's no money, Terrance. Arnie never invested money for you or anyone else.

Mustang Jones — That's not true. He swore my money was separate from the rest of the fund. Jade's too.

Unknown — He lied to you, Terrance. Just like you lied to your friends. Is that so hard to believe? Arnie used you—end of story. And now you're in the middle of his shit storm.

Mustang Jones — Can you really help me?

Unknown — Yes, but we don't have much time. You'll need to cover your tracks. I assume you and Arnie were smart enough never to discuss business electronically. But you'll need to burn everything on paper. Don't shred it. Burn it. Burn any phone you spoke to him on. Burn the phone you're on now. Burn your apartment if you have to.

Mustang Jones — Okay, then what?

Unknown — The feds will come after you. They'll seize your homes, cars, and anything they can get their hands on. They'll bankrupt you trying to repay all the money you helped Arnie steal. How liquid are your assets right now?

Mustang Jones — Very. Arnie told me I'd want as much cash on hand as possible when the real estate market finally bottoms out.

Unknown—Good. I will provide you with account and routing numbers, and you will transfer the money to the Cayman Islands.

Unknown — FILE: Wiring Instructions Cayman National Bank

Mustang Jones — Fuck you. How stupid do you think I am?

Unknown — I don't know, but I know how stupid you've been. Do you have a choice? They will arrest Arnie any day now, and then they will arrest you. Can't you comprehend how big this is, Terrance?

The two of you stole billions with a capital *B*, and once they convict you, you'll never see the outside of a prison again.

Mustang Jones — How does transferring all my money to you save me from prison?

Unknown — It won't, but leaving the country will, and I will help you do that as soon as you've transferred the money.

Mustang Jones — Leave the country? And never come back?

Unknown — Yes, Terrance. Do you truly not understand how much trouble you are in? Barry Minkow only stole one hundred million, and he got twenty-five years. You and Arnie stole five hundred times more. Do you seriously think you could go back to selling grills? Your life as you knew it is over. But if you act now, you can keep most of your money and live out the rest of your days in some South Pacific paradise that doesn't have an extradition treaty with the United States. Or you can stay and rot in jail while government vultures devour everything you've built.

Mustang Jones — You have to tell me who you are.

Unknown — Someone who knows your sins and still wants to help. That should be enough for now, but if a name helps, you can call me Sarah Howe. I'll tell you the next steps after you've made the transfer. If I see they've arrested you on television, I'll know you were too stupid to save yourself.

Three hours later ...

Mustang Jones — It's done.

Unknown — I'm glad you came to your senses.

Mustang Jones — Now what?

Unknown—We have to get you out of the country fast. I've got a boat ready.

Mustang Jones — A boat?

Unknown — You can't fly out of New York. They may already be looking for you. I'll get you to Sikorsky in Bridgeport by boat. A jet is waiting, as is your new passport.

Mustang Jones — Okay, where can I catch this boat?

Unknown — Meet me on Brother Island in one hour.

CHAPTER THIRTY

"Where is Mustang's phone, Izzy?" Kari asked the next morning over a grainy video call on Elton's computer. Since she was banned from visiting, Milo was confined to Tribeca, and we were under lock and key, the A-Team was relegated to virtual meetings where everyone's voices lagged a second behind their moving lips.

"In your backpack," I lied. "Wait, did you lose it?"

It was hard to read Kari's expression in low definition, but I was sure she knew I was lying.

"Dammit. We must have left it on Mustang's desk," I said, then tried to change the subject. "What did you find on the laptop, Milo?"

"Nothing of use to our investigation," Milo said.

I frowned and said, "Aren't you supposed to be some sort of computer genius?"

"I am a computer genius," Milo said, his tone betraying offense, "and with time, I should be able to access any deleted files. Mustang's browsing habits reveal a preference for a particular genre of pornography but do not shed any light on his attempted murder. His email correspondence includes several hundred death threats from clients of Arnie Spencer but no mention of clandestine meetings on Brother Island. My next steps are to identify the whereabouts of each angry investor on December 15th, which will give us a list of possible suspects. This, however, will be time-consuming."

"Thanks, Milo," I said, "and you've got no way of tracing that unknown number?"

"Not without the phone, Izzy," Kari snapped.

"Well, you shouldn't have lost it, Kari," I snapped back.

A bitter silence filled the air, and after a long stare-down with Kari, I asked Milo, "Was there an email from someone named Sarah Howe?"

"No," Milo said, having apparently memorized hundreds of emails in the last twelve hours.

"Why?" Kari demanded.

"I thought I saw that name on one of the letters on Mustang's desk," I lied.

"Sarah Howe was an infamous American fraudster who operated a Ponzi scheme called the Ladies' Deposit Company of Boston in the 1880s," Kari said.

"Wait, how could a lady from the 1880s write Mustang a ..." Axl began, then noticed our expressions and said, "Never mind."

I shook my head at Axl, then turned back to the screen and said, "Don't worry about it, Milo. I guess I saw her name researching Ponzi schemes."

"There are over five hundred women named Sarah Howe in the

New York metro area," Milo said, consulting the phonebook in his head, I suppose. "It will be challenging to determine if any of them invested with Arnie Spencer, but I can—"

"It's okay, Milo. Don't worry about it."

"Very well," Milo said. "I will begin verifying the whereabouts of every investor who wished ill on Mustang via email."

"And I will return to Mustang's apartment and retrieve his cell phone," Kari said.

"No, you can't," I said, for no other reason than I didn't want Kari out there investigating without me. I had the phone, but what if she found something we'd missed and cracked the case?

"Why not?" Kari demanded.

Because I'm not about to let you win, I thought. "Because," I said, racking my brain for a believable and less honest reason before landing on, "it's not safe to go there alone. We should assume whoever stabbed Mustang is several steps ahead of us, and if they catch you there alone ..."

This was all it took to get Elton on my side, and he said, "I concur with Izzy. It is not safe for you to go there alone."

"The two of you would say that," Kari snapped. "You're scared of your mothers. I'm going back for the phone, and neither of you can stop me."

The rest of the morning was miserable. Elton still wouldn't talk to me, and our mothers wouldn't shut up, suggesting every touristy thing they could think of in a futile effort to get us out of the house.

But I told them I didn't feel great, which was true, and that I was going to lie down for a little bit, which was a lie. In my room, I pulled Mustang's BlackBerry from my backpack and read over the texts from the unknown number again. But nothing new jumped out at me, so I cursed and threw the phone across the room.

Typically, the end of Christmas break filled me with anxiety. The two-week break from school and all the shit that went with it never lasted long enough, and by New Year's Eve, it felt like Dick Clark was counting down the seconds to my impending doom. Don't get me wrong, I still didn't want to return to school, but I was ready to go home because this break from life had been worse than life itself. My best friend was pissed off at me for sabotaging his relationship. My boyfriend was hurt that I hadn't reciprocated his declaration of love fast enough. He hadn't texted me since we hung up, and I was starting to worry I'd run off one of the few good things in my life. Mom and Holly didn't trust me enough to go to the bathroom by myself, and things with Axl were weird since I'd caught him snorting pills. There were so many things I wanted to freak out about that my mind couldn't focus on one, and suddenly, the walls in my bedroom started closing in. I ran out to the balcony for air, which wasn't a great idea because the quick transition from my suffocating bedroom to the enormous Manhattan skyline almost made me pass out. So I ducked back inside, and without even thinking about it, took my second pill of the morning—not a good idea—then I hid under the covers of my bed—where I should have stayed. But then the pill kicked in, building on the first one I took that morning, flooding me with a rush of indescribable pleasure. The next twenty minutes were a blur. Thankfully, I didn't leave my room, but I did grab my phone, intending to text

River my plans to kiss him until his lips hurt when I got home. But I couldn't find his name in my contacts, because it was Mustang's phone. Then I had a terrible idea.

Mustang Jones — Hi!

CHAPTER THIRTY-ONE

I watched Mustang's BlackBerry for ten minutes, but nothing happened. It made sense, I suppose. Whoever lured Mustang to Brother Island probably did it on a burner phone they could toss in the Hudson. Still, I was high as a kite and couldn't be deterred.

Mustang Jones — I said, HI!!!!
Unknown — Who is this?

Holy shit! They replied. My heart pounded as I sat up in bed and began banging out texts with my thumbs.

Mustang Jones — This is Mustang Jones.
Unknown — No, it isn't. Terrance Jones is in a coma at Mount Sinai.
Mustang Jones — Wrong! He woke up.

"Dammit," I said with a giggle, then tried to correct my mistake.

Mustang Jones — I mean I woke up. I'm Mustang Jones.

Unknown — Seriously, tell me who this is. If you have Terrance's private phone, you are in grave danger.

A chill finally cut through my Oxy-induced haze, but I wasn't about to let on.

Mustang Jones — Ooo, scary. Who is this?

Unknown — A friend. I told you.

Mustang Jones — Bullshit. Friends don't let friends drive drunk or lure friends to Brother Island and stab them.

Unknown — That was not my intention. I wanted to help Terrance, but someone hurt him before I could. One of his lovers, I suspect.

Mustang Jones — Which lover? I have soooo many.

Unknown — Who knows, though my money is on that jock-turned-preacher's wife. Now, tell me who this is. You're not safe.

Mustang Jones — Why? Are you going stab me on Brother Island too?

Unknown — Fine. Don't believe me. But if I don't know who I'm talking to, I cannot help you, so goodbye.

Mustang Jones — Don't go! This is Izzy Brown. I'm friends with Mustang's son, Elton.

After typing this, I felt a twinge of regret, but I couldn't say why. The feeling was fleeting, though, so I carried on.

Unknown — And Terrance gave you this phone?

Mustang Jones — Nope. Mustang couldn't remember shit when

he woke up except he'd helped Arnie Spencer rip off half the world. He gave us the address to his secret apartment, and we found his secret phone and secret laptop while we were there. We're investigators!!

The science is inconclusive, but I've no doubt there's a link between an opioid high and exclamation point use.

Unknown — Do you have Terrance's laptop with you?

Mustang Jones—Nope! Milo Klink has it at Kanner Academy. All we found on it were a bunch of angry emails from the people Mustang ripped off, but Milo thinks he can access the deleted files with some work. He's a computer genius, like Bill Gates, but somehow more socially awkward. I kept the phone with me because I'm sneaky, and I didn't want Kari Patel to catch the culprit before I did.

I waited. For minutes. Then I couldn't wait any longer …

Mustang Jones — Hello?
Mustang Jones — Gone to stab someone else?
Mustang Jones — Hello??? Stabby McStabberson?
Mustang Jones — Sir Stab-a-lot??!
Mustang Jones — Asshat!
Mustang Jones — Stabbing Asshat!

"Screw you too," I said to the phone, then tossed it across the room. I considered finding Elton and telling him about what I'd done, but he was mad at me, and he'd be even angrier if I told him I'd been texting the suspect by myself. Besides, the second pill of the morning was now pulling me toward the bed, and resting my eyes for a minute seemed the better idea.

I didn't wake up until six hours later when Elton barged into my room and said, "Someone attacked Milo."

Technically speaking, Milo wasn't attacked. An hour after I called our suspect an asshat and told them Milo had Mustang's secret laptop at Kanner Academy, a man in a long coat and ski mask entered the school and took the computer. Milo was pushed and fell during the brief altercation, but apart from a sore butt, he emerged physically unscathed.

That evening, Elton, Axl, and I got on a video call with Kari and Milo. We were shaken up and didn't know what to do next, but we all agreed calling the cops would likely get us all into more trouble.

"Who knew we had Mustang's computer?" Kari asked as we thought through our next move.

"Mustang and whoever saw you go over to his apartment this afternoon," I said, trying to blame Kari while conveniently not mentioning I'd told our only suspect where Mustang's computer was only a few hours ago.

"No one saw me enter the apartment today," Kari snapped back defensively. "Besides, I was there when Milo was assaulted. The timing doesn't work."

"Pushed," I corrected. "Milo was pushed."

"It was an assault, and I'm fortunate to be alive," Milo said, and this time I didn't argue.

"Well, Mustang knows, and I guess anyone who saw us go in the apartment two days ago."

"And who else knows about Mustang's secret apartment?" Axl asked.

When Elton woke me up, I took his father's phone to the bathroom and reread all the texts I'd sent the suspect six hours earlier. All the exclamation points made me cringe, though I did giggle at Stabby McStabberson. But what concerned me most was I didn't remember any of it. That second pill of the morning was a terrible idea, and I obviously couldn't trust myself with that much OxyContin in my system. Still, the suspect had told me something of use.

Unknown —My money is on that jock-turned-preacher's wife.

"I bet Stacey Davis knows," I said. "Your dad says he goes there to get away from Jade, but I guarantee he meant he goes there to spend time with Stacey."

"The apartment is a pigsty," Kari said. "There was a just a mattress on the floor."

"And that's all they'd need," I said, which made Elton squirm uncomfortably. "Maybe Stacey saw us go in and leave with the computer. Or maybe there are security cameras, and she watched us do it later? Either way, she's the only other person we know who has visited that apartment."

"Why would Stacey want the computer back?" Axl asked.

"I don't know. We don't know what was on there or what she thinks is on there. But Stacey has romantic and financial ties to Mustang, potentially giving her two reasons to stab him."

"I disagree," Kari said.

"I'm sure you do," I mumbled.

"Izzy," Milo said, "the person who assaulted me—"

"Pushed," I corrected.

"The person who assaulted me was a man, not Stacey Davis."

"A man who didn't set off the alarm," I said. "Stacey Davis has the money to hire someone to steal the computer, and she could have gotten the Kanner Academy passcode from your dad, right?"

Elton considered this and said, "Affirmative. Mother and Father both receive the updated passcode every Sunday night."

"My father receives the passcode, and he is a man," Kari said.

"Oh good grief," I muttered, then asked Milo, "Did Sachin Patel assault you this afternoon?"

"A ski mask concealed the man's identity. However, I do not believe it was—"

"Exactly," I said, turning off the video call. Then I turned to Elton and said, "It's time we spoke to Stacey Davis."

CHAPTER THIRTY-TWO

"Wait, where are you going?" I called after Elton as he stood to leave my room.

"To my room," Elton said. "I want to build the Lego Fire Brigade I received from Santa Claus."

"You can do that after we talk to Stacey Davis."

"I am not going with you to talk to Stacey Davis," Elton said. "We have no way of contacting her, and even if we did, we cannot leave the apartment without adult supervision. And besides—"

"I've got a plan," I said, but Elton ignored me.

"And besides," he continued, "I think it best I limit the time I spend in your company."

"What? Why?"

"Because, Izzy, I was happy before your visit."

"And?"

"And ever since Principal Baugh asked me to show you around Bardo Academy, my life has been at sixes and sevens."

"What?"

"It is something Mother says," Elton said. "I believe it means utter chaos."

"Elton," I said, "your life has not been chaotic since we met." He stared at me deadpan, and I conceded, "Okay, well, maybe it's been a little chaotic."

"I was happy, Izzy. I have a girlfriend I like very much, but I am forbidden from seeing her, thanks to you. You have ruined everything in one week, and in a few days, you will return to Florida. But I will remain here, trying to piece back together the life you destroyed."

I thought Elton was being a touch dramatic but was ready to apologize anyway if it meant he'd accompany me to talk to Stacey Davis. But before I could, he stomped out of the room, and when I called his name, he didn't look back.

"Listen," Denzel Davis said, answering on the first ring, "I know you kids don't have shit to do but snoop around everybody's business pretending you're the damn NYPD, but I don't have time for this. I've got a church to run, and if you don't—"

"Shut up, Denzel. We need to speak to Stacey."

"Nope."

"I'm sorry, but we do."

"Well, it ain't happening. Now listen—"

"No, Reverend, you listen because you know we know you screwed around and lost seventy million dollars of Village Tabernacle's money to Arnie Spencer. Now, maybe your sheep are so blind they don't care if you spend their tithes on a private jet, so long as you fly around the globe saving souls. And maybe they don't care if you snatch money from the offering plate to pay for your ridiculous Gucci suits, so long as you quote the Bible to all the paparazzi who follow you around. But when these people find out you lost all their money in a pyramid scheme, they're going to want some Old Testament vengeance on your ass. But even if they find it in their hearts to forgive you, the IRS won't. Now, maybe you're thinking, she's just a stupid little teenage girl. She doesn't know anyone at the IRS. And you'd be right. But after all the shit Elton and I have stirred up in the past year, I know lots of people in the media. And as luck would have it, a few of them are local. All it would take is one call to the *New York Times* and—"

"I can give you Stacey's number, but I can't guarantee she'll talk to you."

"Oh, I think you can do better than that, Reverend. You've got more celebrities at your church than regular people. Tell Stacey one of the Kardashians wants to meet her for prayer and pastries at Almondine Bakery in Dumbo at five o'clock this afternoon."

"I'm not lying to my wife," Denzel said.

"Oh please, all you ever do is lie to your wife."

Denzel huffed but didn't argue. "Fine, but the Kardashians don't go to our church. I'll tell her the singer from *American Idol* who visited last week wants to meet. But why the hell does she have to go all the way out to Brooklyn?"

"Because we're grounded and can't go farther than a couple blocks from Elton's apartment without our mothers," I said.

"Good Lord," Denzel muttered. "How did I let this happen?"

"Make the call, Reverend. Because if Stacey doesn't show up this afternoon, everyone in the five boroughs will know what you did."

Early that evening, I sat at a small table in Almondine Bakery, waiting on Stacey Davis and convincing myself it was better that Elton wasn't with me. If he and Axl were here, not back in the apartment playing PS3, it would feel like an ambush, and Stacey might not talk. No, this was better, I decided while sipping my hot chocolate, and there was no need to examine any of the things Elton said before stomping out of my room.

Five minutes past five, Stacey Davis walked in from the cobblestone street and scanned the room, looking for an *American Idol* star, not a meddlesome kid. She was tall, thin, and gorgeous, just like the photos I'd seen of her online. Stacey wore a long red coat and oversized Gucci shades, but put her in a little pleated skirt and hand her some pom-poms, and she could pass for the NFL cheerleader she once was. I dropped my copy of *Page Six* and waved, but she pretended not to see me.

"Mrs. Davis," I said, walking over and offering my hand.

She eyed me suspiciously while still scanning the shop for Kelly Clarkson or whoever Denzel said would be there.

"Do I know you?" she asked.

"No, but I know your husband," I said, "and he arranged for us to meet here today."

Stacey Davis reconsidered me, perhaps wondering if I was one of Denzel's romantic interests and, if so, how much prison time was in his future. She opened her mouth to reply but couldn't find the words, so I slurped down the last of my hot chocolate and cleared the air.

"I know your husband lost a fortune to Spencer Investments. He not only lost your personal money but also your church's endowment. I know your husband is sleeping with Jade Martin, and I know about your decades-long affair with Mustang Jones. What I don't know is who stabbed Mustang Jones, and you're going to help me find out."

Stacey's face hardened, her perfectly plucked eyebrows knitting together. For a moment, the gloss of calm broke. She scanned the bakery, perhaps looking for a hidden camera that would explain this absurd encounter, before returning her gaze to me and asking, "Do I know you?"

"I'm Izzy Brown. I'm friends with Elton Jones-Davies, Mustang's son."

"Oh my God, you're Elton's friend from Florida who solved that murder," she said.

"Murders," I corrected.

"Sorry, murders," she said with a smile. That she'd heard of me put her at ease, though I'm not sure why. "Where is Elton?" she asked, scanning the shop.

"Back in his apartment playing video games," I said. "He's mad at me for telling his mother that his girlfriend is a psychopath. Now, about Mustang—"

"Izzy," Stacey said, putting a soft hand on my arm, "I think it's just precious you're trying to find whoever hurt Terrance. But the last thing he'd want is for you or Elton to get involved in this."

"Whatever. He's the one who sent us to his secret apartment."

"What secret apartment?" Stacey asked.

"Oh, like you don't know," I said, though one look at her face confirmed she hadn't the slightest clue.

"And what did you say earlier about Spencer Investments?"

"Your husband lost all your church's money to them."

"He most certainly did not," Stacey snapped.

I shrugged. People say communication is the key to a healthy relationship, but this relationship was already far from healthy, and communicating this truth wouldn't have helped. "Ask him when you get home," I said.

"I will," Stacey said, and I could hear the uncertainty creep into her tone. But if she didn't know about Denzel losing all their money, she had one less motive for stabbing Mustang, so now I felt more uncertain myself.

"You saw Mustang Jones the day he was stabbed," I said.

"I did not stab Terrance," Stacey snapped, causing several people in the bakery to turn toward the commotion. "And I don't have to stand here while you make wild accusations about my personal life. I don't know about you, but Elton was raised better than this, and I'm shocked Holly lets you within a mile of her son."

Stacey turned to leave, but I stopped her with a hand on her shoulder, which she violently shook off. "Mrs. Davis, I will tell you what I told your husband. If you don't answer my questions, there will be a *New York Times* article about the shady preacher and his wife who gambled away seventy million dollars."

"Denzel never lost a dime of our church's—"

"Would he have lied and tricked you into meeting me here if I didn't have his balls in a vise?"

Stacey swallowed this bitter pill and seemed to concede my point. "Fine," she said, "I saw Terrance the day he was stabbed. I was with him the evening before and spent the night. We talked about getting married. We've talked about it for years, but that night, I thought he was serious. I knew he'd been with Jade, but he told me things with her had been over for months. But when she walked in on us, I could tell by the look on her face he'd lied to us both. So—"

"You decided to stab him."

Stacey rolled her eyes at me and turned to leave.

"Hold on," I said. "If you think I'm being so ridiculous, you won't mind telling me where were you the night Mustang was stabbed?"

Stacey hesitated, then said, "Not that it's any of your business, but I was with my husband."

"And you really didn't know Mustang kept a secret apartment on the Upper East Side?"

"No," Stacey snapped.

And you didn't send a man to Kanner Academy yesterday to steal a computer and assault an autistic boy?"

"Of course not," she hissed, loud enough that every conversation in the bakery screeched to a halt, and those sitting around us quickly looked away, exchanging furtive glances while pretending not to listen. "What is wrong with you?"

"Last question, did—"

"No more questions!" Stacey yelled. "I didn't stab Terrance, but I'm not surprised someone did. Now if you'll excuse me, I'm going to find my husband because he has a lot of explaining to do."

As Stacey stomped out of the bakery, it hit me—she'd been tangled up with Mustang long enough to learn how to hide her secrets. But there'd been a crack in her voice that was unmistakable. For all her practiced deception, Stacey Davis was hiding something big. And I was going to find out what.

"Mr. Jones, good afternoon, my friend. How are things in your world this lovely day?"

"Hey Sachin, I'm good. Listen, we … we, uh … we need to talk."

"We're talking now, I'd say."

"No, in person. We need to talk in person and in private. Actually, no, in public."

"You're starting to scare me, Mr. Jones. Is everything okay?"

"Yeah, everything's fine. But can we meet tonight? Say, Jean-Georges, at 7:00?"

"I'm flying to Boston tonight for an early morning meeting, but I can make that work. However, it's your treat. Remember, my friend, you've got all my money."

Mustang laughed.

Nervously.

Too nervously, Sachin thought.

By now, a plan was in motion. A plan to get Mustang out of the country with most of his fortune still intact. Of course, Mustang had reservations about wiring millions to an unknown caller and then meeting them on a deserted island construction site. And yet, what choice did he have? He could try to take his money and run, or stay and face the coming shitstorm that would bankrupt him and likely put him behind bars. Maybe this person who called themselves Sarah Howe was robbing him blind. Or maybe it was the feds setting him up. Mustang knew the risks, but considering his alternatives, a roll of the dice was as good as he could hope for. Still, he had loose ends to tie and hoped Sachin Patel would help.

Dinner was awkward. The two men talked about their children, the weather, and the New York Jets' chances of clinching a playoff spot. Not until dessert did Sachin finally press Mustang about the reason for their hastily arranged dinner.

"Your money," Mustang said, "it's gone."

The two men locked eyes.

Sachin laughed.

Mustang did not.

"What do you mean it's gone? Eight hundred million dollars doesn't just disappear."

"I'm sorry," Mustang said. "Spencer Investments was a scam from day one."

Sachin's smile vanished as he absorbed this information like a heavyweight boxer taking a stiff jab, then he countered with a flurry of profanity and a professional wrestling-worthy lunge toward Mustang's throat.

"You lying, mother—"

Mustang pushed away from the table before Sachin reached his neck, their commotion bringing the restaurant to a momentary hush.

"I didn't know," Mustang hissed, sliding back up to the table with his hands raised in peace.

"Oh, sure," Sachin said. "How much of your money did you invest with Arnie?"

"None," Mustang conceded, "but only because he wouldn't let me. He lied to me too, though. He paid to bring him clients, but it all went into an imaginary account with Spencer Investments. I'll never see the first penny."

Sachin wiped an imaginary tear from his eye, then flipped Mustang off. "Eight hundred million dollars, Mr. Jones. You're seriously telling me I've lost eight hundred million dollars?"

Mustang nodded. "But big picture, it's just a drop in the bucket. Arnie brought in fifty or sixty billion over the years."

"My God," Sachin said, rubbing his temples.

"Listen," Mustang said in a low voice. "None of this is public yet. You've got a few days."

"A few days until what? My investors storm my office with pitchforks? Do you plan to help me construct a barricade?"

"You lost eight hundred million of other people's money, but you're worth 3.7 billion. Move some money around. No one will ever have to know you lost your investors' money. Sure, you'll take a hit, but you'll still be a billionaire."

"This is what I get for letting a man who got concussions for a living give me financial advice," Sachin said to the sky. Then he turned back to Mustang and asked, "What, do you think, I just have the 3.7

billion sitting in a checking account with Chase Bank? Do you think I can write a check and cover my ass?"

"No, but you're a brilliant man, Sachin, and now that I've given you the gift of time, you can get yourself out of this mess. I just want one thing in return."

Sachin started shouting again, and this time, a waiter materialized out of thin air to ask the two men if everything was okay and if they wouldn't mind shutting the hell up before he called the police.

"The feds are going to eat me alive," Mustang whispered when the waiter hesitantly left.

"Deservedly so," Sachin agreed.

"But my son and my wife—they're going to lose everything too, and they've done nothing wrong. They need somewhere nice to live, something near the park, maybe, and help with college if Elton doesn't get a full ride. A few million is all it would take. That's peanuts to you, Sachin. I could have left the country and let this blindside you, but I didn't. So please, it's the least you can do."

Sachin smiled, but his eyes showed no kindness as he grabbed both sides of the table until his knuckles turned white. Then he stood and flipped the table over, sending dishes crashing and drinks spilling. And while everyone in the restaurant pointed and murmured, Sachin walked out, leaving Mustang alone, sinking in a sea of broken glass and shattered dreams.

CHAPTER THIRTY-THREE

Admitting your mistakes is difficult, even if you can remove all emotion from the situation. I'd gotten high, had a revealing conversation with Mustang Jones's likely attacker via text message, and consequently jeopardized our investigation and poor Milo Klink's life. The instant I mentioned that we'd recovered Mustang's secret laptop to the person calling themselves Sarah Howe, the conversation went dark, and soon after, a man in a ski mask entered Kanner Academy and stole our evidence. This was not a coincidence, however much I wished it were.

Telling the others was the right thing to do. The mature thing to do. But then again, when had maturity ever been my strong suit? Besides, telling the others involved admitting I'd been an idiot and I'd have to bathe in Kari's patronizing superiority, and that was a bridge too far. So I harassed Stacey Davis instead, accusing her of stabbing Mustang and sending a man to Kanner Academy to rough up an autistic boy and steal a laptop. But Stacey swore she didn't know

Mustang kept a secret apartment, and I believed her. There wasn't even a bed or couch in that apartment, so Mustang wasn't taking women back there unless they had a dirty floor fetish. Still, Stacey told me she was with Denzel the night Mustang was stabbed, but Jade Martin told us the same thing. So someone was lying to us.

During our three previous investigations, Elton and I always caught people lying, though mostly to cover up embarrassing shit they'd done, not get away with murder. My hunch was neither Stacey nor Jade stuck a knife into Mustang's chest that night on Brother Island, and I didn't suspect either of them was on the other end of those mysterious text messages. I also didn't really believe we'd been spotted by the killer leaving Mustang's secret apartment with his laptop. Still, I couldn't admit that to the others without also admitting my massive screwup. So, with the stubbornness of a degenerate gambler, I doubled down.

"We need to see your dad again," I told Elton while he and Axl banged away on their PlayStation controllers.

"I do not wish to see Father today," Elton said without bothering to pause his game or even look my way. Without Kari around to drive the investigation, it was clear Elton cared little about finding out who stabbed his father.

"I don't blame you," I said, "but we have to find out who else knew about his secret apartment."

"Why?" Elton asked, giving me the minimum amount of his attention.

Because I said so, I thought, since that was usually enough to get Elton to do my bidding, but apparently not anymore. "Because," I said, "then we can figure out who saw us leaving with the laptop and stole it from Milo."

Elton considered this momentarily, then shrugged and said, "Father's secret apartment looked like a college dorm room. I do not suspect he would have brought anyone there."

I couldn't argue his point, but I wasn't about to give up either. "Well, someone knew about it. Someone who didn't want us to find your dad's computer because they knew it would lead us to them."

"You go," Elton said. "You can tell me what he says when you get back."

"My mother won't let me visit your father alone, you donkey. That's weird. You have to go with me. Right, Axl?"

I pinched my brother hard on the side, and he yelped in pain before saying, "Yeah, right, whatever."

"We can even have Kari meet us there so y'all can spend some time together," I said, the concession making me nauseous.

Elton huffed but relented. "I will ask Mother," he said, "but not until we finish this game."

Kari claimed she was too busy solving the case to meet us at the hospital, and when we got there, Elton insisted on staying in the waiting room while I talked to his dad. By now, Mustang was stable enough to leave the ICU and move into a regular room, though, unlike the other patients in his hall, his room wasn't full of flowers and balloons. It almost made me feel sorry for the asshole, but I suppose he should have been grateful no one had sent him a get-well-soon letter bomb.

"Where's Elton?" he asked when I walked in without a knock.

"In the waiting room," I said. "I don't think he likes you."

Mustang gave me a "What can you do?" shrug.

"The nurses must not like you either," I said, pointing out the window to his less than breathtaking view of a rooftop air-conditioning unit.

"You just missed a couple of New York's finest," Mustang said, changing the subject from people who didn't like him. The color had returned to his face, and he again looked like the version of himself you couldn't miss on late-night television commercials selling grills, apart from the several monitors still tracking his vitals and beeping out their findings every so often.

"They're still camped outside your door," I said. "Here to ask you about the Spencer scheme?"

"Nah," Mustang said, "my lawyers said that won't happen until I'm well enough to walk out of here in handcuffs. Right now, all they want to talk about is the stabbing."

"And?"

"I still don't remember anything," he said, his eyes flicking toward the ceiling. "Where's my laptop and phone?"

"Our friend Milo took your laptop back to Kanner Academy so he could search the deleted files, but a man assaulted him and stole it before he could get to work."

"Dammit, I needed that computer," Mustang snarled, then winced from the effort.

"Milo is fine," I deadpanned, "thanks for asking."

"I don't care," Mustang said, and this time I totally believed him. "What about my Blackberry? Did they take it too? I need it to prove my innocence."

"Or to delete the evidence you were planning to flee the country the night you were stabbed," I said, and Mustang exhaled sharply.

"You read the texts?" Mustang asked, and I nodded. "Look," he said, "it's not what you think."

"Oh, I'm pretty sure it's exactly what I think."

"Fine, but what choice did I have?"

"Stay and take your punishment like a grown-up," I said. Mustang didn't seem to hear this, or at least didn't dignify it with a reply. "Look, I know you're lying. I know you remember who stabbed you. But I also know that while scrambling to save your ass, you planned to live a life of luxury in the Pacific while your son and wife stayed home and paid the price for your sins. That you didn't care about leaving Elton to fend for himself without a dime to his name so long as you didn't have to face the music. I don't care if they ever catch who stabbed you, and if they do, I hope they give them an award. But I'm going to make sure the police see your texts and know you planned to flee the country."

Mustang winced from these blows and shifted uncomfortably in bed to turn from me and face his HVAC views. "That's not true," he said eventually. "Well, it's not entirely true."

I crossed my arms and huffed. Did this man ever stop lying? His voice was calm, but his rapidly beeping heart monitor betrayed him.

"I was leaving, sure," Mustang said, desperate for me to believe him. "If I'd stayed, Elton would have been no better off. But that night, before I was supposed to go to Brother Island, I had dinner with Sachin Patel. Took him to Jean-Georges because it's easier to get a table there now that all the banks have collapsed."

"Wait, you had dinner with Sachin Patel the night you were stabbed?" I asked.

"I wanted to warn him about what was coming down the pipe. He was Arnie's biggest investor. Lord, he was about to lose nearly a billion dollars, most of it other people's money. But I knew Sachin was rich enough to cover his ass if he had time, and that's what I gave him. In return, I just asked him to take care of Elton and Holly after I was gone. You know, pay for college and put them up somewhere nice. I would have never just left …"

I suspected Mustang went on justifying himself to the walls, but I wasn't around to hear it because Sachin Patel had some explaining to do. And this time, I wouldn't leave without answers.

CHAPTER THIRTY-FOUR

"Where are we going?" Elton asked as we waited on the sidewalk outside Mount Sinai, trying to flag a cab. None were stopping.

"Your dad had dinner with Sachin Patel the night he was stabbed," I said.

"On Brother Island?" Elton raised an eyebrow.

"What? No, at some fancy restaurant. That's when your dad told Sachin all the money he'd invested with Arnie Spencer was gone."

Elton stepped in front of me, stuck two fingers in his mouth, and let out a whistle that brought three taxis to an abrupt stop. He held open the door of the closest cab. "So Sachin Patel stabbed my father during this fancy dinner and dragged his lifeless body to Brother Island?" Elton asked, clearly mocking me.

"Well, no," I said as we climbed in. "But Sachin lied to us. He told us he worked late that night, but he was actually having dinner with your dad, finding out a big chunk of his fortune had vanished. Which makes sense because Kari said he came home, threw a tantrum, and smashed the television. Then he lured your dad to Brother Island and stabbed him in the chest."

Elton bit his lip. "Except Sachin Patel flew to Boston that night, and he has flight records to prove it."

"Sachin Patel's worth 3.7 billion dollars," I said. "He could make that flight manifest say he went to the moon with Elvis."

"Occam's razor suggests that if—"

"I don't want to hear about Occam's razor again," I said, cutting him off. Maybe this wasn't the simplest explanation, but I knew it was the right one. "Sachin's the culprit, and I'm about to bust his ass."

Elton shook his head, pulled out his phone, and typed something. "There are several gaping holes in your theory."

If there was one thing Elton was great at, it was poking holes in my theories. And fine, maybe it was necessary, but I didn't enjoy giving him the pleasure. "You're a gaping hole," I muttered, but I was already reexamining my theory, looking for errors.

The earlier texts from the unknown number—Mustang got those before he told Sachin his money was gone, so that didn't line up. Damn it to hell. Unless … Anders! Anders Larsson could've tipped off Sachin if he figured out Arnie Spencer was a fraud first. Maybe he called Sachin, or one of Sachin's accountants caught on. There were a dozen ways he could have known. And his Boston alibi? A net worth of $3.7 billion buys a hell of an alibi. And if Sachin already knew the money was gone, he had time to put his revenge plan in motion.

"We were supposed to go straight home from the hospital," Elton reminded me, since I clearly didn't want to discuss holes in my theory.

"We're already grounded," I said. "What else could they do to us?"

I texted Sachin Patel, asking him to meet us across from his office in Bryant Park. I was going ice skating on this trip if it killed me.

Sachin replied that he was in a meeting and could be down in half an hour. Not wanting to be completely reckless, I texted Mom to say we were stopping to go ice skating on the way home. She and Holly would not be thrilled, but they'd be angrier if we didn't tell them—and besides, they were the ones begging us to do touristy stuff the past few days. My phone buzzed six or seven times with rapid replies, but I didn't look. If I didn't see them, I could pretend I didn't know they were mad.

Bryant Park was alive with skaters and bundled-up shoppers drifting between holiday market stalls, the air thick with roasted chestnuts and hot chocolate. Strings of twinkling lights hung above us, warm and bright against the December chill. The city's hum surrounded us, blending with laughter and chatter, making me wish—again—that I lived on this crazy island. My dueling desires to live here forever and never come here again alternating every hour or so.

We rented skates, and though I was terrible, Elton was even worse, stumbling across the ice like a newborn giraffe. After my tenth or eleventh fall, I spotted Sachin Patel standing by the rail, laughing.

"So you've identified Mustang's attacker?" Sachin asked, smiling as I made my way over and caught my balance on the rail.

"Yep. You," I said.

"Good God, Izzy. You're still trying to blame me? How did you manage to solve those other murders if you're this bad at solving crimes?"

"No, you're right. Blaming you before today was premature. But now we know things. We know you found out about Spencer Investments' fraud before December 15th. We don't know how, but you knew. Then you went to dinner with Mustang, playing dumb, while your revenge plan was already in motion.

Sachin's mouth opened slightly, but he didn't say a word.

"We know you had dinner with Mustang the night he was stabbed. We know you had Mustang's private cell numbers. And I'd bet you convinced him to wire his money out of the country to cover some of your losses, then lured him to Brother Island and stabbed him."

Sachin took a deep breath, exhausted—but not in a guilty way. He looked like a man fed up with dealing with dumb kids. That look I'd seen on my teachers' faces before they disappeared on "medical leave" for two months.

"Yes, I had dinner with Mustang the night he was stabbed. There are only a hundred people in the restaurant who could vouch for it, so it's not something I was trying to hide."

"Don't act like you couldn't afford to make everyone in that restaurant forget what they saw," I said.

Sachin laughed. "A Burger King, maybe, but not Jean-Georges. Hell, I turned a table upside down on Mustang as I left. If you knew any Upper West Side gossip, you'd have heard about it already. I didn't tell Kari because, frankly, would you? With how she's been lately?"

I shook my head no, though Sachin asked rhetorically.

"I didn't know about the Spencer fraud until Mustang told me," he continued, irritation flashing in his eyes. "Yes, we got an anonymous tip earlier that week, so I had my accountants check what a total loss would look like, but I didn't know for certain until Mustang told me at dinner. Then, he had the gall to ask me to take care of his family as he fled the country, so I turned the table over him, went home, and pitched a fit. Then, like I've told you all a million times, I flew to Boston."

Sachin looked past my shoulder and smiled, and I turned to see Kari walking toward us. Elton must have called her. Damn him. Sachin waved her over and said, "And now, against my better judgment, I'm going to tell you all why I went to Boston. Maybe then you'll leave me in peace."

CHAPTER THIRTY-FIVE

Kari walked over to us, though I've no doubt she could have donned a pair of skates and performed several triple axels had she wanted, just to show me she was better than me at everything.

"Hello, liar," Kari snarled in lieu of a normal father-daughter greeting, and Sachin flashed me an exhausted smile.

"Hello, Kadambari. Nice of you to visit me at work today."

Disgusted by the pleasantries, Kari spat on the ice, then stayed on the attack. "You lied to me. You had dinner with Mustang Jones the night he was stabbed." Then she turned to me and said, "And don't think you've cracked this case just because you somehow wrestled this information from Elton's father. I've known my father was guilty from the beginning, and you know it."

Kari looked mad enough to punch me if I used any smart-ass replies that came to mind, so I held my tongue.

"I didn't lie to you. I withheld information," Sachin said, his calm demeanor cutting through the tension.

"Same thing," his daughter snapped.

"No, it's not. I've always been honest with you to a fault—it's one of my few virtues. Occasionally, I withheld information, but it was only for your protection. I didn't tell you about my dinner with Mustang Jones because I knew you'd only jump to more false conclusions."

"Liar!" Kari shouted again, causing a few parents to pull their ice-skating children away from us.

"Fine," Sachin said, raising his right hand and pretending to place his left hand on an imaginary Bible. "Here is the unfiltered truth you so desperately want. I had dinner with Mustang Jones on December 15th at Jean-Georges at his invitation. Over dessert, Mustang informed me that Spencer Investments was nothing but a massive Ponzi scheme, and my entire investment was gone."

"Giving you 800 million reasons to stab Mustang Jones," Kari said.

"I lost a lot," Sachin conceded, "but I'm still worth much more. It's embarrassing, sure, and when word gets out, investors might think twice about trusting me with their money. There will be fines, almost certainly. But you and I won't be sleeping on the street anytime soon, and I'd never risk throwing away the rest of my life trying to murder Mustang Jones."

"But he talked you into—"

"I've already told you once, Mustang Jones did not talk me into anything. The decision to invest with Arnie Spencer was mine, and mine alone. When he told me the accounts were empty, I wasn't even that mad at him. Well, I was furious, but I was angrier at myself. But then Mustang had the nerve to ask me to support his wife and son after he fled the country. That's when I lost it—I flipped a table over on him and earned myself a one-year ban from Jean-Georges. That is why you heard me smashing things and cursing Mustang Jones when I returned home. I wasn't just mad about the money; I was furious at my own stupidity for trusting a lying, conniving bastard."

"So you stabbed him," Kari said, though I think now even she didn't believe it.

"So I flew to Boston," Sachin said.

Kari rolled her eyes, the sarcasm in her expression almost cartoonish as she looked at her father. He sighed and handed her his phone, his voice softer. "Fine," he said, "I never wanted you to know I was behind this, but I can't deal with you anymore. This press release goes out next week."

The sound of skaters gliding across the ice and laughing behind us seemed louder now as Kari's entire body stiffened. I looked over her shoulder at Sachin's phone and began reading.

FOR IMMEDIATE RELEASE

Historic $400 Million Gift Transforms Harvard University

CAMBRIDGE, MA - January 4, 2010 - Harvard University today announced that it has received an unprecedented $400 million anonymous gift, marking the largest donation in the institution's 372-year history. This monumental contribution will empower Harvard to advance its mission of academic excellence, innovation, and societal impact.

The gift, bestowed without restriction, reflects a deep

commitment to higher education and belief in the transformative power of unrestricted philanthropy. "Education is the cornerstone of progress and empowerment," said Harvard University President Dr. Alistair B. Cromwell. "This extraordinary act of generosity affirms confidence in Harvard's ability to strategically allocate funds where they are most needed to inspire and empower the next generation of leaders and changemakers."

"We are profoundly grateful for this remarkable gift," Dr. Cromwell continued. "It will enable us to further our mission of educating and empowering future leaders who will tackle the world's most pressing issues with creativity, compassion, and resolve."

I caught the phone as it fell from Kari's hand and gave it back to Sachin, who smiled and said, "Your place in the Harvard Class of 2015 is secured. You have nothing to worry about."

Kari's face twitched, her mouth tightening to a razor-thin line as she read, the sound of children laughing behind us providing a twisted soundtrack to the scene. She stepped toward her father, who, like me, could see the fault line of rage cracking in her face. Sure, Kari wanted Harvard more than anything, but she wanted to earn it with her own sweat and blood. Now, even if she got in on merit, she'd never escape the doubt. Sachin gave his daughter the medal before she'd even finished the race, and now, she had nothing left to run for. He told me once if Kari ever learned his secret, it would cost her more than she could know, and now I knew what he meant.

Sachin had just lost his daughter forever, and if her shout of "I hate you!" didn't get the point across, the slap that followed—loud and flat in the cold air—left nothing more to say.

CHAPTER THIRTY-SIX

Kari came back with us to Elton's apartment in Brooklyn, where most of the neighboring brownstones still had Christmas trees in their windows, holding on to that last bit of holiday cheer. We were already in trouble for not coming directly home from visiting Mustang in the hospital, so bringing home the girl Holly forbade Elton from seeing probably wouldn't make things worse. Besides, Kari was not in a good place and probably didn't need to be alone.

"Izzy Rose Brown—" my mother began the instant we entered the apartment, but she stopped short after seeing Kari with mascara streaming down her face.

"Kari, dear, are you alright?" Holly asked, stepping in close to Kari, though not entirely sure how much comfort to give her. Kari endured this hug longer than Elton would have, but not by much. After she shrugged off Holly's arm, she tried to talk but only burst into tears again.

"It's her father," I said.

"Oh no," Holly said. "Is he okay?"

"Oh, he's fine," I said. "Well, not fine. He just had the shit slapped out of him. Mr. Patel doesn't understand his daughter very well."

Holly turned to her son, who said, "Mr. Patel donated four hundred million dollars to Harvard University to advance its mission of academic excellence."

"It's not a donation, it's a bribe," Kari snarled through tears.

I suspected this entire situation was beyond my mother's comprehension, but Holly understood and said Kari was welcome to stay as long as needed.

Axl joined the rest of us in Elton's bedroom, and we watched Kari grieve the loss of her dream. After about half an hour, she moved into the anger stage.

"How can I be so brilliant when my father is such an imbecile?" Kari asked.

"Maybe you got your brains from your mother," I suggested, and Elton shook his head.

"My mother is a runway model with the IQ of a lamp," Kari snapped, then after some thought, added, "Perhaps I was adopted."

Axl and I laughed at this, the tension in the room lightened for just a second before Kari shook her head. "My dad just doesn't know me. And if I get into Harvard, I'll never know if it's real."

"Look, Kari," I said, "I know you're mad at your dad, but he obviously cares about you."

"Oh yeah?" Kari said. "How would you two feel if your dad tried to bribe your way into college?"

Axl and I burst out laughing at the thought.

Kari scowled and said, "Seriously, how could that idiot not know me well enough to know I'd only want to go to Harvard if I earned my spot?"

"You could still earn your spot," I said. "Your résumé is ridiculous."

"But I'll never know, will I?" Kari said. "Every time I walk past the chemistry lab, or whatever they build with Father's money, the doubt will creep in."

She was right, I suppose. If Harvard accepted her now, she'd never know if she earned it or if her father bought it. But honestly, I didn't care. That's not true; I was secretly happy. Not that Kari was beyond distraught. I'm not that cruel. But if Kari no longer cared about Harvard, she wouldn't care about solving Mustang's case either, and I was okay with that.

I was okay with quitting the case because I didn't care. In the three cold case murders Elton and I'd solved, I'd become dangerously obsessed with catching the killer. That obsession, which almost got me killed several times, also weirdly helped manage my anxiety. When I only thought about cracking a case, I didn't have time to freak out about all the other shit in my life. But I didn't feel that anymore. Maybe I'd learned to manage my anxiety a little better, or maybe I was taking a few too many pills. Either way, the only reason I even remotely cared about Mustang's case was because I was jealous of Kari. Jealous she'd taken my place in Elton's life, and I wanted to beat her. But I didn't have to solve this case. I could never think about Mustang Jones again, and I'd be happy. Besides, we hadn't gotten shot at yet, or threatened, or kicked out of school. Milo got roughed up a little, but he'd gotten off easy considering how our investigations usually went. If we dropped the case now, we'd all walk away virtually unscathed.

I was about to suggest we ask Mom and Holly to take us somewhere fun and touristy when Kari banged her fist on the floor and said, "I'm going to solve the case anyway."

Dammit to hell.

"I'm going to solve this case," Kari repeated, her jaw clenched with determination, "and I'm going to compile the greatest college application in human history. I'll make Dad take back his gift to Harvard, which will bring my odds of getting in down to zero, and then I will get accepted anyway. I'll get accepted to all the other Ivy League schools too, and then I'll take my acceptance letters, burn them, and post the video on YouTube. And then ... and then I'm going to go to some party school like Arizona State and tell everyone who will listen that the Ivys weren't challenging enough."

While I admittedly appreciated the insane levels of pettiness in Kari's plan, she'd obviously lost her mind, and I wasn't thrilled to know I'd have to spend the last couple of days of our Christmas vacation helping her catch Mustang's attacker.

"You should totally go to Arizona State," I said, knowing Elton's aversion to sweating would keep him far away, "but we're never going to solve the case. There are literally hundreds of people with a reason to stab Mustang. We'd need months and a team of twenty detectives to even talk to them all, and besides—"

The apartment door buzzed, and we all exchanged looks before walking down the hall to see who was there. When we reached the living room, Holly was in the doorway, having a hushed conversation with the agitated concierge. He mentioned the police, and Holly thanked him before closing the door and turning to see us.

"It's nothing," she said, though the look on her face betrayed her. Knowing us well enough to know we wouldn't take "it's nothing" for an answer, she sighed and said, "Apparently, a security guard just caught a man in a ski mask trying to access our apartment by the elevator. When they confronted him, he said something about visiting Terrance Jones, but the man ran when they asked for identification."

"Oh my God," I said, my knees buckling so hard I had to grab the couch for balance.

"Izzy, love, it's okay. The police are already here. They think it was likely someone who lost money to Arnie Spencer trying to scare Terrance. No one can get up here. You're safe."

But I wasn't safe—none of us were—and it was all my fault. With my stomach churning like a washing machine, I sat on the couch, scanning the room for something to puke on that didn't cost more than our trailer in Pineview Villas.

"Oh, Izzy," Holly said, walking over to comfort me.

"I'm going to be sick," I said, running down the hall to my bathroom.

But I didn't puke. I didn't do anything. I just sat on the bathroom floor and cried from the pain. The most common side effect of opioids is constipation, and I'd had my share that fall. I know that's too much information, but it's the truth, and at times that December, my stomach hurt so bad I'd buckle over in pain. This was bad enough by itself, but combined with the hyperventilating panic of knowing my stupid texts had brought the killer to Holly's apartment, it was too much. I splashed cold water on my face and tried slowing my breathing when my phone buzzed. It was River, sending his eleventh or twelfth text of the morning, having apparently forgiven me for hanging up without saying I love you the other day.

Me—Dude, I'll be home in like three days, and we can talk then.

Okay?

River—Okay

Now the shitty girlfriend guilt piled onto all the other emotions I was experiencing, and I started to cry. It wasn't even lunchtime, and I already needed another pill because the one I'd taken with breakfast wasn't working. None of them worked like they used to. They used to hit me with just a little euphoria. A jolt of something that made me happy to be alive. That made me want to seize the day and all that nonsense. Now, though, they just numbed me, which was better than soul-crushing anxiety, I guess. But I didn't want to be a zombie. I wanted to be normal.

I took a pill from my bottle and placed it on my tongue but hesitated. In London, I came up with a plan only to take my pills when the shittiness of life became unmanageable. It was a good plan, I thought, and it got me through some bad times. But there are extreme levels of shittiness that call for extreme measures, right? I kept licking the pill until the coating came off, and then I took the handle of my hairbrush and crushed the pill into powder. From there, I'd like to say I thoughtfully deliberated about what I was about to do, carefully considering the risks. But instead, I bent over the vanity and snorted it, fast and numb, pushing back the emptiness inside.

The day Lakshmi Patel didn't get into Harvard changed every-thing forever. Not for Lakshmi; she was fine. Harvard is a small school with an infinitesimal acceptance rate. Every year, thousands of brilliant students fail to get into Harvard. It's nothing to be ashamed of. Lakshmi went to Princeton—not bad for a safety school—and she graduated summa cum laude with a degree in molecular biology. She now attends The Johns Hopkins University School of Medicine, and in fifteen years, she'll be the world's most famous neurosurgeon with seven million followers on TikTok. For Lakshmi Patel, rejection from Harvard was nothing but a tiny pothole on the highway to success, but for her sister, Kari, it changed everything forever.

Kari's father, Sachin, always drilled into her that hard work paid off, pointing to his own success as proof. But if anyone had earned Harvard, it was Lakshmi. No one had a stronger résumé. No one had worked harder. And yet, Harvard said no. For Kari, the takeaway was clear—Lakshmi hadn't tried hard enough. Kari wouldn't make that mistake.

That day, Kari transformed into an unstoppable machine. A scholastic Terminator with a single goal: Harvard. Every action, every choice, every friendship and every hobby she weighed against her objective, and if something didn't bring her one step closer to Harvard, she cut it. She certainly had no time for a boyfriend, but Elton … Elton could serve a purpose.

Her obsession grew sharper in ninth grade when she read *1984* by George Orwell. The children in the dystopian novel who spied on their parents for Big Brother were supposed to be a warning, but for Kari, they were an inspiration. Orwell's story wasn't a cautionary tale to her; it was a handbook. She watched her father like Big Brother, and she saw in his world the kind of secrets only a daughter could uncover. No one as successful as Sachin Patel reached the top without crossing a line or two. Bringing down her father's empire would make her application untouchable.

Kari stole his passwords and studied his business inside and out. She knew the hoops he jumped through to secure the permit to build on Brother Island. She suspected he'd paid bribes but found no proof. Sachin was crooked … but careful.

Kari likely knew Arnie Spencer was a fraud before anyone else. She scrutinized the numbers in her father's account and found them miraculous—and potentially criminal. From her father's hacked emails, she knew Mustang Jones worked closely with Arnie Spencer, recruiting new suckers for the scheme. Between Arnie, her father, and Mustang, it was obvious Mustang was the weak link—the classic dumb jock, always one step behind. If anyone had left clues that could blow open the whole scheme, it was him. She'd hoped that dating Elton would give her access to Mustang's files but soon learned that Elton hated his father and rarely saw him, and the few times she convinced him to visit, Kari found nothing incriminating in Mustang's office.

Of course, trying to expose massive financial fraud occupied just a portion of Kari's time that fall. She still had lacrosse and cello practice, her medical research internship, endless test prep, and her hair and makeup vlog. She moved her crime-solving ambitions to the back burner—until the night her father came home cursing Mustang Jones and smashing televisions. She'd been right. Spencer Investments was a fraud, and if her father knew, the world would know soon. The clock was ticking if she wanted credit for exposing the scandal. Kari didn't have a minute to spare. Every minute she waited, someone else could get to the truth first, stealing the chance she'd spent months creating.

As her father left that evening, she watched his car pull away, her resolve hardening. Kari had been patient, meticulous even, but now was the time for action. She stepped into the busy street outside her father's apartment and hailed a cab.

"Where to, miss?" the driver asked.

"The Majestic," Kari said. "Central Park West."

Tonight, Mustang Jones was going down.

CHAPTER THIRTY-SEVEN

I'll never forget the first time I took OxyContin. Blaine Park, a first-ballot member of the Shitty Boyfriend Hall of Fame, gave me a little baggie full of them, and I took one on the beach when it felt like my life was falling apart. I'd just had lunch with Blaine and his parents in Seaside, and his asshole father had spent a solid ten minutes strongly insinuating that Axl and I were white-trash charity cases who would never amount to anything. I ran from the restaurant that day, crying and hyperventilating—my go-to method for handling things when life became too much.

Before that day, I'd always thought of drugs as instantly mind-altering—like, one minute you're normal, and the next, you think you're riding a turquoise unicorn down the interstate. But that pill didn't alter my mind—not in the way I expected. It just made me feel, I don't know, that my life was better than it was. All the shit that made me anxious was still there. I just didn't care anymore. My creeping dread was replaced by a feeling that everything was great and getting better, which is much preferable.

No pill ever made me feel like that first one. Each one was just a little more lacking than the last. This wasn't something I noticed on a daily basis. I'm not sure I noticed at all, but it's something I'd understand all too well years later. Back then, I was just taking more when I felt I needed more, not bothering to notice how often that was. No pill ever made me feel like that first one, but the one I snorted in Elton's apartment has an asterisk. That shit hit my bloodstream with the intensity of a freight train, and all I could do was stumble to the floor and smile. The euphoria was so intense I knew it was bad, either because it wouldn't last, and I'd want it again, or it would last, and I'd never leave this bathroom floor. It didn't last, of course, and sitting there on the tile floor, the ecstasy faded into guilt and regret. Guilt for yelling at Axl like a damn hypocrite, and regret because I knew I'd do it again, even though I was already telling myself I wouldn't. It took more effort than expected, but I finally got off the floor and stumbled to my bed, where I'd sleep half the day away.

"Baby girl, you feeling better?" Mom asked as I stumbled into the living room. "We saved you some dinner."

"Dinner?" I asked. I thought it was lunchtime, but then again, I wasn't entirely sure what planet I was on. "Wait, did Kari leave?"

I vaguely recalled her being there, and—oh shit, someone in a ski mask had tried to sneak into the apartment, probably looking for Mustang's phone.

"Kari left several hours ago," Elton said.

I turned to Axl, but when he looked me over, I quickly turned away. He knew. Just one look and he knew what I'd done. Of course, it wouldn't be hard to figure out if I looked as bad as I felt. I couldn't imagine why anyone would want to snort those pills more than once if it made them feel this shitty. But then I remembered how good I felt on the bathroom floor and wanted to do it again. Dammit to hell.

I picked at my food for a few minutes, then excused myself and went to bed early, hoping to feel better in the morning. Sleep was terrible. Just awful. I had such a nasty headache, that even while dreaming, I could feel it throbbing. I hadn't taken a pill before bed, and I was determined not to take one now. Snorting that one earlier was some real drug addict shit, and I had to prove to myself I was still in control, even if I knew I wasn't.

My phone buzzed at 5 a.m., but I was already awake, staring at the ceiling and listening to the sirens blare in this awful smelly city that I never wanted to live in. I blinked at the strange number with too many digits, wondering who the hell would call at this hour. While I contemplated, the call went to voicemail, but my phone immediately rang again, so I answered with a groggy hello.

"Good morning, Izzy. This is Anders Larsson."

It took me a moment to remember who that even was, and then I sat up in bed.

"Where are you?" I asked.

"Sweden," Anders said. "Have I called too early?"

I tried to think of a smart-ass reply, but nothing came to mind. "No," I said.

"Good. Izzy, I'm calling to admit something."

"That you stabbed your boss and fled the country?" I asked.

Anders laughed without humor. "No, I did not stab Mr. Jones, though I suppose I had as good a reason as anyone else. I'm calling to tell you that I was the Spencer Investments whistleblower. I went to the feds, and they leaned on Arnie's son Percy, and the whole house of cards came tumbling down."

"So you knew Mustang was scamming people out of their fortunes?"

"No, not all along. Otherwise, I would not have let Mr. Jones invest most of my salary with Spencer."

"No, I suppose not. So how did you figure out it was a fraud?"

"Here's what happened," Anders said. "After living like a pauper, I decided to finally splurge and buy a car. Well, not just any car. A Ferrari F430 Scuderia. But I was having trouble withdrawing the funds I needed to make the purchase, and when I called Spencer Investments, I got nothing but excuses and stalling. They told me it was a long-term investment, not an ATM, and that I'd have to wait twenty to twenty-four months to access the money. That was my first red flag, because that language wasn't on their website or any of the documents I'd signed. Mr. Jones taught me not to take no for an answer, so I pressed harder, but the excuses only piled up. By now I was panicked, because I had millions invested with Spencer. I started doing my own research, and it didn't take long to realize that Arnie Spencer's supposed returns were impossible. The numbers weren't insane, just steady. Steady all the time, even when the markets were anything but. I calculated the odds of an investor timing the market with Arnie Spencer's supposed level of consistency for two decades, and they were astronomical."

"Like winning the lottery?" I asked.

"Like winning the lottery every day for a year," Anders replied. "That's when I finally confronted Mr. Jones, and he admitted everything."

"Hold up, Mustang admitted he knew Spencer Investments was a fraud?"

"Well, no, not really. He played dumb like always. Said he'd talk to Arnie and straighten things out. Then, a few days later, one million dollars magically appeared in my bank account, along with a note from Arnie calling it a gift for all my hard work. But it was an obvious bribe for my silence, and it's still sitting there because I refuse to touch it."

"Then why'd you leave the country? It's suspicious as hell."

"Because I don't want to die, Izzy."

"Are you afraid the investors will come after you?"

"No, not me. I wouldn't want to meet Master Menace in a dark alley, but even he doesn't scare me as much as she—"

"She who?" I demanded, a chill racing down my spine.

"I'm sorry, I misspoke."

"You did not. She who, Anders? Who are you afraid of?"

"Listen," Anders said, the fear in his voice unmistakable, "I told the feds what I know and what I think I know. The ball is in motion, and if I'm right, you'll see it on the news soon enough. I didn't call to help you with your little investigation. I called so you'd know the proper authorities have all the information they need, and when they have their ducks in a row, justice will be served. But I also called to warn you because we're talking about powerful people, Izzy, and when powerful people feel trapped, they're dangerous." He paused and then, almost as if to himself, added, "Elton is a good kid. He's the only good thing about Terrance Jones, and I would feel awful if something happened to him. Please let the professionals handle it from here, and maybe no one will get hurt."

"Wait, Anders, you've got to—"

Click.

CHAPTER THIRTY-EIGHT

There was a lot to process after talking to Anders. Too much, perhaps, because instead of running into Elton's room and telling him everything I'd just learned, I fell back asleep and slept until almost noon. In my dreams, I was on Brother Island, though instead of a bird sanctuary, it was a creepy abandoned amusement park, like some zombie Coney Island. I was standing in front of one of those fortune-telling Zoltar machines screaming, "Tell me who she is," when Kari stepped out of the shadows with a butcher knife and chased me through a hall of mirrors. Right before she stabbed me, I woke in a cold sweat, my head pounding worse than I could ever remember. I took one stumbling step out of bed and vomited on the floor, which actually improved things slightly. Then I took a pill and lay on the bathroom floor until it kicked in and I felt good enough to shower and dress for the day.

When I finally made it to the kitchen, everyone was already eating lunch, and bright winter sun flooded through the windows. I'd tried my best to make myself presentable, but I must have still looked like hell, because everyone stared back at me with concern etched on their faces.

"Baby girl, we should take you to see a doctor this afternoon. You might have come down with the flu."

"I'm fine," I said, waving off Mom's concern and sitting at the table. "It was just a migraine. I haven't had one in ages, but that one knocked me for a loop. But I never had a fever or anything."

Mom was skeptical but accepted that I must feel better after watching me scarf down my lunch in record time. After dessert, which I also inhaled, I asked Elton and Axl to follow me to my room.

"Anders Larsson called me last night," I told them once I'd shut the door. "Well, technically, he called early this morning, but I fell back asleep. Anyway, he said—"

"Izzy, are you really okay?" Axl asked, interrupting me.

"Yeah, I'm fine."

"You do not look fine," Elton observed.

"You don't look fine either," I snapped back. "Now, both of you shut up and listen. "Anders was the Spencer whistleblower," I said. "He told the feds everything. Apparently, your dad invested most of his salary with Spencer Investments for years, and Anders thought he had millions in his account too, but when he tried to pull out some cash for a car, Spencer gave him the runaround."

I took a breath. "So he started digging and figured out that Spencer's supposed returns were impossible. He confronted Mustang about it, and a few days later got a million-dollar bribe from Arnie."

"Did Father know about the bribe?"

"I don't know, but Anders left the country because he was scared."

"Scared of who?" Axl asked.

Axl's question rattled around in my brain, looking for an answer, but not finding one. Our conversation now felt like it happened five years ago, and all the details were hazy.

"Izzy, who is Anders scared of?" Elton asked when I didn't answer.

"Your girlfriend," I blurted out before I even knew what I was saying.

Axl laughed and rolled his eyes, but Elton took me seriously enough to say, "Explain."

"She's freaking psycho," I said, the memory of my drug-hazed conversation with Anders and my nightmare about Kari blurring together into what felt like the inescapable truth. "She was obsessed with getting her father arrested because she thought that would impress Harvard. That in itself is insanity defined. But here's the thing. Kari is crazy, but she's brilliant. And if I had to guess, when she started snooping through her father's financials, I bet she figured out Spencer Investments was a fraud too. So she sees an opening, right? She can kill Mustang and pin it on her father. And everyone would believe it because Mustang cost Sachin Patel a fortune. But then, unbeknownst to her, her dad left town that night, and now she can't figure out how to blame him."

"Izzy," Axl said, "I don't think—"

"I know you don't think, so you shouldn't talk either," I said. Then I turned to Elton. "Dude, I'm sorry your girlfriend is an attempted murderer, but them's the breaks. You're young; you'll find someone else."

On some level I realized I sounded a little insane, even to myself, but the pieces fit—or at least, they felt they fit in my fogged-up head. Maybe I hadn't fully slept off the night before. Maybe my brain was just grasping at shadows.

Elton put a hand on my shoulder, which he never did. I looked at it, confused, then back at him. He smiled at me like you'd console a crying child and said, "Izzy, I think you need to lie down for a minute."

I shook his hand off my shoulder and jumped to my feet. "Hey, Big E, I get it; I've dated shitty people too. Blaine Park turned me in to the cops. Sterling Masters bet his friends he could sleep with me. I mean, none of them stabbed my dad, but still, I can commiserate."

Elton looked to Axl for help, but my brother could only shrug.

"Izzy, Kari did not stab Father."

"I'm afraid she did. Why don't you call and ask her? She's probably as terrible at lying as you are."

"I never thought I would say this," Elton said, walking toward the door, "but I think I will be happy when you return to Florida."

CHAPTER THIRTY-NINE

After Elton left my room, Axl and I sat marinating in the awkward silence. I wanted to cry, but I wasn't about to cry in front of him, so I just bit my quivering lip and waited for him to leave.

"Seriously," Axl said, apparently in no hurry to leave, "what's been wrong with you the past few days? Girl stuff?"

"Sure," I said. "Girl stuff. Now, can you leave me alone?"

"I'm worried about you."

"Don't be," I said and rubbed my nose. It was something I'd seen Axl do a lot in the past six months, though I'd never put two and two together. I'd only snorted one pill, so the nosebleeds, sinus infections, and funky-colored snot were still down the road. But that morning, I'd convinced myself some pill dust was still in my nostrils, and now I couldn't stop reaching for my nose. Even Axl, dumb as he is, could figure this one out.

"Oh shit," he said, his voice flat with dread, "you're snorting."

"Shut up."

"You are," he said, looking sick. In frustration, he pulled on his hair and started pacing the room, swearing under his breath. "How long's this been going on?"

I started to lie again, but what was the point? He knew. "I'm not snorting, I snorted, once, yesterday, and it was a huge mistake I will never repeat."

"But why?" Axl asked.

"Same reason you do it, I guess," I said, which landed like a stiff jab.

"Damn it," Axl said, resuming his pacing. "I should have never given you the idea."

"You didn't invent snorting pills, Axl. I could have just as easily figured that out on my own."

"But you didn't," he said. "You saw me do it once, and a week later, you're doing it yourself. It's messed up, Izzy. This isn't like you."

"Dude, calm down, I said I won't do it again."

"Yeah, I only tell myself that every time," Axl said, slamming his fist on the bed in frustration. "Fuck!"

"Dude, chill," I said.

He looked me over and shook his head with pity, which really pissed me off, then asked, "Why now? Why this time?"

"Same reason you do," I repeated.

"You hurt your ankle playing football?"

"Not everyone who sprains their ankle is snorting oxycontin two years later," I said, a sharp edge creeping into my tone. "I told you, I only take pills when life's shittiness feels unmanageable, and yesterday, the shittiness reached critical levels."

Axl scoffed. "We're on Christmas vacation in New York City. How could the shittiness possibly be unmanageable?"

"And you snorted a pill five fucking days ago right down the hall," I shot back, a little too loudly. Axl immediately shushed me, glancing toward the door like he expected Mom to hear every word.

"My leg was killing me the other day," Axl said in an intense whisper. "What's your excuse?"

"The shittiness was unmanageable," I whispered back. "We've been over this."

Axl huffed in frustration. "Well, if you hadn't spent your entire Christmas vacation trying to solve a crime, maybe you'd have enjoyed yourself and not felt the need to snort pills."

"I didn't come here to solve a crime. I came here to hang out with Elton, but if I hadn't helped him and Kari, I'd have never seen him. I don't care about that case. I don't care who stabbed Mustang. I could never think about any of it again and be happy."

This was true enough and a stark departure from the three cases Elton and I solved before, when catching the killer consumed my every waking thought. It should have been a warning sign that the pills I was taking too many of had begun zapping the motivations that used to define me. The realization crept over me: what if, someday, all I cared about was the next hit? I wasn't there yet, but I was on that road, and there weren't many exits left.

"I just … I just felt super shitty when security said some guy in a ski mask was trying to get into Holly's apartment."

Axl looked at me puzzled. "Why would you feel shitty about that?"

I took a deep breath and came clean. "Because I sort of swiped Mustang's phone out of Kari's backpack the other day after we searched his secret apartment."

"You had the phone?" Axl asked.

I nodded sheepishly and said, "And I sort of took too many pills the other morning and started texting the person who lured Mustang to Brother Island."

"Izzy, what the hell?"

"And I sort of let on that Milo had Mustang's computer at Kanner Academy, and I had the cellphone in Holly's apartment."

Axl's face betrayed a range of emotions from bitter disappointment to teeth-grinding anger. He opened his mouth to tell me how stupid I'd been. To tell me I could have gotten Milo, Holly, or Elton killed. To tell me that I'd screwed everything up. That I always screwed everything up, and I always would. But he'd already told me those things a dozen times, so what was the point. Instead, he just shook his head and slammed the door as if he'd decided he didn't need my drama in his life anymore.

Half an hour later, after I stopped crying, I tried calling River. Since I'd now screwed everything up, I hoped maybe I could start fixing some things. But the phone rang once and then went to voicemail. I hung up and tried again with the same result. And though there are a few explanations for this, I couldn't help but imagine him seeing my name and hitting the decline call button so hard he jammed his finger. It felt like even the one person who'd always accepted me, warts and all, had finally had enough.

I couldn't stand another second in my room, so I went to the balcony to breathe. A crisp breeze off the Hudson cut through the winter quiet, carrying with it the distant hum of the city below. As I took in the sight, I noticed Mom, already lying on a lounge chair like it was summer and she was poolside. She looked over and saw me before I could duck back inside.

"Come here, baby girl," she said, patting the chair for me to sit with her. I did as I was told, and she said, "I feel like I ain't seen you in three days. You feeling better?"

I'd feel a lot better at the bottom of that river, I thought. "Yeah," I lied, the smell of Mom's favorite cheap perfume taking me away from the penthouse and back to Pineview Villas. "Sorry I ruined the vacation."

"You didn't ruin nothing. I'm happy just sitting out here looking at that city all day."

I smiled weakly. "I figured you were mad at me like everyone else."

"Well, I wasn't thrilled you and Elton tried to get mixed up in Mustang's mess after all the trouble you've caused in the past, but I guess y'all just can't help yourselves. And nothing came of it, so no harm done, I guess. Now, what makes you think everyone else is mad at you?"

I shrugged. "Elton's mad because I keep pointing out all the ways his girlfriend sucks."

Mom laughed. "Jealous much?"

"I'm not jealous of Elton's girlfriend. I just …"

"Why's your brother mad?" Mom asked, graciously changing the subject.

"Because he's always mad at me," I said. "He thinks I screw up everything."

Mom squeezed me tight and said, "Baby girl, he don't mean that. He's doing what big brothers do."

"Little brother," I corrected.

"That's right, little brother, and don't you let him forget it." I smiled, and Mom took me by the shoulders and said, "Izzy Rose, you ain't screwed nothing up. You and your brother have both worked so hard. I couldn't be prouder of you." She wiped a tear away and held me at arm's length. "That don't mean I don't get mad at you. Sometimes I get so mad at you I can't see straight. Like when you solved those murders. You put yourself in so much danger, and I was furious with you, but I was proud of you too. We ain't there yet, baby girl, but we're gonna get there."

"I know, Mom."

"I'm always proud of you, baby girl."

"I know," I said, wiping away my tears. I hugged her once more, then went back to my room and took another pill.

CHAPTER FORTY

I sat on my bed, feeling like shit, scraping at the pink coating of my next pill with my fingernail. If Mom could see me now, she wouldn't be proud. If she had any idea the sort of person I'd become, she'd put me up for adoption, if that's even something you can do with a seventeen-year-old. But I could solve crimes. I was good at it. Well, maybe not good, but I got results. Or at least I used to, before half-assing my way through this case.

I could still crack it, bring Mustang's attacker to justice—maybe even keep Holly and Elton from losing everything while giving Mom one small, not-pathetic thing to be proud of. The dramatic thing would have been to throw the pill across the room, but I knew I'd take it eventually, just not now. Right now, I had work to do, and the last time I took two in one morning, I got loopy and had a way-too-revealing text convo with a violent criminal. I put the pill back in its bottle and got to work.

But after ten minutes of staring at my suspect list, I was ready to give up again. There was Sachin Patel, who couldn't have stabbed Mustang because he was in Boston bribing his daughter's way into Harvard. The lover's triangle of Stacey Davis and Jade went nowhere. Denzel Davis had an alibi. And if I was honest, Kari was only on my list because I didn't like her and had a weird dream about her after snorting drugs.

The truth was, literally hundreds of people had a reason to stab Mustang Jones, and a case like this would take an entire department of detectives months, if not years, to solve. If they even tried that hard, because it's not like the public was clamoring for Mustang's assailant to be brought to justice. Honestly, most people would probably rather throw them a parade than lock them up. Maybe this case was just beyond my pay grade as a wannabe detective. Or maybe I'd taken so many pills that my brain would never work right again. That thought sent a chill down my spine, so I quickly banished it.

Usually, these things were like a knot of fishing line. I'd keep pulling at different strands until the whole thing unraveled. What had I missed? What strand had I not pulled hard enough?

Jade. Jade told me she was with Denzel the night Mustang was stabbed, but Denzel and Stacey told me they were with each other. Of the three, Jade's alibi didn't line up. I'd known this, but I wrote it off as dumb grownups hiding their stupid affairs. But maybe not. I had Jade's number. I'd gone through Elton's phone and copied all his contacts because that's the sort of friend I am.

Me—Hey Jade, this is Elton's friend Izzy. We found a secret bank account of Mustang's we thought you'd want to know about. There's a lot of cash still in it. Call me.

My phone rang in six seconds.

"That money belongs to me," Jade said by way of hello.

"Hey Jade, great to hear from you. There's no secret bank account; I was lying." Jade called me a "little bitch," among other things, but before she could hang up, I said, "But while I have you on the phone, would you mind telling me why you lied and said you were with Denzel the night Mustang was stabbed?"

"I didn't lie. I was with Denzel," she said, now sounding her usual annoyed self.

"Then why did Denzel and Stacey tell me they were together?"

"Because they were together," Jade said.

My face scrunched in confusion, like I was doing long division in my head, and then it hit me.

"Oh … ohhhhhh. Gross." My stomach twisted in a mix of revulsion and disbelief. "That's … messed up."

"I've had better nights," Jade deadpanned. "It was all Anders's idea."

"Wait, Anders was there too?"

"No, Anders wasn't there. The threesome with Denzel and Stacey, and secretly filming it, was his idea. We both needed money. Anders spent eight years working for Mustang with nothing to show for it. I spent eight years in Mustang's bed with nothing to show for it. So Anders came to me with a plan to blackmail the Davises. He knew Denzel had already lost his personal fortune with Arnie, but their church still had money—or so we thought. And they hated Mustang for their own reasons, so talking them into a night of revenge sex didn't take much convincing. That note you found was to Denzel. I handed it to him the next morning in Mustang's office while showing him our little home movie. He said he'd pay whatever it took to make it disappear, but it turned out he was just as broke as I was. We didn't know it, but he'd gone back to Arnie and invested all the church's money too. So I had a night of uninspiring sex for nothing."

"Holy shit," I mumbled.

"But Elton's little friend Kari already knew all of this," Jade said.

"Wait, what?"

"She showed up at the apartment that night looking for Mustang. Elton must have given her a key, and she got an eyeful when she walked in unannounced. She didn't tell you?"

"No," I said, "she didn't tell me. Thanks for your help, Jade. I've got to go."

"If you do uncover a secret bank account, you'd better—"

Click. Oh my God, I was right. Kari left her house looking for Mustang the night he was stabbed. Sure, I'd only accused Kari because I didn't like her, but I was right. Maybe I did have a knack for this stuff. Elton wouldn't like this one bit, but he couldn't argue with facts. I was about to tell him the news when my phone rang. It was Ruby Spencer.

"Uh, hello?" I said.

"Izzy, this is Ruby Spencer. Is now a good time?"

"Uh, yeah," I said.

"Great, please fill me in on your investigation. I haven't heard from you since you visited, and I wanted to know if you'd uncovered the plot to set up my poor Arnie?"

Holy hell. How this woman still hadn't accepted the truth about her husband was beyond me.

"No, ma'am," I said, "but I do think I know who stabbed Mustang Jones. It was Kari Patel, Sachin's daughter."

Ruby Spencer was quiet for a long moment. "Yes, that makes sense. It all makes sense," Ruby said, with a confidence I did not share.

"Wait, it does?"

"Kari Patel is a diabolical young woman. She's donated her father's money to my Audubon Society for months, hoping to sabotage his Brother Island project. I spoke to her at one of our meetings, and her obsession with getting into Harvard is beyond the pale. I've no doubt she would stab a man and try to make her father take the fall. But not only that, she's dating Terrance's son, Elton, am I right?"

"Yeah, she is."

"Which means she had access to Terrance's computers, and thus, the Spencer Investments servers."

"I suppose—"

"I can't believe I didn't see it sooner. Izzy, time's running out—and this has to stay between us. The police are already conspiring against my Arnie, so let's handle this ourselves. I've got a plan, and if you'll listen to me, we'll come out of this smelling like roses."

11:27 PM
DECEMBER 15, 2009
THE DAY OF THE STABBING

Ruby Spencer came from money and always expected to have it. But after twenty years of marriage to Arnie, she was broke. Well, maybe not broke. In the early eighties, Ruby and Arnie Spencer's net worth was roughly ten million dollars. They had a nice place on the Upper East Side, sent their kids to the right boarding schools, and vacationed in the right Italian villas. You'd have to search long and hard to find someone to pity the Spencers. But Ruby's father once spent ten million dollars on a single thoroughbred horse, and he paid more than twice that for a Monet. Sure, Ruby lived a life most of the world would envy, but by the standards she grew up with, she might as well be homeless.

Ruby's father didn't like Arnie. Didn't want his little princess marrying some poor kid from Washington Heights.

But Ruby was stubborn.

And Ruby was in love.

And Ruby didn't think her father was serious when he threatened to cut off her money.

He was.

And he did.

Every night for the first five years of her marriage, sleeping next to Arnie on a foldout couch in their shoebox apartment, Ruby fought the urge to run back home to Daddy's money.

Things got better when Arnie went out on his own in 1970. He opened Spencer Investment Securities with a big loan from Ruby's father, who gave Arnie favorable terms but still wanted his money back with interest. Arnie worked hard, made a lot of money, and provided his family a life almost anyone would be happy with. But not Ruby.

Ruby turned forty in 1985. It was not a pleasant occasion. When Ruby's mom turned forty, her father threw her the biggest party Manhattan had ever seen and bought her a mansion on Further Lane in the Hamptons. Arnie gave Ruby a watch.

Arnie's problem, Ruby decided, was that he was too honest. She recalled childhood games of Monopoly with her father and how he'd cheat like the devil to win. "When it comes to money," he'd say, "rules are excuses for the losers." Ruby helped Arnie doctor the first batch of falsified statements in the fall of '85. Nothing crazy. Clients saw a steady return during a rocky three-month stretch when most of their friends had broken even. Business picked up as word spread that Arnie was winning when other firms were settling for draws. Then came October 19, 1987—Black Monday. The largest one-day percentage drop in Dow Jones history.

Arnie probably spoke to a hundred investors that day, feeding them lines directly from Ruby.

"We're hedged against this."

"You think I'd lose your money in this little crash?"

"I'm Arnie Spencer. Trust me."

When word got out that Arnie had produced steady returns right through the biggest crash since 1929, life would never be the same. The dam broke, and investors flooded in by the thousands, making Arnie richer than he ever dreamed possible. Richer even, than his father-in-law. When Ruby turned fifty, Arnie bought her another watch, and a fifty-million-dollar mansion in the Hamptons.

The celebrity recruiting scheme was Arnie's idea. An idea Ruby strongly advised against. Publicity brings scrutiny, and that was the last thing the Spencers needed. But now, some gangster rapper called Master Menace was namechecking her husband on his latest album.

"I give props to Arnie, that dude with Midas hands,
Turned my shit into gold, now I'm stacking rubber bands.
Market's always crashing, but we ain't ever took a loss,
Spencer got me winning, got me hustlin' like Rick Ross."

"He's just a dumb football player," Arnie would say whenever Ruby questioned him about how much Mustang knew. "Don't worry about him."

But Ruby did worry. Football players weren't meant for high finance, but Arnie trusted him like one of the old-money crowd. And after a few glasses of wine at dinner, Arnie was liable to tell you about his colonoscopy or the giant Ponzi scheme he'd run for twenty-five years.

She worried because Spencer Investments had long since passed the point of ever being able to pay back their investors. New money slipped through their fingers as fast as it came in. And now that even glossy magazines like *People* were profiling her husband, she feared that before long, some ambitious financial reporter would take a hard look at Spencer Investment's returns and realize they were impossible.

So Ruby made a plan. A brilliant plan, if she dared to say so herself. A plan that would see Ruby get away with more money than she could ever hope to spend. A plan that would let Ruby live out her golden years in a sunbaked paradise. A plan that started with Ruby, waiting for Mustang Jones on Brother Island.

Waiting with a sharp blade.

CHAPTER FORTY-ONE

I dug Mustang's secret BlackBerry out of my backpack and powered it on, tapping the clunky keys until I saw the last texts I'd sent to the assailant, who called themselves Sarah Howe. Of course, Kari knew who Sarah Howe was when I'd mentioned the name to Milo; it was her alias. I cringed a little, scrolling through my pill-inspired text spree. You remember the one where I broke out such classics as Stabby McStabberson, Sir Stab-a-lot, and Stabbing Asshat. I shook my head as I reached the bottom of the thread, then typed out a new message.

Mustang Jones — Hi Kari.

The little pencil icon on the screen began moving as Kari typed her reply, and I felt my heartbeat accelerate.

Unknown — Who told you? I know you didn't figure it out on your own.

Holy shit! Kari stabbed Mustang Jones. Elton's girlfriend stabbed his father. I allowed myself a quick fist pump and celebratory dance around the room, silently narrating my victory to an invisible crowd cheering my genius. A billionaire's daughter stabbed Mustang Jones, and I busted her. Even if the feds took everything for Mustang's role in the Spencer scam, he'd win a fortune when he sued Sachin Patel and his daughter for damages, and Elton and Holly wouldn't have to live on the streets. Ladies and gentlemen, the great Izzy Brown has done it again.

Mustang Jones — No one told me, Kari, I solved it on my own, just like Ricky Lee, Davy Taylor, and Vance Fuller. Crazy thing is, this one took less than two weeks. A personal best, despite the fact the culprit was "helping" me investigate by insisting we focus on her red herring father.

Unknown — You think you're so smart.

Mustang Jones — Nope, just nosy to a fault. But hey, I didn't figure it all out. Ruby Spencer solved part of the puzzle.

Unknown — And what part is that?

Mustang Jones — The part where you used Elton to access his father's computer and the Spencer Investments servers. You cooked the books to make it look like Arnie Spencer had spent decades stealing from his client. You fabricated the crime of the century and then solved it in hopes of using your newfound fame to get into Harvard.

Admittedly, I wasn't so sure about this set of accusations, but Ruby Spencer was, and she was my best chance to catch Kari, so I tossed them out at her request. Besides, it all sort of fit. Anders Larsson told me he was the Spencer whistleblower, but Kari could have used him. Or, more likely, he was working with Kari, and once she got what she needed from him, she tried to dispose of him, only Anders fled the country before she could. He told me he was scared of someone, a certain she, but he wouldn't tell me who. Kari made the most sense. Kari was diabolical.

Mustang Jones — Kari?

Unknown — What?

Mustang Jones — What are you thinking?

Unknown — That I'm going to prison if I don't go jump off the roof first.

Mustang Jones — Don't do anything stupid. Ruby Spencer wants to help you.

Unknown — What? Why?

Mustang Jones — Because she's a bird freak. And your dad is building a giant condo on that bird island. But she's willing to help you cover your tracks if you can talk your dad into abandoning his Brother Island project.

Unknown — He'd never do that.

Mustang Jones — He would to save his precious Kadambari from a scary women's prison. Ruby wants to talk to you both tonight on Brother Island. Can you be there?

The line went quiet for twenty minutes this time, but when Kari returned, she was ours.

Unknown — We'll be there.

"One last favor, and you're off the hook."

Denzel Davis cursed under his breath and sighed heavily as if crushed under an avalanche of bad decisions. I'd heard that sigh a lot over the past two years.

"Yeah, sure," Denzel said. "One last favor. Why do I feel like I'll be doing 'one last favor' for you every week for the rest of my life? What if I tell you to go to hell instead?"

"That's your prerogative, Reverend. But I've got an interesting home video of you, Stacey, and Jade Martin that I thought you might want."

"You have the tape?"

"Yep," I lied. "The one and only copy. Jade gave it to me since you're broke and blackmailing you wouldn't get her anything. I told her I still might have some use for it, and now, if you help us, I'll give it to you, and I'll give you my word never to bother you again."

"What do you need?" Denzel asked.

"Doesn't Justin Bieber attend your church?"

Two hours later, Elton, Axl, Milo, and I were in Denzel's Jesus Jaguar, heading across the river into Manhattan. I glanced out the window as we crossed the Brooklyn Bridge. The bridge's towers loomed over us, and in the distance, I could see the Empire State Building lit up for New Year's. The whole city was getting ready to watch the sky explode—but Times Square had nothing on the fireworks we were about to see.

"Watching fireworks from the roof of Denzel's church does not make sense," Elton said for maybe the twelfth time since our invitation. "The surrounding buildings will severely hinder our view, and I do not even want to meet Justin Bieber."

He was right, of course. His mother's balcony would provide panoramic views of the midnight fireworks show, but our Brother Island confrontation promised to be equally explosive in its own right.

"You're right," I said, "but Kari is meeting us at the church, and your mom wouldn't let you invite her over. Don't you want to kiss her at midnight?"

"Affirmative," Elton said begrudgingly.

"That's what I thought."

"But I still don't understand why I had to leave my watch in Elton's room," Milo said.

"Because your parents track your every step," I said.

"True," Milo replied, "but they would likely have allowed me to attend a church function. Well … not likely, but conceivably."

"We couldn't risk it," I said. "I've got to meet Justin Bieber. This way, your little tracking dot will stay at Elton's apartment all night, and your parents will have a relaxing evening. What they don't know won't hurt them."

Our driver merged onto FDR, and I stared back across the East River at the twinkling Brooklyn lights.

"You hate Justin Bieber," Axl said when he caught my eye.

"I don't hate anyone," I said, "except maybe Blaine Park. And Sterling Masters."

His eyes narrowed, but he didn't press me. It wasn't until we'd passed the Queensboro Bridge that Elton looked up from his phone and realized something was up.

"Driver. Excuse me, driver, you missed your turn."

"Don't mind him," I said to the driver, who was struggling to stay in one lane after turning to look back at us.

"But he missed his turn," Elton said, growing agitated. "We are in Midtown, and Village Tabernacle is at least three miles south in the East Village. Driver, we will be in Connecticut soon if you do not turn around."

"Elton," I said, with a firm hand on his shoulder that he shook off, "we're not going to Village Tabernacle."

"Damn it, Izzy," Axl said, "I knew it."

"But you said Kari is meeting us at Village Tabernacle," Elton said.

"No, she isn't," I told him. "She's meeting us on Brother Island."

CHAPTER FORTY-TWO

As part of Sachin Patel's deal with the city to build condos on Brother Island, he was granted permission to construct a temporary floating bridge connecting it to Port Morris in The Bronx. If you're picturing something like an inflatable toy kids would play on in a lake, think bigger. Much bigger. This bridge was wider than the West Side Highway and could easily accommodate all manner of construction vehicles needed to build the Blades of Brother Island.

Because of the bird dispute, none of those construction vehicles had made their way across the bridge yet, and the island looked pretty much like it had for the last several decades—in a word, terrifying.

Even across the dark river, we could see the outline of the old boiler room and its towering smokestacks slowly being consumed by vines. A shiver went down my spine, and I silently cursed Ruby Spencer for not suggesting we meet at a Starbucks.

"Izzy," Axl said, as the four of us reached a six-foot chain-link fence covered in sternly worded signs, "what do all these no trespassing signs mean to you?"

"That if someone really wanted to keep people off the island, they'd pay for a guard," I said, and started climbing the fence that thankfully didn't even have barbed wire on the top. I landed on the other side in time to see the three boys exchange what-can-we-do shrugs, and then begin climbing with various levels of success.

After we rescued Milo from the top of the fence where his belt loop had hung up, we began walking across the bridge toward the island.

"Come on, Izzy, what are we doing on this creepy island?" Axl asked. "Mom is going to ground us until we're thirty, then murder us."

"No, she won't," I said, my pace slowing as we neared the end of the bridge and the wilderness beyond.

"In my experience," Elton said, "whenever Izzy has solved, or thinks she has solved a case, she begins making bizarre decisions and withholding information until she finds herself being held at gun-point by a murderer."

"Wonderful," Milo said. "Can I not wait in the car?"

"No one is going to point a gun at us tonight," I said. "This time, I'm several moves ahead of the culprit. It's checkmate, and she doesn't even know it."

"She who?" Axl asked, but I ignored him.

Ruby Spencer wanted us to meet on the first floor of the abandoned Riverside Hospital, but getting there from the bridge involved a three-hundred-yard trek through an overgrown jungle. We passed the boiler room first, a red-brick building tangled with kudzu. Rusted metal panels clung to the structure, partially hidden beneath vines, while old gauge panels sat covered in grime, their dials frozen in place. It was creepy enough without Axl suggesting this was where they burnt all the bodies of the patients who died of smallpox.

"They didn't burn the bodies, did they, Elton?" I asked, but he was too busy looking at his phone to answer. I figured he was trying to text Kari, but I knew she had way too much going on at the moment to reply.

The rest of us used our phones as flashlights and followed an overgrown trail toward the island's north shore, where the hospital sat. The building was so covered with vines that we almost ran smack into it before we even saw it, four stories of ornate brick and shattered windows.

We had to fight through a tangle of vines to reach the old main entrance, where the doors had long since rotted and fallen off. Inside what was once the lobby, the floor was littered with debris. Collapsed furniture lay scattered like bones, and an old, overturned metal chair creaked ominously as Axl accidentally nudged it. Stumbling into the room, Milo kicked an old bedpan, giving us all a good jump scare. Water dripped from the ceiling in rhythmic, haunting drops, adding to the spooky soundtrack as if the setting needed any help being terrifying. The paint-chipped walls and long, dark corridors leading to who-knew-what more than sufficed. Thankfully, Ruby Spencer said to meet her here.

"Good job, Izzy," Axl said, "you found the creepiest place on Earth. Can we leave now?"

Axl was scared, and I couldn't blame him. This was the set of every horror film.

"Yes, I would also like to leave," Milo added. "Our chances of contracting smallpox are low but greater than zero. Right, Elton?"

"Affirmative," Elton said, "though tetanus is much more likely."

My arrogant side wanted to wait until Kari and her father arrived to have my ta-da moment when I pulled the mask off the real criminal. Still, I could sense a mutiny was at hand, and if I didn't want the boys to leave me on creepy smallpox bird island alone, I'd have to tell them what I'd figured out.

"Kari stabbed Mustang Jones," I said.

"Wait, what?" Axl said.

"It was Kari," I said. "I don't know how I didn't see it before. You remember how Kari was always so adamant that Jade, Denzel, and Stacey had nothing to do with your father's attack, even when they did things that made them look suspicious as hell?" I asked Elton.

"Affirmative," Elton said. "From the beginning, Kari has focused on only one suspect, her father."

"Well, she knew they didn't have anything to do with it because she walked in on the three of them together in your father's apartment the night he was stabbed."

"Jade Martin had a threesome with Denzel Davis and his wife?" Axl asked, biting his lip and trying to picture the scene.

"Yes, and stop imagining it," I said, hitting him on the arm. "Anders found out Mustang had lost all his money to Arnie Spencer, so he and Jade decided to blackmail Denzel and his wife in hopes of at least getting some cash, but it turns out Denzel had lost all of his money to Spencer too."

"You've lost me," Milo said, "and I have an IQ of 162."

"Kari walked in on them because she was out looking for Mustang."

"Why would Kari be looking for my father?" Elton asked.

"So she could stab him," I almost shouted.

"Why would Kari want to stab my father?" Elton asked, his calm questioning starting to annoy me.

"Kari wanted to get into Harvard, right? She's put together this crazy résumé, but she knows it might not be enough because it wasn't enough for her sister. She meets you in August and finds out you helped solve three cold case murders, and she thinks, if I could do that, I'd be a shoo-in for Harvard. But finding solvable cold case murders isn't easy, and even if she did, there's no guarantee she'd solve it before applying to Harvard. So she starts snooping through her dad's finances, looking for something she could bust him on, but Sachin is clean, or at least so careful that Kari can't find any crimes. But she did find his investments with Spencer. So Kari decides she'll fabricate a crime and solve it herself. Thanks to you, Elton, Kari had access to your father's laptop, which meant she had access to the Spencer Investments servers."

I'd hoped by now a lightbulb would have flipped on, but all three looked like dumbfounded toddlers being asked to explain quantum physics. Of course, Axl always had that look on his face, but the other two were allegedly brilliant.

"So," I continued because these dummies wouldn't get there on their own, "Kari hacks into the Spencer server. She goes crazy deleting files, hiding cash, and making it look like all the investors' money is gone. Arnie calls Mustang in a panic; Mustang tells Sachin because he's the biggest investor. Kari stabs Mustang, frames Sachin, solves the case she fabricated, and voilà. Hello, Harvard."

Elton removed his glasses and rubbed his eyes like some of my teachers did at Dandridge right before they quit. "Izzy, my father had a secret laptop for Spencer business, and we only just discovered it a few—"

"Look," I said, "I know she's your girlfriend, but she—"

A rustling in the jungle outside stopped me short, and the four of us turned to the entrance, holding up our flashlights to see Kari fighting her way through the vines.

"Elton," Kari said, flailing to free herself from the weeds, "there'd better be a good reason you brought me to this stupid island."

"Wait, where's your dad?" I asked when Kari finally stumbled into the abandoned hospital lobby, and I realized she was alone.

"Home, I guess, or maybe he's in New Haven, trying to bribe my way into Yale."

"But you told me you'd bring him," I said, and Kari looked at me like I'd suddenly started speaking one of the few languages she didn't know.

"I did not."

"Yes, you did."

"When?"

"When we were texting earlier."

Kari and Elton exchanged glances, and Kari said, "Elton texted me half an hour ago and said you were acting strange and taking him to Brother Island. I told him I'd be there as fast as I could. We never texted earlier, Izzy. I don't even have your phone number."

I didn't enjoy being spoken to like a child, but I was baffled, and they all could see it.

"Check your phone and see who you texted," Axl said, which was a logical suggestion, except …

"I didn't text her on my phone," I said, then cringed and added, "I texted her from Mustang's phone."

"You had my father's secret phone?" Elton asked.

I nodded sheepishly. "I didn't want Kari taking it back to Kanner and solving the case before I could, so I snuck it out of her backpack on the car ride home. Then I …"

"Then you what?" Kari demanded.

"Then I got a little loopy one night after taking too many pills for my headache and started texting the unknown number that lured Mustang out here."

There were gasps of shock and groans of disappointment, and then Milo asked the obvious question. "Did you tell this person I had Mustang's laptop at Kanner Academy?"

My silent admission was met with a chorus of rebukes and hyperbolic accusations that I could have gotten Milo killed.

"So hold on," Kari said, enjoying this a little too much, "why did Izzy bring you all here?"

"Izzy believed you stabbed my father," Elton said.

"Because you did," I added, trying to sound confident. "After your father came home and smashed his television, you went out looking for Mustang so you could stab him and frame your father."

"How do you know I was looking for Mustang?" Kari asked, and I felt a glimmer of hope that I was still on the right track.

"Jade told me. She said you walked in on her and Denzel and Stacey."

"That's true," Kari admitted

"So you were looking for my father?" Elton asked.

"Yes," Kari admitted.

"And you found him on Brother Island," I said.

"Wrong. I never found him," Kari said. "So I returned home and resumed my ACT preparation."

"Good lord," Axl muttered, but Kari ignored him.

"It wasn't until the next day, when we learned Mustang had been stabbed, that I realized my father did it. Then I switched from exposing his financial misdeeds to exposing his knife-related misdeeds."

I felt sick. I'd been so sure and was so wrong. But worse than that, everyone was now in danger because of me. I told whoever stabbed Mustang we'd be here. I told them we'd be here because Ruby Spencer told me to.

"Oh my God, Ruby Spencer," I said.

"What does Ruby Spencer have to do with this?" Kari asked.

"Everything," Ruby said, finally stepping out of the shadows.

CHAPTER FORTY-THREE

"See," I said, turning to Kari, "I told you it wasn't your dad."

"Oh, shut up, Izzy. You thought I did it, you moron."

"Well, you were out snooping around trying to find Mustang the night he was stabbed," I said.

"Girls," Ruby Spencer interjected, her soft voice failing to cut through.

"So what?" Kari shot back. "It's a free country."

"Sure is," I said. "And you're free to tell us why you were looking for him."

"Girls, please!" Ruby's voice rose sharply.

"Fine," Kari snapped. She turned to Elton, took a deep breath, and said, "Whenever we visited your father's apartment, I would sneak into his office to search for incriminating evidence. Later, after you gave me the key I asked for, I went back alone when I knew your father and Jade were out of town but still found nothing. Of course, I didn't know then about his secret apartment."

"You were trying to take down my father?" Elton asked, his voice tense.

"Not at first. I was trying to take down my father, but then I learned your father and Arnie Spencer were the real criminals, and I wanted to go after them instead. I focused on your father because I assumed he'd done the worst job of covering his tracks."

I could see Elton's mind working. His sense of right and wrong had no problem with his father facing punishment for his crimes, but I could tell he didn't love the idea of his girlfriend bankrupting his family and putting him and his mother on the streets. His jaw clenched, and he looked down, his face tight with conflict as he studied the floor.

"Accusing Arnie Spencer and Mustang Jones of running the biggest Ponzi scheme in history was a big deal. I had to make sure I was right, but while compiling evidence, my father came home cursing Mustang Jones. I knew then the cat was out of the bag, and I didn't have much time. I went looking for Mustang to get a confession, but he wasn't home. The next day I learned Mustang was stabbed. Violent crime is always more sensational than financial crime, so I decided to solve that case instead, since I was sure my father did it."

"But he didn't do it, and you didn't solve anything," I said.

"Oh, shut up, you didn't solve anything either," Kari snapped.

"At least I didn't sneak around my boyfriend's dad's office trying to bankrupt his entire family."

"At least I didn't take a bunch of pills and text a violent criminal."

"Girls, shut up!" Ruby Spencer's voice cracked, cold and commanding. We finally looked toward her and realized she was accompanied by two henchmen, and they were both pointing pistols at us.

"Dammit, not guns again," I murmured, and Ruby hissed at me to be quiet.

"Stephen, check them for weapons." One of the men continued aiming his gun at us while the other patted us down. When he was finished, Ruby said, "You two are foolish girls, who had no idea what was really going on. Yes, Kari, the books at Spencer Investments were cooked. Any person of reasonable intelligence and a basic understanding of accounting could see it. But do you know who cannot see?"

"Blind people?" Axl guessed, and Ruby glared at him, not expecting an answer to her obviously rhetorical question.

"Blind people," Ruby continued, "and do you know what blinds people?"

"Refractive errors? Cataracts?" Elton started to answer, and Ruby cut him off.

"Greed," Ruby Spencer spat, her eyes wild. "Greed blinds people. Arnie has been giving people unbelievable returns for fifteen years, and not once did a client question the numbers. Why?" Ruby raised a finger to keep Elton from answering another rhetorical question and said, "Because they wanted the numbers to be true. They needed them to be true."

"Hold on," I said, taking a step forward, then immediately retreating when one of Ruby's bodyguards turned his pistol on me. "You said Arnie was set up. You told me this afternoon it was Kari."

"How would I even do that?" Kari asked me. "Arnie Spencer started ripping people off ten years before I was born."

"I don't know," I said with a shrug. "It made more sense when Ruby explained it." At least it did when I was high on opioids, but I didn't add that last part.

"No one set Arnie up," Ruby said, "but I persuaded him. Arnie never truly understood human nature. He thought his clients wanted honesty, and surely, a few did. He worked hard and produced steady, unremarkable returns for his investors. The same crap any schmo with a finance degree could produce. But most people don't want honesty. Not really. They want to be rich. They want to think the game is rigged in their favor. And once I talked Arnie into embellishing his statements to give his clients a taste, he saw that I was right.

"He was hesitant, yes—it was illegal for sure. But after the crash in '87, the clients and money came so fast there was no turning back. Spencer Investments became a rocket we could ride into old age, and they'd only catch us after we were dead. Or, at least that's what I told Arnie. I knew the risks—a financial reporter or some meddlesome kid might take a closer look at the numbers and call someone at the SEC. That's why I've been hiding millions for decades. In the Caymans. In Switzerland. My money has gone through so many shell companies and banks that it would take a thousand accountants a thousand years to trace it back to me. One day, I knew Arnie would take the fall, and all I had to do was play the grieving, ignorant wife. Alternate between apologizing and spewing crazy conspiracy theories about my husband being set up. The world would agree I, too, was an innocent victim of my conniving husband." Ruby smirked, celebrating her touchdown before she crossed the end zone. "Then, when the smoke cleared, I'd leave the country and live out my years in Monaco, or the Maldives, or wherever the hell I wanted to."

I turned to the others while trying to process everything Ruby Spencer had said. "It's a solid plan," Kari said.

"Yeah, if you don't love your husband," I replied.

"But I did love poor Arnie," Ruby said.

"Did?" I asked.

Ruby nodded solemnly. "I did, and Arnie loved me too. In his right mind, he'd never throw me to the wolves. But the arrest took a mighty toll on him. He seemed to have aged twenty years in a week. At trial, under intense questioning, there's no telling what he'd say. So tonight, filled with grief, Arnie went to the offices of Spencer Investments and took his own life. I'll report him missing in the morning, and the cleaning crew will find him on January 2nd."

"Oh my God, you're insane. Dozens of people at Spencer Investments have to know you were involved. You can't kill them all."

"Wrong," Ruby said. "I am very sane, and only three people at Spencer knew I could even use a calculator. It doesn't take a lot of manpower to run an investment firm with no actual investments. Most of our employees were on the real estate side under our son, Percy. Arnie knew about me, but he won't be talking. Sandra, Arnie's whore of a secretary, likely suspected me, but she's dead too, and I wouldn't let him hire a new one." Ruby saw the looks on our faces and added, "Cancer. I didn't have a thing to do with it, though I wish I did." Ruby cackled at her own joke, then said, "And finally, Terrance 'Mustang' Jones."

I turned to Kari and said, "Was Ruby Spencer on your list?"

"No," she admitted.

"Mine either," I said.

"The tragic part is," Ruby said, rubbing her chin like she was mulling over dinner plans instead of attempted murder, "Mustang didn't even know. He and Arnie were close. Too close, if you ask me. I always assumed by now Mustang knew all our secrets. I mean, Arnie would tell a stranger on the train about his enlarged prostate.

It wasn't much of a leap to think he'd spill the truth about the Ponzi scheme to his partner. But either Arnie had more discretion than I gave him credit for, or Mustang was too stupid to put one and one together.

"Either way, when he met me here on this island and I laid it all out, he was genuinely shocked. Not as shocked, of course, as when my friends held him down and I sank a knife into his chest."

"But he lived," I said.

"But he lived," Ruby repeated, throwing a disgusted look at each of her henchmen like it was *their* fault Mustang had a pulse. "We left him here in the woods, certain it'd be weeks before anyone found the body. But I'll give your father this, Elton—he's a tough man. How he made it off this island with a blade in his chest, I'll never understand. But he did. And when I saw the news the next morning that he'd been admitted to Mount Sinai, I knew I had a problem. A loose end.

"Fortunately, I also knew Mustang wouldn't talk to the feds. Not when he was stabbed trying to flee the country to avoid prosecution. Accessing his hospital room hasn't been easy with all the security, but this morning we finally secured a keycard. Soon, a very helpful nurse will give Mustang Jones a syringe full of strychnine."

She was going to get away with this. She was going to kill Arnie. Kill Mustang. Kill *us*. Then vanish with more money than she could spend in a thousand lifetimes. I wanted to throw up. I wanted to slap the smirk off her face so bad it made my teeth ache.

My mind scrambled for something—*anything*—until it landed.

"Anders," I blurted. "Anders Larsson knew the accounts were fake. He was so scared of you, he fled the country."

"I discovered the fraud first," Kari said, because even facing death, she had to win the gold medal in accounting.

"Which might've been worth mentioning earlier," I snapped.

"And *you* might've skipped stealing Mustang's BlackBerry from my backpack and dragging us all here to die."

"Girls, please," Ruby hissed. We both shut up.

"You're right, Izzy. Anders is a problem. We tried paying him off. No dice. So yes, I've sent men to Sweden. He'll be handled—just like Mustang. Which leaves the five of you. Five nosy kids who could've spent Christmas break at the movies or the mall, but instead decided to play detective.

"Of course, I saw this coming. I knew about your exploits, knew you'd poke around. I hoped you wouldn't, prayed even. But when you called, I invited you over and pointed you toward Denzel Davis, hoping that wild goose would keep you busy long enough for me to disappear. But no. You had to be clever. And now? Now, you have to die."

She turned to Kari with a cruel little grin. "But you know, sweetheart, this might work out well for both of us. Your father seems determined to bulldoze this bird habitat and put up his little vanity project. But if his daughter's murdered here? He might just let the whole island rot from guilt."

"That *is* possible," Kari said, breezing past the part where she had to be dead for the plan to work.

"Okay, whoa, Mrs. Spencer," I said, holding up a hand. "There has to be a better option. We found out who stabbed Mustang. That's all we wanted. You leave the country, we go home, everybody wins."

Ruby chuckled. "Oh, darling. Like I'd trust any of you as far as I could throw you. Start with the tall one," she said, pointing to Elton.

Her henchmen raised their pistols.

My stomach dropped. My skin went white-hot, like it had been hit by lightning. This was it. This was *really* happening.

Everything slowed.

Midnight fireworks cracked outside, casting flashes of color through the shattered windows like some twisted kaleidoscope.

"No!" I screamed, leaping in front of Elton—ready to take a bullet for the boy who'd saved my life more times than I could count.

The gunshot cracked louder than thunder. A white-hot flash exploded in the room. The hospital filled with searing light.

Then came the thumping. Heavy. Rhythmic. Like the naval helicopters back home in Pensacola.

Voices shouted from the jungle. Distant but gaining fast.

And then—

Just like that—

The world plunged into darkness.

CHAPTER FORTY-FOUR

Here's the thing about Milo's parents: they weren't just overprotective; they were methodically, obsessively, thoroughly overprotective. They tagged him in every way imaginable—his watch, his backpack, even his shoes. They hoped he'd never try to sneak off, but if he did, they'd know exactly where he was, which is precisely what happened that night. When Milo's GPS blip started moving across the Brooklyn Bridge into Manhattan, his dad initially thought he'd snuck off with friends to celebrate in Times Square. He called Milo, ready to ground his son for eternity, but no one answered, and the GPS dot kept moving—straight up into the Bronx, across bridges, and finally over the dark stretch of water that separated Brother Island from the city.

That's when Mr. Klink knew something was wrong. That's when Mr. Klink knew his son had been kidnapped.

Instead of dialing 911, Mr. Klink—a very important man with very important connections—called the mayor, who in turn called

SWAT. Within minutes, a fleet of vehicles was on its way, with heli-copters slicing through the firework-laden sky to descend on Brother Island.

Just as Ruby's little speech ended, and her henchmen raised their pistols toward Elton, the first stun grenade exploded, knocking us all on our asses and momentarily blinding us with brilliant white light. The scene dissolved into chaos, full of flashing lights, commands shouted over radios, and the heavy thud of boots. Men in Kevlar and helmets stormed in, pointing rifles and barking orders. Ruby's body-guards—who apparently had a total of zero loyalty—dropped their guns so fast you'd think they were on fire.

We all yelled at once, trying to explain, our voices tumbling over each other.

"She's the mastermind of the Ponzi scheme!"

"She killed her husband! He's dead in his office right now!"

"She sent people to kill Mustang Jones and Anders Larsson!"

"She's stashed millions in overseas accounts! She was going to flee and start a new life ... with a bunch of pool boys or something!"

Then, a guy in a dark suit entered, his gaze surveying the chaos. He put a hand on my shoulder, helping me up. "We know," he said, nodding as Ruby was dragged to her feet and handcuffed. There was a calm authority to his voice, like he'd seen way worse than a gang of crooked finance goons. "Arnie Spencer flipped on Ruby the minute we brought him in. We've been building a case for days. We would have arrested her soon. You kids are lucky to be alive."

"But Mustang and Anders...?" I asked, heart pounding.

"They're safe," he said calmly. "One of Ruby's men was arrested at Mount Sinai five minutes ago, and Interpol will meet two others when they land in Stockholm. It's over."

He looked at us, his face a mix of relief and exasperation. "Now, come with us. There are a lot of worried people waiting for you at the station."

A New York police station at two a.m. on New Year's Day was the afterparty you didn't want to be invited to. People were slumped over on benches, sleeping off the night, and a man in a top hat and face paint was arguing loudly with a cop about the theft of his pet iguana. Across the room, a woman in nothing but glitter-covered underwear and mismatched high heels was pacing furiously, demanding they track down her stolen tiara, while a guy dressed as a leprechaun laughed hysterically in a corner, his arm red from what looked like a self-drawn tattoo.

We were ushered through this bizarre parade into a cramped office—a small upgrade from the interrogation room—where we were left to wait for what felt like hours, listening to the muffled voices and occasional bursts of laughter echoing down the hall.

Finally, our parents entered, and the entire thing turned into the world's worst parent-teacher conference. Holly and Mom were there, as were Mr. and Mrs. Klink and Sachin Patel, and they all listened in stunned silence as we detailed everything that had happened over the last week. Kari admitted she'd discovered the Spencer scheme while trying to find dirt on her father to get into Harvard, and I reluctantly recounted the parts about Mustang's secret phone and the tangled mess of Denzel and Stacey's affairs. I explained how I'd suspected Kari was the killer, only to realize that Ruby was manipulating all of us into a trap. I didn't exactly highlight the parts where I'd spent half the time high on pills, but the guilt sat heavy in my stomach.

One of the detectives looked at me and raised an eyebrow. "You're the same girl who solved those cold cases last year?"

"Yeah," I muttered, cheeks red. "This wasn't my best month."

"Elton solved those cases!" Kari blurted out, rolling her eyes at me.

"You thought your dad stabbed Mustang, you idiot!" I shot back, our argument escalating until two detectives had to pull us apart.

In the relative calm that followed, The Klinks and Sachin took the opportunity to insist on one thing: that their names be kept out of the headlines. They looked about as desperate as any two men could be to vanish into thin air. Then, when the police left us all alone, the real yelling began. First me at Kari, but we were soon drowned out by Mr. and Mrs. Klink screaming at Milo, then Mom and Holly lit into Elton and me. It was a cacophony of angry voices, each of us getting our turn in the hot seat, while Sachin just rubbed his temples and muttered to the other parents, "Welcome to my world."

They let us go around seven a.m., just as dawn was breaking over the city. We stumbled out into the morning light, bleary-eyed and defeated. The Klinks whisked Milo away without a word, covering his ears as we tried to say goodbye, like we were a bad influence or something. Honestly, they weren't wrong. I had a feeling Milo's days at Kanner Academy were probably over, and the A-Team would disband forever.

I pulled Sachin aside, giving him an awkward apology. "I'm ... really sorry about all this," I said, feeling surprisingly guilty.

He just shrugged. "You saved me a rather large donation to Harvard. Maybe I owe you one."

Then there was the matter of Elton and Kari. Their breakup was one of the most painfully awkward things I've ever witnessed. Elton stood there, arms crossed, his voice stiff as he said, "I do not think I can be romantically involved with someone who would try to bring down my family."

"Understandable," Kari replied, her tone icy but unflinching. "However, your family will be bankrupt soon, ending your enrollment at Kanner Academy. We likely would have broken up anyway."

"That is true," Elton conceded, his gaze shifting to the sidewalk. "Still, for the record, I am breaking up with you now."

I wanted to squeal and hug him, but I didn't, mostly because I didn't want to fight Kari on the sidewalk and end up back in the police station.

They both stood there, looking everywhere but at each other. Finally, Kari broke the silence. "Do you still want to play League of Legends later?"

"Affirmative," Elton said.

"I'll see you online," Kari said, shaking Elton's hand with all the warmth of a business deal before walking away with father's arm around her.

After all that, the five of us who remained—Mom, Holly, Elton,

Axl, and I—went to some bagel place for breakfast. It was awkward and quiet. The waiter didn't even ask for our order; he just set down five coffees and we all stared at them for a while, letting the silence sink in. The tension hung over the table like a fog, thick and hard to shake.

Eventually, I mumbled, "I didn't want to do any of this, you know."

"She didn't," Elton said, sticking up for me. "It was my fault."

Holly shook her head, not really seeming to hear us. "It doesn't matter now," she said, almost to herself.

I glanced around the table, but my eyes kept returning to Holly. She'd always been so optimistic. The person who could see a silver lining in the worst storm cloud. But now… now she just seemed tired and defeated, like she was bracing herself for the worst.

"You don't have to worry about Denzel," I said, guessing at what had her so upset. "I know we kind of blackmailed him and made him mad, but he'll still testify against Mustang at the divorce hearing. I can make sure of it."

Holly gave a weak smile, her voice barely above a whisper. "Terrance and I won't have anything to fight over soon, Izzy."

I stared at her, confused. "You … you knew?"

She nodded, her face tired and resigned. "My lawyer told me the minute the news about Arnie Spencer broke. I didn't want to upset Elton. Not at the holidays. I thought it might … well, I don't know what I thought."

"So what will you do now?" I asked, my voice barely above a whisper.

She gave me a weary smile. "We'll figure it out. We always do, don't we?"

But what if we don't this time? I thought. "Yeah, we do," I said, without conviction.

The table fell into silence once more, and in that stillness, a sense of clarity emerged. Leaving New York might be the best thing for all of us. "Maybe it's best if we head back to Florida a little early," I suggested, glancing up at Holly to see if I'd hurt her feelings.

But Holly just sighed and nodded, her eyes far away. She didn't argue, didn't even try to convince us to stay longer. She just sat there, staring out the window, like she'd already seen a future none of us were ready for.

EPILOGUE

Ruby Spencer was charged with murder on New Year's Day, shortly after Arnie's body was found in his Manhattan office. The Ponzi scheme charges followed, though it took forensic accountants months to untangle the full financial mess. In the end, Spencer Investments' victims lost an average of 98 percent of their money. Ruby was eventually sentenced to 765 years in prison, though she served only one before hanging herself in her cell.

Mustang Jones was never charged criminally—turns out being clueless isn't illegal—but that didn't stop the avalanche of civil suits from every investor he'd ever sweet-talked into trusting Arnie Spencer. Public outrage helped fast-track the hearings, and within months, Mustang was flat broke. He lost everything: the grill sponsorship, the condos, even Holly's parents' house in Graves—which he'd conveniently titled in his own name. A benevolent judge awarded Holly half of everything in the divorce, but half of nothing is still nothing.

And Mustang, who once played charity golf with celebrities and senators, was last seen on late-night cable, shirtless and oiled up, selling testosterone boosters to men who used to be somebody.

In the end, Sachin Patel's Brother Island bribes came to light, as did his misappropriation of investor funds. The fines were steep, as Sachin had predicted, and his reputation was ruined, but the man had good lawyers, and they kept him out of jail. The Blades project was scrapped, the investors were reimbursed, and Brother Island remained a bird sanctuary—still creepy, but now officially protected. Kari got into Harvard but turned it down, opting instead for Arizona State, where she partied hard enough to end up on academic probation her freshman year. These days, she's a reality TV star with her own E! show, *Kari Gone Wild*, where she stages dramatic interventions for the ultra-wealthy—calling out environmental crimes between gala fundraisers and yacht tours.

The scandal worked in reverse for Denzel Davis. Somehow, his church exploded in size after Jade drunkenly posted his sex tape and it went viral. Soon Village Tabernacle began holding Sunday services at Madison Square Garden whenever the Knicks were on the road. Stacey stuck by his side, and soon enough, the church blessed them with matching his-and-hers private jets. Meanwhile, Jade Martin returned to modeling, married an NFL quarterback, divorced him, and now runs a skincare line aimed at preteen girls.

Holly, on the other hand, was left with nothing—no money, no friends, and no one left to call. Mustang had bled everyone dry, including her parents, who lost their retirement and were now crammed into a one-bedroom flat in Kent. She was broke, humiliated, and utterly alone. By summer, she and Elton were reduced to asking us for help, bless their hearts.

As for Axl and me, we were chained to the tracks of a runaway train. That spring my pill habit only grew. I was up to 40 mg twice a day, though I still hadn't snorted again. Axl and I hardly spoke. He missed school, skipped spring football practice, and drifted through the rest of junior year like he was half-asleep. I didn't ask about his pill habit because I didn't need to. It was that obvious.

Things with River were back to normal—or whatever version of normal he believed in. But to me, it felt hollow. He loved me—maybe too much—and every time he looked at me, I felt the weight of that love pressing down. His trust. His hope. And the creeping certainty that I didn't deserve any of it. He didn't know the truth—the pills tucked behind every smile, the wreck of a person hiding just beneath the surface. The more he insisted I was perfect, the more I felt like I was drowning in a lie. I prayed every night he'd be the one to end it, because I wasn't strong enough to break his heart.

The world kept spinning, but I was stuck—frozen in a version of myself I hardly recognized. My life had become a routine—a bad one, but a routine all the same. School in the mornings, drifting from class to class, just scraping by with average grades. After school, I worked at Piggly Wiggly, scanning barcodes and bagging groceries to pay for my pills. It wasn't much of a life, but it was mine.

"While I was in New York, River had told me about the fire on Rattlesnake Road. The Hoochie Hut, a strip club just outside town, had gone up in flames. At first, no one thought much beyond the usual Dandridge gossip—just another dive lost to insurance fraud. But weeks later, the police announced that a body had been found inside, the remains of an exotic dancer who'd been killed before the fire started.

Now, it was all anyone in Dandridge could talk about. At every grocery line and gas station, people swapped theories like they were local detectives. A year ago, I would've been right there with them, picking apart clues before anyone else knew where to look. A year ago, I'd have cracked the case before the Dandridge Police had wiped the donut crumbs from their mustaches.

But now, I watched it all from the other side of a glass wall, everything muffled and dull. Somewhere in the back of my mind, I remembered how I'd once worried that life would start to revolve around the next hit, that one day I'd wake up and realize that was all there was. Now, the fear felt distant, but the reality was settling in.

I was already there.

THE END

Izzy and Elton will return in
RATTLESNAKE ROAD
2026-ish

For updates visit www.chadalangibbs.com

ACKNOWLEDGEMENTS

Writing this book wasn't easy.

I mean, it wasn't hard work. I didn't sweat—well, okay, I sweated a little, but I live in Alabama and our decades-old air conditioner can only do so much. The writing just didn't come as easily this time, not compared to the first three Izzy and Elton books.

At the end of *Ashes in the Pines*, there's a note promising that Izzy and Elton will return in *The Blades of Brother Island*, 2024. Yeah... I waved at that arbitrary deadline as it sailed past.

The truth is, I got a little tired of writing the same characters. I wasn't sure anyone would really notice—or care—if they didn't return. But some of you did care. You emailed, messaged, or even asked me at the pool, "Where's my fourth book?" It wasn't exactly like readers with pitchforks outside George R. R. Martin's house demanding *The Winds of Winter*, but I appreciated it all the same. Your questions and your patience encouraged me to finish this one and get it into your hands.

So, thanks to you, the readers, for sticking around—and for choosing to spend your precious free time with something I wrote. That still humbles me.

Thanks to my wife, Tricia. Some people claim our world is a simulation, and after twenty years of marriage, I'm starting to agree. No way I'd be lucky enough to marry you in real life.

Thanks to my sons, Linus and Oliver. You've filled our home with so much love, laughter, and incredibly smelly socks.

Thanks to my editor, Becky Philpott. The first draft of this book was basically one giant plot hole. Thanks for helping me fill it—and for all your hard work through the years.

Thanks to Robert Finkel for the Photoshop help. I promise to repay you in Korean wings from Chimac.

The next Izzy and Elton book will be the last. I hope to give them the kind of ending that feels right—and doesn't result in angry letters. I've got another project I want to work on first, but then I'll get to work on *Rattlesnake Road*. I'm thinking 2026... but I make no promises.

Also by Chad Alan Gibbs

<u>Standalone Novels</u>

Two Like Me and You
The Rome of Fall

<u>Izzy and Elton Mystery Series</u>

Bardo by the Sea
Graves Upon Bones
Ashes in the Pines

TWO LIKE YOU AND ME

"A Smashing debut that's
both intimate and epic."
—Kirkus Reviews
(Starred Review)

Best Books of 2019
Kirkus Reviews

Rubery Book Award
2019 Winner - Fiction

CHAD ALAN GIBBS
TWO LIKE ME AND YOU
A NOVEL

The Rome of Fall

*"A highly readable...
nostalgia-incuding novel"*
—Kirkus Reviews

*"A classic yet delightfully
quirky rock n' roll novel."*
—IndieReader

THE ROME OF FALL
chad alan gibbs